Gothic Originals

Gothic Originals

Published so far

Charlotte Dacre, *The Passions* (1811), edited by Jennifer Airey

Elizabeth Gunning, *The Foresters. A Novel* (1796), edited by Valerie Grace Derbyshire

Dion Boucicault, *The Vampire* (1852) and *The Phantom* (1873), edited by Matthew Knight and Gary D. Rhodes

The Female Vampire in Hispanic Fiction: A Critical Anthology of Turn-of-the-Twentieth-Century Gothic-Inspired Tales, edited and translated by Megan DeVirgilis

In preparation

Mary Elizabeth Braddon, *The Factory Girl* (1863), edited by Bridget Marshall

Washington Allston, *Monaldi: A Tale* (1841), edited by Kerry Dean Carso

Gothic Originals

The Female Vampire in Hispanic Literature

Gothic Originals

With full introductions and explanatory notes to the text, Gothic Originals *consists of scholarly editions aimed at readers, teachers and students of the gothic. Each text is a definitive scholarly edition, edited by an expert in their field. The series consists of texts from the eighteenth century onwards, and includes hidden classics to forgotten anthologies of terror. The series is an essential collection for any serious scholar of the gothic.*

General Editor
Anthony Mandal, *Cardiff University*

Series Editor
Andrew Smith, *University of Sheffield*

Editorial Board
Carol Margaret Davison, *University of Windsor*
Jerrold E. Hogle, *University of Arizona*
Marie Mulvey-Roberts, *University of the West of England*
Franz Potter, *National University*
Laurence Talairach, *University of Toulouse Jean Jaurès*
Dale Townshend, *Manchester Metropolitan University*
Lisa Vargo, *University of Saskatchewan*
Angela Wright, *University of Sheffield*

The Female Vampire in Hispanic Literature

A CRITICAL ANTHOLOGY OF
TURN-OF-THE-TWENTIETH-CENTURY
GOTHIC-INSPIRED TALES

edited and translated by Megan DeVirgilis

UNIVERSITY OF WALES PRESS
CARDIFF
2024

A Lola

© Megan DeVirgilis, 2024

Typeset in Minion 3 and SchwarzKopf New
at the Centre for Editorial and Intertextual Research, Cardiff University.

All rights reserved. No part of this book may be reproduced in any material form
(including photocopying or storing it in any medium by electronic means and
whether or not transiently or incidentally to some other use of this publication)
without the written permission of the copyright owner. Applications for the copyright owner's written permission to reproduce any part of this publication should
be addressed to the University of Wales Press, University Registry, King Edward
VII Avenue, Cardiff CF10 3NS.

www.uwp.co.uk

British Library CIP Data
A catalogue record for this book is available from the British Library.

ISBN 978-1-83772-168-9 (hardback)
      978-1-83772-169-6 (ePDF)
      978-1-83772-170-2 (ePUB)

The right of Megan DeVirgilis to be identified as Editor and Translator of this work
has been asserted in accordance with sections 77 and 79 of the Copyright, Designs
and Patents Act 1988.

Contents

Acknowledgements ix
List of Abbreviations xi
Introduction xiii
   The Sympathetic Female Vampire: A Transhispanic
     Gothic Literary Phenomenon at the Turn of the
     Twentieth Century xiii
   Introductory Essays to the Tales in this Collection . . xxviii
   Select Bibliography. lxv
Note on the Texts lxxiii
   Textual History of the Tales. lxxiii
   The Present Edition lxxvii

THE FEMALE VAMPIRE IN HISPANIC LITERATURE
The Female Vampire (1899). . . . . ·3
   Leopoldo Lugones
The White Farmhouse (1904) . . . . ·7
   Clemente Palma
Mr Cadaver and Miss Vampire (1910) 19
   Antonio de Hoyos y Vinent
The Cold Woman (1922). 27
   Carmen de Burgos
The Vampire (1927) 53
   Horacio Quiroga

Explanatory Notes 69
   The Female Vampire 69
   The White Farmhouse 70
   Mr Cadaver and Miss Vampire 73
   The Cold Woman 76
   The Vampire 82

vii

Acknowledgements

THIS BOOK HAS GROWN from a chapter I wrote on female vampires in my doctoral dissertation, so I would first like to thank my dissertation committee for their valuable suggestions on the corpus and content of that chapter. Specifically, I'd like to thank my advisor, Hiram Aldarondo, for kindling a curiosity of the gothic, the fantastic and monstrous women in me. Also, Víctor Pueyo, for his continued support and friendship over the years.

The completion of this project would not have been possible, at least not at this point in my life, without a Faculty Award from the National Endowment for the Humanities. The award relieved me of my teaching and service responsibilities at Morgan State University for the 2021–2022 academic year, during which time I completed the majority of this project. It was a gift to be able to write for long periods of time, uninterrupted, and for that I am forever thankful. My appreciation also goes to my department chair, Helen Harrison, who is a bottomless well of support and kindness. I know that my leave wasn't easy on her or the department, and I will always be grateful that she encouraged me to pursue this opportunity. Thank you also to the University of Wales Press for their support of my project, in particular Sarah Lewis, and to Anthony Mandal. Farin Kamangar also deserves a mention here for his gracious support while I navigated the NEH award on my institution's side, as does Luke Swinson, for his keen editing eye and really helpful suggestions.

A special thanks goes to Abigail Lee Six for generously providing her insightful comments on the essay that discusses Carmen de Burgos and her novella. Also, for her pioneering work on Spanish gothic, and one article in particular that brought Antonio de Hoyos y Vinent's female vampire tale, included here, to my attention.

I would also like to thank my friends who had a hand in the completion of this book. Lina Ruíz Guzmán, for her support and comments on my translations. Renata Pontes, for graciously helping me acquire sources. Lorraine Savage, for her encouragement and for finding quiet spaces for me to write. Harold Morales, for his friendship and guidance at various crucial points during the last few years. My 'Baltimore family', Matthew and Laura Durington, for their generous support and guidance as well. Dawn Episcopo, for her steadfast encouragement and affection that nourished me while I was writing this book. Joseph Hasenaur, for his gorgeous painting gracing the cover of this book. Thank you for so thoughtfully bringing the sympathetic female vampires in the selected tales to life (again).

Lastly, I am grateful to my family. My mother, Bertha Luaces Weldon; my tía, Hortensia Luaces; and my in-laws, Rodie Alvaré-Henson and Tom Hen-

ACKNOWLEDGEMENTS

son, for all of their support. And most especially, I am endlessly thankful to my husband, J. DeVirgilis, for always listening patiently as I talked through my ideas and my concerns, no matter if it interrupted his workday or his sleep. His expertise on film also proved invaluable when it came time to translate the most technological parts of Horacio Quiroga's tale. This book, like my life in general, is so much better because of him.

List of Abbreviations

ACC   Antonio Cruz Casado, 'La novela erótica de Antonio de Hoyos y Vinent', *Cuadernos Hispanoamericanos*, 426 (1985), 101–16

AG   Aníbal González, *A Companion to Spanish American modernismo* (Woodbridge and Rochester, NY: Tamesis, 2007)

ALS   Abigail Lee Six, 'The Last of the Vamp(ire)s: Two Spanish Stories at a Semantic Fork in the Road', *Horror Studies*, 10.2 (2019), 173–88

JASR   José Antonio Sanz Ramírez, 'Antonio de Hoyos y Vinent: genealogía y elogio de una pasión' (unpublished doctoral thesis, Universidad Complutense de Madrid, Madrid, 2010)

JOJ   José Olivio Jiménez, *Antología crítica de la poesía modernista hispanoamericana* (Madrid: Hiperión, 2011)

NMK   Nancy M. Kason, *Breaking Traditions: The Fiction of Clemente Palma* (Lewisburg: Bucknell University Press, 1988)

Introduction

THE SYMPATHETIC FEMALE VAMPIRE: A TRANSHISPANIC GOTHIC LITERARY PHENOMENON AT THE TURN OF THE TWENTIETH CENTURY

CCORDING TO BARBARA CREED, '[a]ll human societies have a conception of the monstrous-feminine, of what it is about woman that is shocking, terrifying, horrific, abject.'[1] The female vampire—from her origins in mythology and folklore, to her iterations in contemporary cultural production—is but one figure in the profound milieu of monstrous women across human societies. And she is indeed a fascinating one. This study of the female vampire is, at its core, a celebration of 'monstrous' women, for who better to rely on to draw attention to—and in more progressive cases, challenge or dismantle—patriarchal society's inconsistencies, vulnerabilities and inequities? The acute reappearance of the literary female vampire at the turn of the twentieth century is not happenstance, but rather a direct response to shifting ideological, political and economic concerns, and even more precisely, a response to growing tensions over women's roles and behaviours in the public and private spheres in light of rising first-wave feminisms on a global scale. This is the first critical study to suggest that mounting global fears concerning female autonomy and women's bodies as sites of immorality and disease significantly affected late nineteenth- and early twentieth-century gothic literary production in Spain and Latin America, and that these narratives should be recognised and valued in relation to their US and European predecessors. I contend that the Spanish and Latin American short narratives compiled here are not simply imitations of imported models, but rather unique iterations that meaningfully deviate from the European and US gothic literary traditions, resulting in trends and traditions of their own.

The sympathetic female vampire—or vampiric *femme fatale* when she does not engage in blood drinking—has been overwhelmingly understood as a more contemporary phenomenon by anglophone gothic scholars, her emergence being attributed to the works of Angela Carter (UK, 1940–1992) or Anne Rice (US, 1941–2021).[2] Abigail Lee Six, however, suggests that the first sympathetic female vampires appeared as early as 1910 and 1922 in works by Spanish authors Antonio de Hoyos y Vinent (1884–1940) and Carmen de Burgos (1867–1932), respectively.[3] The primary aim of this study is to build on Lee Six's pioneering work, establishing that Latin American authors were also producing disruptive models of the female vampire up to two decades earlier than de Hoyos y Vinent's and de Burgos's cases, and possibly inspiring them. The five tales included here, written by five different authors from either Spain or Latin America, embrace female agency, consider genre and gender disruption, and question the sanctity of marriage and the moral compass of society. The female 'vampire', they seem to suggest, is not the cause of society's ills, but rather a victim herself of patriarchal fears and oppression and/or outdated moral codes.

While presenting the first known cases of sympathetic and complex literary female vampires is the primary purpose of this critical anthology, there are other significant, interrelated aims as well. As the study's title suggests, I consider these tales to be 'gothic-inspired', a doubly loaded term. As several scholars of the burgeoning fields of Spanish and Latin American gothic studies have noted, the gothic is especially marginalised in Spanish and Latin American literary studies: while the gothic itself has been historically marginalised for being too 'low brow', too 'emotional', too 'immoral' and, worst of all, too 'feminine', its appearance in Spanish and Latin American letters has tended to either be ignored or flat-out rejected. Instead, scholars and authors themselves have opted for designations such as literature of the 'unusual' in the Spanish case, 'magical realism' in the Latin American case and 'fantastic' in both cases, to categorise literature that contemporary authors and scholars are increasingly beginning to approach through a gothic lens.

In their paradigmatic study, *Latin American Gothic in Literature and Culture*, Sandra Casanova-Vizcaíno and Inés Ordiz note how the *Antología de la literatura fantástica* [Anthology of fantastic literature], edited by renowned Argentine authors Jorge Luis Borges (1899–1986), Adolfo Bioy Casares (1914–1999) and Silvina Ocampo (1903–1993), established the first definitions of the fantasy mode in Latin America. By purposely excluding gothic fiction, they reinforced the marginalisation of the gothic in comparison to the fantastic.[4] In his comprehensive study of the gothic in Spanish literature and film, Xavier Aldana Reyes notes a similar tendency in Spanish letters, as well as its implications: 'the predominance of [the term "fantastic"] to describe what would be more intuitively characterised as terror or horror denies the Gothic its eminently transhistorical, transmedial and transgeneric nature.'[5] In anthologies and edited volumes on gothic literature, mention of Spanish or Latin American texts is incredibly sparse. Without a doubt, the gothic has been traditionally understood as an Anglo-European phenomenon, as a reaction to Protestant Enlightenment thought or a symptom of counter-rational reason.[6] As a genre, the gothic pertains to the specific ideological coordinates of the rise of the bourgeoisie and the division between the public and private spheres. It is the space that occupies and expresses the vulnerabilities, excesses and horrors of modernity. Thus, while the reasons for its refutation in Spain and Latin America are arguably entrenched in the same logic that marginalised European gothic literature,

xiv

THE SYMPATHETIC FEMALE VAMPIRE

it can be suggested that they are also rooted in their peripheral statuses as Catholic, non-anglophone regions with very different paths to modernity.

In the Spanish case, the path to modernity entailed a slower transition to a capitalist economy and a gradual consolidation of a bourgeois epistemology.[7] The Spanish nobility maintained dominance over the political terrain, delaying the development of the public/private divide, a crucial ideological function that favoured the bourgeoisie.[8] Under these conditions, how could a strong gothic tradition emerge? Who would fear the return of labyrinthine castles, aristocratic villains and 'barbaric' Catholic rituals if they were not things of the past? Spain, it was understood, was more a setting for gothic novels than a producer of gothic fiction itself. And yet, Hispanists have recently begun to explore Spain's rich gothic tradition. According to Miriám López Santos, this tradition dates back to *Noches lúgubres* [*Lugubrious Nights*] (1789) by José Cadalso (1741–1782) and the liberal translations of French, English and German gothic literature, wherein the authors could conform to the strict censorship of the day by dropping much of the subversive content, saturating the scenes with religious images and taking a moralising turn.[9] Original Spanish gothic novels were soon to follow in the latter half of the nineteenth century.[10] Lee Six's groundbreaking *Gothic Terrors: Incarceration, Duplication, and Bloodlust in Spanish Narrative* (2010) convincingly sets the stage for exploring post-Romantic and realist works through a gothic lens, suggesting that authors employed gothic elements in a selective fashion in order to keep the label at arm's length.[11] More recently, scholars such as Ann Davies and Aldana Reyes have explored the wide usage, as well as the regional and broader implications, of the gothic in contemporary Spanish literature and film.[12]

Where Latin America is concerned, its path to modernity is linked to that of Spain's through violent colonial processes, but distinctive in that it was a conglomerate of colonies with a different kind of feudal past. Spanish settlers did establish feudal-type economic structures in Latin America, such as the *encomienda* system,[13] and agricultural sectors in some colonies continued to be dominated by feudal relations of production and exploitation of the peasantry well into the nineteenth century.[14] Accordingly, a case can be made for a Latin American feudal or semi-feudal past, one that, like Spain's, lingered to the point of delaying a strong consolidation of the bourgeoisie. In terms of the development of a gothic tradition, Latin America lacked the necessary iconography that nourished the genre, most notably in its deficit of castles in ruins. That said, like Spain, Latin America has managed to produce an interesting and unique gothic tradition that meaningfully adapts European and US models to suit their own needs, as well as, in the early days, to possibly avoid censorship. A curious example to note with respect to the overarching theme of this edition is the translation of German writer Johann Wolfgang von Goethe's (1749–1832) poem 'Die Braut von Korinth' ['The Bride of Corinth'] (1797) by Cuban poet José María Heredia (1803–1839). Whereas the original includes the verse, 'And I

XV

have sucked the lifeblood from his heart,[15] Heredia's 1825 translation modifies the verse to read: 'You won't live long, my husband'.[16] A. Owen Aldridge suggests that with this modification, Heredia's poem, possibly the first iteration of the literary vampire—male or female—in Latin American letters, 'is not a vampire poem at all'.[17] Yet, as evidenced in the tales compiled in this anthology, female 'vampires' can take on many forms, and do not necessarily drink blood.

As the nineteenth century progressed, Latin America's gothic tradition strengthened, continuing to adapt earlier models in ways that respond to its own particular fears and horrors, especially regarding gender, modernisation and urbanisation, and even nation-building processes.[18] In the twentieth and twenty-first centuries, the gothic becomes an apt medium through which to explore, and sometimes rewrite, colonial and imperial traumas, as a number of scholars have recently observed in their scholarship on Latin American gothic.[19] The present critical anthology is indebted to the works of these scholars, as well as to those of Spanish Peninsularists Lee Six, López Santos, Aldana Reyes and Davies. Indeed, one of the main objectives of this study is to contribute to their scholarly dialogue by expanding research on the gothic in these regions to include an in-depth study of the female vampire. In the introduction to their influential volume, *Doubles and Hybrids in Latin American Gothic* (2020), Antonio Alcalá González and Ilse Bussing López encourage other scholars to analyse the presence of distinct gothic motifs in Latin American cultural production.[20] This book takes up their call to action.

Now that the use of the term 'gothic' in the subtitle of this critical edition has been contextualised, on to the second part of that loaded term. I refer to these texts as 'gothic-inspired' after much consideration, and knowing that it requires some explanation; for as I just described, have convincing and unique gothic traditions in Latin America and Spain not already been established by Latin Americanists and Peninsularists? And if so, why not simply refer to these as 'gothic texts'? The main reason behind this choice of phrasing lies in the gothic's evolution and plasticity, and more specifically, in its manifestations at the turn-of-the-twentieth-century Spain and Latin America. Once solely used to define a particular genre of novels that spanned a sixty-or-so year period—beginning with the publication of Horace Walpole's *The Castle of Otranto* in 1764 and ending with the publication of Charles Maturin's *Melmoth the Wanderer* in 1820—the gothic now tends to be understood as an ever-evolving, genre-disrupting, global cultural process that, while responding to past and present regional/national anxieties, also dialogues with, adapts and reappropriates early European and US gothic models. The gothic is still a literature of nightmares—as the manifestation of fear, either in the reader or a character, is what distinguishes it from its fantasy cousins—but gothic novels and tales produced after 1820 tend to be described as adhering to the 'gothic mode'. The term *mode* lets the gothic coexist with other genres and modes without judgement. Yet, as Davies posits, it is of value to understand the gothic as a 'nexus', in that 'there is a sense of cross-pollination' inherent to the gothic, a 'circulation and cultural flow [that does] not assume a Gothic that is ever on the move but one that comes to rest here and there.'[21] The gothic, therefore, is not an insulated or continuous process, but one that experiences acute manifestations at specific times, arguably in accordance with moments on the verge of social change or during political or economic unrest. I suggest that the gothic comes to 'rest' in Spain and Latin America in similar ways, even an interconnected way, at the turn of the twentieth century. Since the gothic was essentially an imported and adapted literary phenomenon that existed tangentially in their contemporaneous cultural frameworks, Hispanic authors on either side of the Atlantic were not prone to subtitling their works 'A Gothic Tale' or following strict gothic formulas. Instead, authors drew inspiration from their gothic predecessors and contemporaries, implementing borrowed tropes (such as the vampire) and narrative devices (for example, Poe's 'unity of effect')[22] to appeal to a wider readership by exploring subversive themes and cultivating suspense. In this scenario, the gothic coexists with, draws from and responds to other literary trends. The turn of the twentieth century was an especially ripe time for this flow to occur, as literary trends that lent themselves to a gothic sensibility were on the rise.

One prominent example is the short-lived yet influential Decadent movement, born in France during the closing decades of the nineteenth century. According to Hannah Thompson, the movement's foremost concerns were 'an abiding fascination with questions of non-normative gender, sex, and sexuality and an interest in a self-conscious aestheticism.'[23] In terms of the representation of women, Thompson argues: 'The Decadent heroine is almost invariably represented as a dangerous, even deadly creature who wields an attractive yet terrifying power over the submissive, frequently masochistic hero.'[24] The Decadent heroine thus bears a stark resemblance to the female vampire, to the point where, as explored below and in the accompanying essays in this volume, they meet in the figure of the vampiric *femme fatale*. For Matei Calinescu, Decadence is compatible with a high degree of technological advancement: 'The fact of progress is not denied, but increasingly large numbers of people experience the *results* of progress with an anguished sense of loss and alienation. Once again, progress *is* decadence and decadence *is* progress.'[25] Advances in technology, alongside urban development, also fuelled the emergence of science fiction, while a rising fascination with the occult and spiritualist practices inspired its offshoot, pseudo-science fiction. Pursuing a spiritual approach to explain what science could not during a time when a religious society had given way to a secular one was common in the pseudo or occult sciences of the time. The Decadent imagination and the emergence of science and pseudo-science fictions thus lent themselves nicely to the dark ethos of the gothic universe, as can be observed in several of the tales compiled here.

INTRODUCTION

Another prominent example of a late nineteenth-century literary movement that has marked influence on the evolution of the gothic in Hispanic letters is Latin American *modernismo*. José Olivio Jiménez defines *modernismo* as a style that placed particular emphasis on beauty, lyricism, purity and harmony; as a protest against sociohistorical conditions that reduced writers to mere producers; and as a refuge where writers could explore ontological problems (JOJ). *Modernismo* is typically associated with poetry, but the phenomenon also extended to prose (JOJ, 9). It was an experimental literature that aimed to break from the confines of the past and launch a new era for Latin American literature. According to Aníbal González:

> Spanish American writers and intellectuals set out to deliberately create a literature that would be just as solid and aesthetically valuable as that of their European counterparts. The *modernistas* were well aware of the boldness of their move, for it was a bid by writers from nations that were still striving towards modernity in other spheres, to achieve full literary modernity (AG, 1–2).

While not overtly dark in sensibility, the movement's interest in exploring the nature and limits of beauty, its taste for destabilising genre and conventional literary conventions, its political impetus, its penchant for psychology (AG, 54), as well as its underlying sense of despair, even fear, prompted by the limits of both religion and science (JOJ, 22–29), can be argued to have made gothic strategies appealing. Evidence can be found in the short-story production of Nicaraguan Rubén Darío (1867–1916) and Argentinian Leopoldo Lugones (1874–1938), both heralded as pioneers of *modernismo* and both having published several tales of terror.

Decadence and *modernismo* developed almost simultaneously in Latin America, and it is not a mere coincidence that the gothic experienced its first fertile appearance during this time. In her groundbreaking study on Peruvian author Clemente Palma (1872–1946), Gabriela Mora suggests that there is a particular gothic–decadent vein in Latin American *modernismo*, one that builds on the conventions of the past but also breaks from them, revealing an anti-bourgeois sentiment through an experimentation with language and forms. This inclination towards the gothic helps explain the literary tendencies and intertextuality at play in Palma's works, including an affinity with Poe.[26] Mora is not the first Latin American scholar to note nineteenth- and early twentieth-century Latin American authors' admiration for and adaptation of Poe's works.[27] However, her suggestion of a particular gothic–decadent vein in *modernismo* is a significant contribution to Latin American gothic studies, and Latin American literary studies more broadly. The present collection aims to expand Mora's theory to include both Latin American and Spanish authors of the time. To my knowledge, mine is the first critical study to note *modernismo*'s influence on the gothic as a transhispanic phenomenon.[28] I ground my argument in a long transhispanic gothic connection that can be evidenced in publication history, as well as in Alejandro Mejías-López's theory on Latin American *modernismo*

xviii

THE SYMPATHETIC FEMALE VAMPIRE

as a kind of 'inverted conquest'. He boldly notes: 'With the advent of *modernismo* in the Peninsula in the 1880s, Spanish Americans brought about a radical transformation of Spanish letters and, in doing so, they completely reversed the location of literary and cultural authority.'[29] This book therefore brings Mora's and Mejías-López's scholarship into conversation to suggest that a gothic–decadent vein of *modernismo*—or a gothic-inspired one, to bring this discussion full circle—infiltrated the Spanish literary landscape at the turn of the twentieth century, to the point of resulting in the first trend of sympathetic female vampires.

The transatlantic gothic connection between Spain and Latin America dates back as early as the 1730s with the publication of what Carlos Abraham refers to as 'periódicos gótico-políticos' (gothic political newspapers). These four-page periodicals were political satires narrated by goblins or witches, although devils, owls and vampires also appeared as narrators, and are thus outside the realm of what we have come to understand as gothic horror. They appear to have been first penned by the Portuguese friar Manuel Freyre de Silva (1690–1770), who criticised the monarchy and was soon arrested.[30] His satirical writings circulated in Madrid, and later in Spanish America, where imitators abounded.[31] Abraham notes that in its most common form, which circulated in Argentina between 1818 and 1879, the newspapers are 'narrated by a magical creature of nature that infiltrates unsuspected places, where no one would think there to be a spy; as a result, it manages to learn extremely hidden secrets.'[32] While lacking proper gothic strategies, including the crucial purpose of inspiring fear, both the front-page illustrations and the titles themselves convey gothic inclinations.[33] Example titles include 'Duende resucitado' [The resuscitated goblin], 'El diablo en Buenos Aires' [The Devil in Buenos Aires] and 'La bruja o la ave nocturna' [The witch or the night owl]. These gothic precursors may have influenced later eighteenth-century European gothic satire directed at the monarchy and clergy, such as Voltaire's (1694–1778) entry on vampires in his *Dictionnaire philosophique* [*Philosophical Dictionary*] (1764), where he claims that 'true suckers lived not in cemeteries, but in very agreeable palaces.'[34] Spanish painter Francisco de Goya (1746–1828) also employed the vampire as a metaphor to criticise the institutions and processes that ignored or exploited society's labouring classes and most vulnerable. For example, in *Sueño 16: crecer después de morir* [Dream 16: rising after death] (1797–1798), a tall corpse-like noble—gaunt, eyes shut, mouth open and dressed in antiquated clothing—is being propped up by several smaller, struggling men. To the left of the men appear two ecclesiastical figures, one possibly preaching while the other reads from a text. According to Roberto Alcalá Flecha, this scene contains a sharp criticism of both the nobility and the clergy, wherein both groups enjoy numerous privileges while the labouring classes are left to carry out all the back-breaking work.[35] At the same time, this scene could be read as a commentary on a dying feudal order that Spain and its peoples continue to support through ideological and

xix

INTRODUCTION

political institutions. Either way, the etching clearly draws attention to class conflict through the noble vampire and the struggling men. The vampire is also a recurring figure in Goya's *Desastres de la guerra* [Disasters of war], a series of etchings created between 1810 and 1820 that reveal the horrors of political violence and economic injustices during that period in Spain.

The transhispanic gothic connection continued into the nineteenth century as gothic satire mostly surrendered to gothic horror and the gothic novel yielded space to the gothic tale. Argentine writer Juana Manuela Gorriti (1816–1892) published tales in Madrid,[36] while Lugones was increasingly read in Spain.[37] Peruvian Clemente Palma sent his collection of short stories, *Cuentos malévolos* [*Malevolent Tales*] (1904), to Miguel de Unamuno (1864–1936), a renowned Spanish writer of the time. Unamuno responded by writing Palma a letter celebrating (for the most part) his collection, and Palma included the letter as the prologue to the collection. Moreover, Palma dedicated tales in his collection to Emilia Pardo Bazán (1851–1921) and Benito Pérez Galdós (1843–1920), contemporaneous Spanish writers whose works also exhibited gothic strategies.[38] Pardo Bazán herself published in Latin America,[39] and she was aware of Gorriti, referring to her as part of a 'distinguished group of brilliant' Latin American women authors.[40] Meanwhile, Spanish author Carmen de Burgos y Seguí (1867–1932), whose novella is included in this anthology, followed in Pardo Bazán's footsteps by adapting gothic tropes to challenge the status quo and by joining transatlantic organisations such as the Women's Council of the Ibero-American Union. Pardo Bazán and de Hoyos were both admirers of Darío (AG, 6; JASR, 323), and de Hoyos dedicated a section in his collection of short stories, *Del huerto del pecado* [From the garden of sin] (1910), to him. As such, this was a time when both male and female Spanish writers were paying attention to what their Latin American contemporaries were up to, staying informed of their literary works and, in some cases, publishing on their side of the Atlantic. I expect that more archival research will bring further evidence of a transhispanic gothic connection to light, but as Abraham poignantly observes, the weak archival traditions of Latin America have made it difficult to locate literary works. Of Argentina's tradition, he notes that when a writer dies their family tends to either throw away or, best case scenario, store their unfinished works and other papers in an attic to gather dust, thus denying their critical study. If Eduardo Ladislao Holmberg's (1852–1937) papers had been conserved, Abraham suggests that today we might have access to his currently lost novels, one of which was intriguingly titled *El vampiro negro* [The black vampire].[41]

The final major aim of this study is to introduce Latin American and Spanish gothic traditions to a wider anglophone readership. Of the tales included in this edition, three have never before been translated into English, while two were previously translated by independent publishers.[42] This is the first instance, however, where all five tales originally written in Spanish have been translated into English with extensive annotations and critical

xx

THE SYMPATHETIC FEMALE VAMPIRE

notes for the purposes of introducing the stories to a scholarly audience. It is also the first time Lugones's tale 'La vampira' ['The Female Vampire'] (1899) appears in an edited collection, having previously only been accessible through a facsimile of original newspaper clippings compiled by the author's son, of which only a handful of copies is available worldwide. The translations will allow English-reading gothic scholars access to these texts for the first time in most cases, feasibly leading to new comparative studies. My hope is that the accompanying notes and essays will provide scholars of Latin American and Spanish literature and culture with a constructive new framework to approach early twentieth-century Hispanic literary production. I have also written and arranged this anthology with upper-level undergraduate as well as graduate students in mind. I am optimistic that the translations and critical essays will prove useful in UK and US English classrooms, where gothic fiction is taught almost exclusively in English and the nineteenth- and early twentieth-century female vampire is understood as a primarily Anglo, German and French cultural phenomenon.

Before moving on to contextualising the rise of the female vampire in *fin-de-siècle* culture, it is important to note that this is not an exhaustive study. Scholars of the gothic or the fantastic in Spain may detect 'El claro del bosque' [The clearing in the woods] (1922) by Wenceslao Fernández Flórez (1885–1964) missing from this anthology, while Latin Americanists may note the absence of 'Thanathopia' (1893) by Darío, 'Tristan Cataletto' (1893) by Julio Calcaño (1840–1912) and 'Vampiras' (1906) by Palma. These cases do not fit into the larger trend of sympathetic, complex female vampires I have identified. Palma's 'Vampiras' does invite an against-the-grain reading that suggests the male protagonist's 'vampiric' girlfriend is understandably demonstrating natural female sexual desire through her 'attacks', but its overtly parodic tone and tongue-in-cheek ending distances it from the tales of terror included here, all of which decisively break from their European and US predecessors by shifting the locus of horror from the woman's body to social structures and outdated moral codes. There is arguably much value in continuing to study more status quo-affirming representations of monstrous women, as well as expanding the possibilities of these texts by adopting a gothic framework, especially in the underdeveloped case of Hispanic literature and its transhispanic trends. Yet these representations appear to belong to the minority. Instead, it is the sympathetic female vampire that emerged in a more dynamic way at the turn of the twentieth century. The main purpose of this study is to highlight this emergence, its political, economic, social and literary contexts, and its greater implications.

The female vampire is closely linked to her literary counterpart, the male vampire, but she is her own beast. Like the male vampire, she is produced in the shadows of the Enlightenment, entangling questions of autonomy, immigration, race, secular morality, the nuclear family, gender roles and 'appropriate' sexual practices. At the turn of the twentieth century, however, her iteration as a vampiric *femme fatale* is a product of specific ideological,

xxi

INTRODUCTION

political and economic concerns fuelled by the rise of first-wave feminisms and the emergence of the New Woman. During that time, European and American women were lobbying for the right to vote and run for political office, for access to education and equal opportunities in the job market. Some feminists even went as far as to call for the elimination of the double standard, for the right to have sexual relationships outside marriage, for the right to divorce and own property, and to be considered legitimate members of society without necessarily conforming to the current male-imposed models of domesticity and motherhood. Growing economies, immigration, the rise of the print economy (in which women were both consumers and producers), feminist movements and the transition from the model of labour and production to that of supply and demand gave way to fears of mass consumption, the spread of disease and degeneration, and the collapse of gender hierarchy.[43] The public/private divide, bourgeois institutions and the futures of nations were seen as under attack, fuelling opposition from state, religious and medical institutions, and society at large. According to Jennifer Smith:

> The new authority of medical discourses on sexuality was especially effective in keeping down the rising female emancipation movement, which had gained force since liberal theory seemed to promise that all human subjects, regardless of their gender, were equal and therefore deserving of the same rights.[44]

The link between female sexual and economic autonomy was strengthened through dominant medical, state and literary discourses, which encouraged women to stay inside the comfort and protection of their own homes, to exercise impeccable moral judgment and ethical responsibility to their family and their country, and to manage the household income.

Concerns over growing economies and the rise of the New Woman were not particular to Europe, as Spain and the newly independent nations of Latin America were contending with economic change, the consolidation of the bourgeoisie, and a re-evaluation of gender roles and the concept of morality within the framework of an evolving public/private divide. Different brands of feminism began to rise in accordance with liberal values, the possibility of social mobility and, due in part to immigration, the dissemination of information on a regional and transatlantic level. Christine Arkinstall argues that even though feminism was less radical in Spain than it was in France and the United States, feminist ideas were beginning to be realised in the last decades of the nineteenth century.[45] For example, an amendment offered in the Spanish parliament presented the idea of restricted female suffrage in 1877, while feminist conferences took place in Palma de Mallorca and Barcelona in 1883.[46]

Across the Atlantic, democratic values and the print economy played important roles in the rise of the politically conscious Latin American female writer. According to Nancy LaGreca:

> Women writers of the 1880s and early 1900s witnessed the disruptions of power that arose from the processes of modernization. The rhetoric of

xxii

equality and education that accompanied ideals of democracy planted the seeds in the minds of women across the region to question the bases of their social and legal inequality.[47]

In *fin-de-siglo* Peru, women's issues overlapped with larger national concerns:

> Liberal and conservative tendencies in the late 1800s meant that women intellectuals and activists such as [Mercedes Cabello de Carbonera] and her early feminist friends Clorinda Matto de Turner and Juana Manuela Gorriti would fashion their pro-woman arguments in dialogue with liberal discourses of progress.[48]

According to Maxine Molyneux: 'The writings of some [European anarchist feminists] were already being published in Argentina in the 1880s, and in the anarchist press critiques of the family appeared together with editorials supporting "feminism", by then a term in current usage.'[49] Anarchist–communist feminism was a working-class brand born of the anarchist–communist movement of the late nineteenth century; a section of the anarchist press was sympathetic to their cause, resulting in some clandestine pamphlets and even a proper journal, *La voz de la mujer* [Women's voice].[50] Later, the emergence of socialist feminism in Argentina allowed women to tackle more practical issues, such as equal rights, better educational opportunities and reforming the Civil Code.[51] Feminism thus bore nascent movements in industrial Latin American nations that began to grow against the backdrop of a changing political and economic landscape, and while the press enabled the circulation of ideas, both male and female writers took it upon themselves to confront these issues in their narratives.

An interesting case in point is Argentine writer Leopoldo Lugones's 1893 essay on women, 'La educación de la mujer: lo que es y lo que debe ser' [Women's education: what it is and what it should be], which illustrates how critical women were to nation-building processes. He writes: 'Far from dishonouring, work dignifies; far from impoverishing the soul, it fecundates and beautifies it. Any woman who has withstood it will surely be more industrious and administrative.'[52] Here, Lugones suggests that a woman with work experience outside the home will be better able to understand the operations of society and of the domestic economy. His argument is not advocating for single women who would rather work than raise a family, but for the importance of training and educating the nation's future mothers, conforming to a standard nineteenth-century view of women's role in the nation-building process. In Argentina, the incipient public school system and the emergence of vocational and professional schools conformed to this project: 'These institutions endeavoured to make future Argentine mothers into intelligent, industrious, skilled people conscious of their part in building the nation.'[53]

Women's roles began to shift, however, as Argentina started to grapple with fast-growing economic and industrial sectors, as well as a heavy influx of both welcome and unwelcome immigrants. According to Cynthia Jeffress Little: 'During the period 1860 to 1926, rapid urbanization, high

INTRODUCTION

foreign immigration, and thoroughgoing economic changes combined to alter many aspects of Argentine life. Even the role of women, long considered a constant, began to change due to these pressures.[54] Argentina became a major trade and commercial centre in the 1880s, and the nation needed women to work in sales and other white-collar jobs.[55] That said, women were still underpaid and underserved, and as a result, equal pay, better working conditions and the opening of daycare facilities became major feminist causes. Such causes, in addition to the rapidly changing labour landscape, began to foster negative views of this 'New Woman'. According to Francine Masiello, 'in a society where the family was equated with the national good, women who left the private sphere and moved into the public domain were often considered saboteurs of the unified household, promoting activities that undermined larger state interests.'[56] In Argentina, as in other growing Latin American economies, women needed to work, but only certain women, and only until they were married and became devoted educators of the nation's future citizens.

As critics have noted, there is a clear connection between the visibility of women in the public sphere and representations of wicked women characters in the late nineteenth century. According to Carol A. Senf, 'the growing nineteenth-century interest in powerful women characters may have stemmed from its concern—even obsession—with women's actual power, an obsession that increased as the century progressed.'[57] Similarly, Heather Braun proposes: 'The Decadent Movement, which united familiar tropes of courtly love with allusions to female vampires, revealed concerns about the encroaching power and visibility of the New Woman.'[58] Argentina experienced a similar reaction: 'Given the growing mass movement among anarchist and socialist workers and the demands by middle- and upper-class women for rights of suffrage and divorce, the masculine imagination identified women with subversion.'[59] Thus, while this nineteenth-century literary trend of identifying women with subversion—often representing them as iterations of monsters, such as snake-women or vampires—originated in Europe, it was later adopted by male Argentine writers such as Lugones and extended to other regions as well. This can be evidenced in the tales of Peruvian Clemente Palma, Uruguayan Horacio Quiroga (1878–1937) and Nicaraguan Rubén Darío. The phenomenon also extends to Spanish letters, in the writings of Gustavo Adolfo Bécquer (1836–1870), Ramón del Valle-Inclán (1866–1936), Fernández Flórez and de Hoyos.

In the earliest literary representations of the female vampire, they are prone to deviant and subversive desires and behaviours, can be greedy and untrustworthy, and/or are guided by their instincts rather than their intellect. Examples include: 'Die Braut von Korinth' ['The Bride of Corinth'] (1797) by Johann Wolfgang von Goethe (Germany, 1749–1832); 'Christabel' (1797–1800) by Samuel Taylor Coleridge (1772–1834); 'Lamia' (1820) by John Keats (England, 1795–1821); 'Laßt die Todten ruhen' ['Wake Not the Dead'] (1823) by Ernst Raupach (Germany, 1784–1852); 'Berenice' (1835),

xxiv

'Morella' (1835) and 'Ligeia' (1838) by Edgar Allan Poe (US, 1809–1849); 'La Morte Amoureuse' [The dead woman in love; translated into English as 'Clarimonde'] (1836) by Théophile Gautier (France, 1811–1872); 'Les Métamorphoses du vampire' (1852) by Charles Baudelaire (France, 1821–1867); 'Carmilla' (1872) by Joseph Sheridan Le Fanu (Ireland, 1814–1873); 'Olalla' (1885) by Robert Louis Stevenson (Scotland, 1850–1894); *The Blood of the Vampire* (1897) by Florence Marryat (England, 1833–1899); and *Dracula* (1897) by Bram Stoker (Ireland, 1847–1912), among others. While female victims vary in representation, female vampires tend to be beautiful but dangerous, charming but immoral, and ultimately represent the possible collapse of hierarchy in bourgeois patriarchal society.

On the surface, female vampires of the Romantic and Decadent imaginations were akin to their predecessors in mythology and folklore, as they were all monsters of the night that attacked men, usually in their sleep. They differ, however, in a simple yet significant way: while succubi were night demons, excluded from the human community and outside symbolic classification, the female vampires of the European literary tradition occupy a peripheral space of belonging and non-belonging; they are dead yet undead, alluring yet repulsive, and thus abject, in the Kristevan sense.[60] More importantly though, is that they could be one thing during the day (prospective wife and mother) and another thing at night (sex- and blood-hungry vampire). Who is *Dracula*'s Lucy Westenra, for example, if not a woman torn between being a wife and being free to carry on relations with several men? The horror that sustains this nineteenth-century monster lies in her ability to go along undetected, worm her way into the hearts (and beds) of men, then bare her fangs and drain men of their energy (semen), life force (blood) and/or finances, a particular capitalist fear that highlights the connection between female sexual desire and economic instability that was encouraged by the dominant medical, state and literary discourses of the time.

During the late nineteenth century, the female sex drive was regarded by many physicians and psychologists as a problematic behaviour that required treatment. Examples include *Psychopathia Sexualis* (1886) by Richard von Krafft-Ebing (1840–1902), *Studies in the Psychology of Sex* (1897) by Havelock Ellis (1859–1939) and works by Sigmund Freud (1856–1939) on dreams, hysteria and sexual theory from 1893–1905.[61] Female sexual desire was a concern even with respect to married women. In 'Excessive Sensuality or the Woman Vampire', a section from his book *Married Life and Happiness: Or, Love and Comfort in Marriage* (1922), Dr William J. Robinson writes: 'Some make excessive demands upon their husbands from ignorance, but some continue their practices even after being informed that it means impotence, sickness and a premature grave for their husbands.'[62] All five of the vampiric *femmes fatales* that appear in this collection manifest this fear, albeit in a parodic way that redirects culpability to the male characters and implicitly challenges outdated sex and gender norms.

INTRODUCTION

What is curious about most late nineteenth- and early twentieth-century Spanish and Latin American literary representations of the female vampire is that the narratives dismantle the model of their European and US predecessors through irony, parody and a sympathetic gaze towards the female protagonist. The trend first appears in Lugones's 'The Female Vampire' (1899), in which a young man is haunted by his love for an unattainable and beautiful spendthrift widow. On the surface, the text appears to define the female protagonist within the parameters of the vampiric *femme fatale* tradition, but a close reading reveals that female sensibilities are pitted against male impulses in a way that suggests the illusoriness of gender constructions while challenging the idea of feminine desire as destructive. Published five years later, Clemente Palma's 'The White Farmhouse' (1904) draws attention to the vulnerabilities of the private sphere, including a secularist moral code and the bourgeois institutions of marriage and the nuclear family: by the end of the story, the wife disappears, the child dies horrifically and the marital home is literally set ablaze. In a clear departure from European and US models, the wife's vampiric qualities garner reader sympathy while the anachronistic morality of the patriarchy implodes against a *fin-de-siglo* backdrop of nihilism and contempt.

This trend of depicting sympathetic female vampires extends to Spanish letters just a few years later, making its first appearance in Antonio de Hoyos y Vinent's 'Mr Cadaver and Miss Vampire' (1910). In the tale, a male narrator who admires a woman from afar, always spotting her about town with a different exsanguinated-looking man, becomes the very object of her affection. On the surface, the tale appears to align with the traditional model of the vampiric *femme fatale*, yet a close reading suggests a more nuanced portrait of sex and gender norms that questions the double standard and unreasonable expectations of women. Lee Six has noted the dialogue between this story and Carmen de Burgos's novella 'The Cold Woman' (1922), and how both texts speak to the vulnerable and precarious position of women in Spanish society of the time (ALS, 185). In 'The Cold Woman', Fernando is torn between his attraction for Blanca, a beautiful widow with a dark and mysterious past, and the attentive and virginal Edma, yet the text suggests that these characterisations correspond more so to his (and society's) ideals of women than to the women's actual realities. In Blanca's complex representation that questions customary archetypes of women characters, she shatters the nineteenth-century dialectic of the angel of the house/*femme fatale*. Moreover, she is a product of several literary currents, styles and modes: Romanticism, melodrama, *modernismo*, the gothic, the fantastic, Decadence and the *avant-garde*. This reappropriation and blending of styles to serve progressive concerns could be a factor in how the text moves away from horror and towards parody. Here, the reader is not persuaded to fear Blanca, but to fear *for* her in such a way that calls attention to the oppressive systems that determine both her worth and that of female authorship.

THE SYMPATHETIC FEMALE VAMPIRE

In the final tale of this volume, Horacio Quiroga's 'The Vampire' (1927), one pseudoscientist seeks out another with the aim of extracting life from a film. After a series of botched experiments and the murder of an actress in Hollywood, the spectre of the actress is finally realised, but as the narrator feared, she leaves his friend Rosales 'without a drop of blood' in his veins. Yet, is she really the seductive vampire the narrator determines her to be, or is she instead the victim of Rosales's own seduction and symbolic exsanguination? Like the other tales in this collection, the problematics of the male characters' and narrator's assumptions and actions reveal a more complicated, pitiable portrayal of the female 'vampire'. Other common themes and implications abound between these texts, revealing a curious connection that arguably points more to processes of influence and adaptation than to mere coincidence. They include iterations of the vampiric *femme fatale*, a female character who tends to be beautiful, mysterious and dangerous for men to be around, but who does not literally drink the blood of her victims. In all the tales compiled here, the metaphorical processes of exsanguination or suffering extend to the male characters to differing degrees, displacing the locus of horror and altering the expected gendered implications of her representation. The reader is therefore encouraged to look beyond her body and behaviours as the source of immorality or exploitation. Female sexual desire is presented in such a way that questions social norms, expresses a disillusionment with societal or ideological structures, or challenges gender differences, stereotypes and hierarchy. Moreover, whereas original gothic novels tended to set their plots in distant times or places to play out fears over the return (or lingering) of the 'barbaric' past, these tales are set in the here and now and, either explicitly or assumedly, in their countries of origin, thus forming a clearer connection between modern processes and society's problems.

Another common theme in the tales is that of sickness and contagion. This is of course typical of vampire literature, a trend that at the turn of the twentieth century revealed fears over race and degeneration, but also fears over sex and gender, as Alexandra Warwick has noted.[63] Yet, the illnesses developed in these tales parody earlier female vampire models. Illnesses ranging from the 'romantic' (Lugones's and de Burgos's tales) to the physical (Lugones's, Palma's and de Burgos's tales) to the psychological (Palma's, de Hoyos's and Quiroga's tales) all reposition the source of the illness outside the vampiric *femme fatale*; in some cases, they even affect her and result in her own death or suffering, furthering her sympathetic portrayal.

All in all, whereas challenges to the bourgeois ideal of wife- and motherhood usually perish alongside the perverse gendered imaginary that is the female vampire's body, these five stories show sympathy towards the figure, directly challenging the bourgeois moral code that encompassed gender relations, sexuality and appropriate 'spaces' for men and women. And precisely where these tales do differ, such as in their degree of feminist inclination, gothic influence or mixing of other literary modes or trends—from

xxvii

INTRODUCTION

modernismo to melodrama to science fiction—they all point to unique attributes of Latin American and Spanish gothic traditions: they are subversive, disruptive and interrelated traditions that break from European and US models in meaningful and innovative ways. In doing so, they carve out a space for themselves as both distinctly modern and distinctly Hispanic, as the two are not mutually exclusive.

INTRODUCTORY ESSAYS TO
THE TALES IN THIS COLLECTION

The Female Vampire (1899)[64]

Leopoldo Lugones (1874–1938) is arguably one of the most influential, respected and critically studied authors of modern Latin American literature. He has been heralded as one of the leading figures of *modernismo*, a pioneer of science and pseudoscience fiction, and a major influence on the fantastic mode that would develop in the River Plate later in the twentieth century. Some of his most important works include the poetry collections *Las montañas del oro* [The mountains of gold] (1897) and *El libro de los paisajes* [The book of landscapes] (1917), and the short story collection *Las fuerzas extrañas* [*Strange Forces*] (1906). According to Jorge Luis Borges: 'The literature of America is still nourished by the work of this great writer; to write well is, for many, to write like Lugones.'[65] That said, his legacy is also marked by extreme and swift-changing political ideologies.

Lugones was born on 13 June 1874, in Villa María del Río Seco, a small town in Córdoba, Argentina.[66] By the age of eighteen, he had published his first work and was directing his first journal, the anticlerical and libertarian *El pensamiento libre* [Free thought]. He soon began to tackle social causes such as student strikes, and later founded a socialist organisation and literary journal.[67] After World War I, his perspective on socialism changed and he began to embrace an anti-democratic political ideology grounded in nationalism and, eventually, militarism.[68] David Rock argues that Lugones emerged as a 'leading Nationalist figure', although he eventually became disillusioned with his party and was rumored to have embraced religion near the end of his life.[69] On 18 February 1938, Lugones poisoned himself in a hotel room in Tigre, Argentina. The factors that contributed to his death continue to be debated by scholars.

Prior to this anthology, the sole place 'La vampira' ['The Female Vampire'] could be accessed was in a rare collection of facsimile reproductions of original newspaper clippings, *Las primeras letras de Leopoldo Lugones: reproducción facsimilar de sus primeros trabajos literarios escritos entre sus dieciocho y veinticinco años* [The early writing of Leopoldo Lugones: a facsimile reproduction of his first literary works written between the ages of eighteen and twenty-five].[70] Yet, as mentioned above, Buenos Aires experienced a periodical 'mania' that began as early as the mid-nineteenth century,[71] suggesting that this story was read widely at the time of its origi-

xxviii

THE TALES IN THIS COLLECTION

nal publication in 1899, and that readership may have extended to other Latin American countries and even to Spain. The collection of facsimile reproductions as a whole evidences that Lugones was steadily engaged with contemporary debates on socialism and 'the woman question'. He was not a feminist *per se*, but his two essays on women, published in the same decade as 'The Female Vampire', reveal sympathetic attitudes towards women and their struggles. For example, in 'La cuestión feminista' [The feminist question] (1897),[72] Lugones argues that Woman is not organically inferior to Man but has been made inferior by socio-historical processes. While 'The Female Vampire' encourages a sympathetic reading of the female vampire character on its own, the implications of which are elaborated below, it can be suggested that his essays on women only further support such a reading.

'The Female Vampire' tells the tragic love story of Adolfo and an unnamed female character whose description aligns with Pre-Raphaelite and *modernista* images of women, as well as the vampiric *femme fatale*.[73] In line with Pre-Raphaelite artistic conventions, she is passive and at times expressionless, while the description of her eyes as golden and her body as both marble-like and sumptuous aligns with *modernista* aesthetics. Her *femme fatale* characteristics include her tall and majestic stature, beauty, piercing eyes and seductive nature, as well as being a wealthy widow with a mysterious past. Several of these characteristics also align her with the female vampire, as do her animal-like qualities and her draining men of their life-force. Adolfo feels possessed by this 'terrible woman' who has managed to provoke feelings of both love and fear in him: 'Indeed, her love was a demon that consumed both his mind and his soul. He had battled it for a year to no avail.'[74] She is also a constant theme in local gossip owing to her conduct: spendthrift with her husband's money and a heartbreaker with a history of spurned lovers. She is, thus, the ultimate consumer—of both men and their money—a representation that aligns with fears of the time concerning women as both sexually and economically threatening. As the story unfolds, however, her characterisation becomes more complex, ironic and even sympathetic. While for the narrator the woman is 'terrible', the reader is encouraged to consider her a victim—not just of the men in her life, but of greater social standards and power dynamics. The implications of this are multifaceted. While 'The Female Vampire' is possibly the first sympathetic female vampire narrative, it relies on a combination of literary conventions and traditions to contend with marital, relationship and broader social anxieties, thus serving as an effective case study of how gothic forms have been successfully adopted and adapted outside European and Anglo literary traditions.

Although Adolfo's death is not at the hands (or at the bloodied mouth) of a fanged vampire, 'The Female Vampire' clearly belongs to the late nineteenth-century female vampire tradition. She is violent, engages in energy-sucking behaviour and, like many vampiric *femmes fatales* before her and after, possesses animal characteristics that highlight her proximity to the

xxix

INTRODUCTION

savage, natural world. She is referred to as a sphinx and a lioness, and also presented as a snake-woman. As she is about to kiss Adolfo in the final scene, the narrator describes how her masculine side takes over her senses, provoking a film to cover her eyes. This trait is typical of the snake-woman legend, but also of the vampire right before she attacks her prey.[75] Interestingly, '[o]ne of the earliest female vampires on record is the Babylonian snake-goddess Lilitu, who was later borrowed by the Hebrews for their own traditional lore and renamed Lilith.'[76] There is also a correlation between her and the moon, typical in vampire literature of the Romantic and Victorian eras,[77] yet here the author's lexical choice of 'crepuscular opal' aligns with *modernista* aesthetics as well.[78] The titular character also coresponds with Poe's images of mysterious and beautiful women: 'In Poe, the idea of beauty is fused with those of femininity and death. Femininity materialises in a mysterious being, sensual yet lifeless and deathly pale.'[79] The tale therefore dialogues with both the mythological and literary vampire traditions, but it also challenges them in interesting ways.

The most significant way that this tale subverts the vampiric *femme fatale* tradition is through its treatment of consumption, which can be understood in relation to the late nineteenth-century fascination with the occult. Blavatskian Theosophy was a major influence on occult beliefs; moreover, Lugones himself was a devout believer.[80] He was admitted to the Theosophical Society of Buenos Aires in 1898,[81] contributed to *Philadelphia*, a Buenos Aires newspaper that diffused this type of thinking,[82] and concluded his otherwise fictional collection *Las fuerzas extrañas* with 'Ensayo de una cosmogonía en diez lecciones' [An essay on cosmogony in ten sections].[83] Modern occultists believed in a natural cosmic harmony, and soul transmigration offered the possibility of attaining it. As Beth Pollack notes: 'Transmigration is not simply rebirth into another body, it is an opportunity to perfect one's essence. One lifetime is insufficient to learn everything and attain cosmic harmony.'[84] Curiously, gender plays a significant role in this process: 'One physical form is not sufficient because "the psycho-physical experience of a male is totally dissimilar to that of a female, and it is essential to have both if half of a fundamental experience is not to be missed"'. Here lies the crux of 'The Female Vampire': if transmigration allows for the possibility of natural cosmic harmony, and he is the one executing the action,[85] then he is continuing to live in and ultimately control the body of his wife. This prompts a series of important questions, such as who is responsible for Adolfo's death, she or her husband, and what does this suggest of gender formation and identity? If she is not responsible, and therefore does not represent the typical anxieties concerning female sexual and economic autonomy, then what *does* she represent? And if soul transmigration is conceived of in a positive light in occultist circles, why does it go so tragically wrong in the story? As Pollack observes—in reference to *Las fuerzas extrañas,* but equally applicable here—'Lugones' characters reflect his belief in a series of lives as a means for attaining oneness with the

XXX

THE TALES IN THIS COLLECTION

universe.'[86] But this 'oneness', in the case of the story at hand, in addition to recognising alternative conceptions of the natural and supernatural worlds, confirms the absurdity of the masculinisation and feminisation of feelings and behaviours, and even draws attention to the vulnerable and exploited state of women that Lugones articulates in his essays from 1893 and 1897.[87]

Her character's association with consumption is one of the most significant ways that the text illuminates the blurring of boundaries between victim and vampire. The correlation between sexual and economic consumption has been discussed in several studies on the representation of women in the *fin-de-siècle* literary landscape. For example, according to Lana L. Dalley and Jill Rappoport, '[w]hether women were represented as preying upon blood or consuming extravagantly in general, their presumed failure to manage their households with restraint was seen as threatening the stability of the bourgeois family.'[88] When the female vampire is initially described, she is portrayed as being spendthrift with her husband's money, but is she really the ultimate consumer in the story? It could be suggested that even though she is at first portrayed as such—hyperbolically, which only highlights the superficiality of her image—she conforms more to the idealised bourgeois woman than to the female vampire:

> For Ruskin and other commentators on the Victorian discourse of proper womanhood, the idealized woman does not, vampirelike, clamor for her fair share of comestibles. She is instead a source of consumption for others—a fertile, maternal, lactating body, with a free-flowing supply of fluid sustenance.[89]

The titular character may be cold and beautiful with a mysterious and deadly past, but she is also motherly, not solely in the sense that the vampiric relationship is akin to that of intrauterine existence (as victim and vampire are bound by the sharing of blood),[90] but also in the sense that her body is a source of comfort and serves as a 'home' for her husband, one which he 'occupies' after his death. Her husband forces her to abandon the traditional role of wife for a non-traditional role of mother, wherein her free-flowing supply of sustenance is her body, her thoughts, her happiness and ultimately her consciousness, as the narrator reveals that she suffered an epileptic attack from which she has yet to recover after strangling Adolfo.[91] Given that her body hosts her husband, allowing him to influence her thoughts and behaviours, it seems more appropriate to consider her a victim of consumption or vamping rather than a consumer or vampire herself.

In addition to being a source of consumption for her husband, she is also one for society at large. Through her, the townspeople create their own versions of reality, but even more troublingly their own versions of her, projecting onto her what they believe constitutes a rich widow. Ironically, in the same sentence that describes her spending as wasteful and unprecedented, the narrator reveals that she is also a victim of gossip: 'Her behaviour was fodder for gossip in certain circles' (p. 3). She is therefore an image that does not correspond to an actual reality: a stereotype perpetu-

xxxi

INTRODUCTION

ated through gossip for which there is no proven foundation. By portraying her as both the consumed and the consumer—the idealised wife/mother and the vampiric *femme fatale*—Lugones creates a grey area for both expression and understanding that challenges the idea of binary oppositions as an unequivocal truth.

The final scene supports the idea that her husband, a colonel, is the real vampire. The story begins to hint at this in the descriptions of their love, his illness and his soul's transmigration, and later, during the scene in the garden, where right before she asks Adolfo to leave, she feels her husband's presence taking over as a result of his jealousy and rage. She and Adolfo are in love, but her husband's feelings are in stark contrast to this: he sees her as his possession instead of an equal, which juxtaposes women's and men's feelings and behaviours. It is in the final scene, however, where the battle of the sexes comes to a head. Adolfo's death is violent and unexpected, solidifying the tragic and ironic tone of the story, but it is also the point in which the colonel finally takes over his wife's body. She decided to lean in and kiss Adolfo because '[t]hat moment's peace overcame her repugnance' (p. 6). Here, Woman (peace) has triumphed over Man (hatred)—but not for long enough: 'The hostility she harboured within suddenly overcame her with the force of a hurricane. Her eyes filmed over.' (p. 6) This hostility arguably derives from her husband, who activates a rage within his wife that provokes a film to cover her eyes, anticipating his attack. In this scenario, it is not she who strangles Adolfo but her husband. As such, the title of the story is as problematic and illusory as the image first constructed of her.

'The Female Vampire' juxtaposes masculine and feminine desire in an ironic way, challenging the idea that feminine desire is destructive while questioning the ideological constructs of Man and Woman. Even though the initial descriptions seem to conform her to the late nineteenth-century image of the vampiric *femme fatale*, these are later exposed as part of a parodic representation that conveys the illusoriness of gender constructions. Traits such as her tortuous allure, coldness, animal-like characteristics and fatal past are overshadowed by her warnings to Adolfo, love as the motivation of her actions, the exploitation of her body and her continuous suffering as a victim. Elisabeth Bronfen writes that 'Woman comes to represent the margins or extremes of the norm—the extremely good, pure and helpless, or the extremely dangerous, chaotic and seductive. The saint or the prostitute; the Virgin Mary or Eve.'[92] Curiously, Man also comes to represent the extremes of the norm in 'The Female Vampire': the extremely aggressive, impatient and exploitative (the husband/colonel), and the extremely weak, lovesick victim (Adolfo). In an ironic turn of events, a woman strangles a man, but the most absurd aspect about this is that it was her husband's aggressions that made her do it, therefore dismantling the image of the *femme fatale* altogether. The story communicates that, while this beautiful and sexually experienced, rich widow may be flawed, she is not the cause of late nineteenth-century society's problems. The text also

xxxii

THE TALES IN THIS COLLECTION

clearly dialogues with Theosophy, and soul transmigration in particular. The constructs of Woman and Man are exaggerated in a battle in which Man eventually triumphs, but this triumph leads to death and disorder, articulating the idea that the exploitation of women, albeit through soul transmigration, leads to disharmony, not natural cosmic harmony. In this tale, a *modernista* fascination with beauty, harmony and the occult intersects with a gothic fascination of the vampire in such a way that challenges the vampiric *femme fatale* tradition and broader norms and stereotypes inherent to bourgeois patriarchal society.

The White Farmhouse[93]

Clemente Palma (1872–1946) was a Peruvian writer, founder of a literary journal, cultural magazine and newspaper, a library curator, Peruvian consul to Barcelona and a doctor of letters (1897) and law (1899).[94] Since his writings were so difficult to obtain outside of his native Peru, he was practically unknown beyond its borders until the late twentieth century. Yet even within his native country, he had always been overshadowed by the literary career of his famous father, Ricardo Palma (1833–1919). Clemente was also a political activist. A fervent supporter of Augusto B. Leguia during his second term as president of Peru (1919–1930), he was politically persecuted by Luis Sánchez Cerro, the colonel who overthrew Leguia, and eventually exiled to Chile in 1932, where he continued to work in journalism (NMK, 19). In 1933, Sánchez Cerro was assassinated, so Palma returned to Peru, living the rest of his life largely out of the political spotlight.

Palma's literary contributions span themes and genres: from political and sociological essays, poetry, literary theory and criticism, and a text on Peruvian culture,[95] to short stories and novels that demonstrate a *fin-de-siglo* affinity for the gothic and the occult. As Mora observes: 'The Peruvian's dead beauties and their vampire traits align him with the Gothic cultivated by Poe as well as Baudelairean Decadence.'[96] His most well-known literary contributions are two collections of short stories, *Cuentos malévolos* [Malevolent Tales] (1904 and 1912) and *Historietas malignas* [Evil vignettes] (1925), the novella *Mors ex vita* [Death from life] (1918) and the science fiction novel *XYZ* (1934). As is the case with all the tales in this anthology, many of Palma's stories also fall into the realm of the fantastic, and Palma is widely considered the founder of the fantastic short story in Peru.[97]

'La granja blanca' ['The White Farmhouse'], which appeared in both the original and reprint version of *Cuentos malévolos*, opens with a dedication to Emilia Pardo Bazán, a Spanish author and feminist, and a contemporary of Palma's. This paratextual element draws attention to the transatlantic dialogue between Latin American and Spanish writers of the time,[98] and anticipates the similarities between this story and so many of Pardo Bazán's gothic-inspired tales. The tale also adheres to a *fin-de-siglo* mood typical of French Decadence. For example, in its expression of anxieties over existence and mortality through a pessimistic attitude, grounded in a disillu-

xxxiii

INTRODUCTION

sionment with modern-day science, which was unable to fill the void created by the transition from a religious to a secular society. Cordelia's sickness, coupled with her pallor and coldness, adhere to the Pre-Raphaelite models of beauty later adopted by the Decadents, further aligning Palma's story with their penchant for death and decay. Nancy M. Kason suggests that this attitude, present in Hispanic modernism in general, reflects the changing philosophical currents dominated by Nietzsche, Kierkegaard, Tolstoy and others, which influenced the literary and spiritual crisis of the late nineteenth century (NMK, 33). Kason's point draws attention to the overlap between Decadence and *modernismo*, literary movements that developed almost simultaneously in Latin America. Similarly, José Miguel Oviedo describes Palma as a Decadent and a *modernista*, noting that his taste for satanism, esotericism, horror and abnormal psychologies set him apart from his contemporaries.[99] It is Mora, though, who suggests there is a particular gothic–decadent vein in Latin American *modernismo* that better explains the literary tendencies and intertextuality at play in Palma's works.[100] In several of her articles, Mora casts *Cuentos malévolos* as a direct challenge to bourgeois art and ideology, urging the reader to recognise female sexuality as a lesser evil than the cruel and more harmful behaviours alongside which it appears in the collection. Referring specifically to 'The White Farmhouse', Mora suggests that the subversive exploration of necrophilia and female sexual desire question social norms.[101] The present analysis contributes to this scholarly dialogue by suggesting that the text is an early example of a sympathetic female vampire character that draws on European and American vampiric *femme fatale* models in ways that challenge social institutions and outdated moral codes.

The story is divided into ten sections that span more than two years, beginning with a philosophical debate into whether humans exist as autonomous beings or solely in the dreams of 'some eternal sleeper'. This theme is addressed in the last section as well, thus framing the narrative, which explains why studies on this story have focused so much attention on dreams, mental states and questions of life and death. From the second section on, the story revolves around the narrator and Cordelia, his cousin and fiancée. The two share an intense romance and appear to live only for each other. One month before their nuptials, Cordelia becomes ill with malaria and dies. Notice of her death causes the narrator to faint and hit his head, prompting a possible delusion where Cordelia returns to health, and they marry. They move into the titular white farmhouse together, an old mansion belonging to his family that had gone uninhabited for over two centuries, and have a daughter, also named Cordelia. They appear to live a happy life, but strange events begin to occur. One night, Cordelia disappears, and the arrival of a philosophy teacher the following day casts doubt as to whether she had ever lived at the farmhouse at all. When the narrator shows him their child as proof, they both become convinced that she is Cordelia reborn. Then, the philosophy teacher, fearing a possible future incestuous relation-

xxxiv

THE TALES IN THIS COLLECTION

ship with her father, throws little Cordelia out the window, where she is later devoured by the encroaching wolves. The next morning, the narrator sets fire to their home with their deaf servant still inside, and rides away alone. In setting the marital home ablaze, Palma directly attacks the bourgeois ideological construct of the home as a symbol of stability, family, marriage, love and morality. Moreover, by linking the home with vampirism, incest, insanity, delusion and murder, the story appears to encourage the reader to ask: can marriages survive under a new moral code, outside the confines of a religious society? And is the marital ideal even possible, or simply illusory? In a break from earlier female vampire tales' concern with immorality, disease, race and so forth, 'The White Farmhouse' challenges the status quo by rendering the social structures of marriage and family obsolete, and it does so without proposing any alternatives.

The tale nods intertextually to its vampiric *femme fatale* predecessors, inviting a reading of Cordelia as a female vampire. Cordelia exhibits traits that liken her to Dracula's wives and Carmilla: beautiful, manipulative, sharing possible ties to the Devil, sensual—with 'red lips' and a 'feverish sparkle' to her eyes—and a voracious sexual appetite. Moreover, her husband observes that 'there was something strange in her remarkable beauty' (p. 8). Mora suggests that Cordelia's blonde hair and delicate nature are a departure from the more common dark-haired vampire, with which Poe's Ligeia aligns, but notes that the two female characters are similar in their 'strangeness'.[102] The idea that Cordelia and her daughter might also be one in the same could be a nod to Poe's 'Morella',[103] while the various references to Cordelia's likeness to the eponymous girl in Gerbrand van den Eeckhout's painting *La resurrección de la hija de Jairo* [*The Resurrection of Jairus's daughter*] (c. 1663), invites a parallel between her and Le Fanu's 'Carmilla'. According to Laura, the narrator in 'Carmilla', the titular character looks very much like the woman in a painting in her home dated almost two centuries prior, but not until Carmilla's true motives are revealed to the narrator does she understand that they are in fact the same woman. It can similarly be understood that the various references to Jairus's daughter not only serve to anticipate Cordelia's resurrection, as other critics have noted,[104] but also suggest that the two are one in the same. Cordelia's illness and possible resurrection also hark back to earlier representations of female vampires, such as the titular characters in several of Poe's female vampire tales and *Dracula*'s Lucy Westenra. Indeed, Cordelia gives the impression that she 'was dead, that she was incorporeal' (p. 9). Cordelia may also be cold-blooded; at one point, her husband feels 'a current of ice-cold blood pass through her veins' (p. 13). While this garners her a reptilian quality that further aligns her with Lucy, who is associated with Medusa, it also inserts Cordelia into the longstanding tradition of associating female vampires with reptiles that dates back to the Babylonian snake-goddess Lilitu.

While Cordelia appears to align with her female vampire predecessors, 'The White Farmhouse' also portrays her sympathetically. The narrator

XXXV

INTRODUCTION

lovingly notes how she would initiate hide-and-seek games that ended in 'long' kisses, and he is not fearful of her sexuality after they are married. By permitting Cordelia sexual agency, her representation dismantles the virgin/seductress dichotomy more commonly associated with male-authored vampire literature of the time.[105] According to Amanda Raye DeWees: 'A bride's innocent appearance may only conceal a tendency to sexual predation or a character unfit for motherhood, probably the two cardinal sins for nineteenth-century females.'[106] Yet in this case, the narrator seems more pleased than horrified by his wife's sexual nature, challenging the idea that marital sex is merely for reproductive purposes. Cordelia is also described as a loving wife and a tender, doting mother, therefore fully realising both her socially assigned and 'natural' roles as a woman in bourgeois patriarchal society, further complicating the virgin/seductress and victim/vampire dichotomies. Even the scene in the tale where the narrator senses 'ice-cold blood pass through her veins' complicates her representation. Upon learning it was their second wedding anniversary, she shuddered, suggesting that Cordelia could be terrified of what is happening to her, and thus, not fully in control. This lack of control can also be noted in her physical and emotional reactions to her self-portrait, suggesting an inversion of the roles of vampire and victim. As José Miguel Sardiñas suggests: 'The described effect that Cordelia's dedication to painting has on her coincides with the victim of a vampire: she retreats pale, exhausted, melancholic.'[107] A nod to Poe's 'The Oval Portrait' (1842), what is most interesting about this exchange is that she reluctantly agrees to paint herself at her husband's request. His insistence therefore ties him to the vampiric act, which is in turn tied to the dissolution of their marriage. While Cordelia thus shares many traits with her female vampire predecessors, the tale's vampire logic can be argued to extend far beyond Cordelia's body and behaviour.

In its blurring of the lines between victim and vampire, the story does not appear to take a clear stance on Good versus Evil. While this is typical of Decadence and the pessimistic attitude it so often projects, it is rare for a vampire tale at the turn of the century. Numerous critics have argued that there are suggestions of a pact between both Cordelia and the Devil, and the narrator and the Devil. The narrator's mention of Cordelia whispering to an invisible someone, possibly pleading for more time, does suggest a pact between her and the Devil, as does Cordelia's terrified reaction upon learning the date (namely, because her time here is up). In the case of a pact between the narrator and the Devil, Cordelia's sickness pushes him to both curse and plead with the powers that be:

> My lips formed curses and blessings, blasphemy and prayer, demanding Cordelia's return to health. It did not matter whether it was God or the Devil who granted it. All I wanted was Cordelia healthy. I would have bought it with my soul, my life, my fortune. I would have committed the most foul and criminal acts. (p. 10)

xxxvi

THE TALES IN THIS COLLECTION

Thus, the Devil could have granted him his wish, resulting in his mental breakdown and demise, but the pessimistic attitude and ambiguity suggest otherwise. Whereas, within feudal and Catholic society, the Devil was blamed for humans' immoral or harmful behaviour, within secular society regulated by capitalist modes of production, the blame has turned inward, understood as a manifestation of man's animal nature.[108] While this idea of an inherent animality helps explain how the narrator could have made such an abrupt shift from a loving, sentimental husband and father to an 'empty' (souless) murderer, the concept is arguably extendable to the structures that sustain contemporary civilisation, especially within the framework of a *fin-de-siglo* disillusionment with society and modernity. The concept also helps explain Cordelia's sensuality, which, while not in line with moral standards of the day, is permissible because it is natural and pleasurable.

Whereas the vampire figure in earlier gothic fiction tends to support a moral code, Palma's text seeks to question or even dismantle the moral code embedded within bourgeois ideology. Mora argues that the text warns of the dangers of conceiving Good and Evil as fixed concepts that do not change over time.[109] Indeed, and this helps explain why the text treats the female vampire trope sympathetically: she questions an outdated moral code and its restrictive dichotomies. As a result, the social institutions that rely on these dichotomies to function, particularly marriage and the nuclear family, are challenged. In the end, it appears that the marital ideal is as illusory as Cordelia herself.

Mr Cadaver and Miss Vampire (1910)

Antonio de Hoyos y Vinent (*c.* 1884–1940),[110] though a widely read and highly regarded Spanish author during the first few decades of the twentieth century (ACC, 102), is currently not nearly as well known as the other authors included in this anthology. Literary critics have reckoned this is due to his 'erasure' after the Spanish Civil War (1936–1939) and during the conservative, nationalist Franco Regime (1939–1975) (ACC, 102). De Hoyos was not only an openly gay man (JASR, 61, n. 40), but also an anarchist who wrote scathing articles for the journal *El Sindicalista* [The Unionist]. He was jailed by the Nationalists after the war and died shortly thereafter in prison (ACC, 105).

De Hoyos was a prolific author who wrote criticism, essays, plays, short fiction and novels, with his novels receiving the most attention in the small cluster of scholarship (mostly dissertations) that focus on his life and literary works. He was born into the Spanish aristocracy, which 'left an indelible mark on his spirit and the nature of his esthetic inclinations' (JASR, 23; my translation). Fascinated by the cosmopolitan and luxurious lifestyle of the aristocracy, he was equally fascinated by the lower strata of society, particularly the urban underworld (ACC, 108), often bridging the two in his literary works to create scenes of excess and subversion. As María del Carmen Alfonso García observes, de Hoyos's literature aspires to unite op-

xxxvii

INTRODUCTION

posites such as good and evil, brutality and pleasure.[111] His novels have mostly been categorised as erotic and/or Decadent, while Lee Six has gone beyond the established position of relating early twentieth-century Spanish literature to French models by reading two of his tales through a global gothic lens via the vampire metaphor (ALS, 173–88).

'El señor Cadáver y la señorita Vampiro' ['Mr Cadaver and Miss Vampire'] appears to have first been published in the collection *Del huerto del pecado* [From the garden of sin] (1910), and not previously in a literary magazine. *Del huerto del pecado* was the first of two short story collections penned by de Hoyos, the second being *El pecado y la noche* [Sin and the night] (1913). During this period, the treatment of sin permeates his work and conforms to the contemporary sensibilities of the erotic novel prevailing in Spain (ACC, 102), as well as the vestiges of Decadence visible in Spanish and Latin American literature of the early decades of the twentieth century. As mentioned above, de Hoyos was widely read, but he was also broadly celebrated amongst his renowned literary peers. Emilia Pardo Bazán (1851–1921) wrote the prologue for two of his books, Juan Valera (1824–1905) wrote a review of one, and Vicente Blasco Ibáñez (1867–1928), Jacinto Benavente y Martínez (1866–1954) and Miguel de Unamuno (1864–1936) all wrote prologues for different novels (ACC, 102). Given de Hoyos's popularity, it is likely that his first collection of stories, published seven years after his first novel and including a prologue written by Pardo Bazán, was well received and widely read.

In this collection, de Hoyos makes it clear that he was well read while situating himself within global and local literary traditions. Many of the tales contain epigraphs from famous literary works by the likes of William Shakespeare (1564–1616) and Edgar Allan Poe (1809–1849), and the epigraph for the tale at hand is a verse from Charles Baudelaire's (1821–1867) poem 'Le Vampire' from *Les Fleurs du mal* [Flowers of Evil] (1857). The collection is divided into sections, and de Hoyos dedicates one of them to Pardo Bazán, another to Ramón María del Valle-Inclán (1866–1936) and, even more relevant to this study, another to Nicaraguan author Rubén Darío (1867–1916). Darío was one of the pioneers of Latin American *modernismo*, a writer of several tales of terror, including the female vampire tale 'Thanathopia' (1893), and a considerable influence on de Hoyos. De Hoyos once stated that he admired Darío so much that *Prosas profanas* (Profane hymns, 1896), Darío's influential and highly acclaimed book of poems, was his 'breviary' (JASR 323, n. 346). This connection is important because it encourages a shift from a Spanish and Eurocentric gaze on de Hoyos's literary production to a transhispanic one, thus helping situate de Hoyos within a specific gothic-*modernista* trend of depicting sympathetic vampiric *femmes fatales*.

While not a characteristically gothic tale, gothic strategies nonetheless abound in 'Mr Cadaver and Miss Vampire'. These include the author's lexical choices: 'haunting', 'macabre', 'lugubrious', 'monstrous', 'shudder', 'myste-

xxxviii

THE TALES IN THIS COLLECTION

rious', and so on; the cultivation of the sublime aesthetic through phrasing and resulting imagery such as the 'crunching of bones' (p. 23); nightmarish theatrical scenes of disfigured bodies and other disturbing images; direct references to Poe and E. T. A. Hoffman (1776–1822); death-like states; and the association of vampirism with sex, exsanguination and death. The tale's title underscores the female vampire trope and even suggests her alignment with earlier models, but the text itself complicates reader expectations and produces what could be the first sympathetic female vampire in Spanish literature. As Lee Six suggests, the tale is left open to interpretation as to whether it was all 'a cruel game she enjoyed of ruining men's lives or maybe, just maybe, a life of serial desertions by men whom she throws into a panic and scares off unintentionally' (ALS, 182). Lee Six argues that the latter interpretation is supported by a 'perceptible gulf between the internal narrator's interpretation of the characters and events on the one hand, and a subtler, more ambiguous picture that is discernible over his head'. This in turn is supported by considering another one of de Hoyos's tales that clearly sympathises with the plight of vulnerable women in pre-welfare-state Spain (ALS, 185).

On the surface, Miss Vampire appears to conform to the previous century's literary female vampire model. She is beautiful and alluring, yet linked to death and rot; has a hypnotising quality and a mysterious past; appears to be motivated by sexual desire and money; and travels from one cosmopolitan setting to another (Venice, Madrid, Paris)—thus encoding fears of the time concerning immigration, sickness and contagion, including sexually transmitted diseases. Lee Six notes how the tale also appears to align with preoccupations concerning male disempowerment, so evident in earlier representations such as Raupach's 'Wake Not the Dead' and Gautier's 'Clarimonde':

> To liken human women to supernatural ones such as these suggests that the men who fall in love with them feel (whether justifiably or not) that they are victims, prey and the horror effect resides in their believing themselves robbed of their masculine agency by the women's seductive power. (ALS, 174)

Yet let us not forget about the 'perceptible gulf' between the narrator's interpretation and the bigger picture at hand, which can be defended not only with extratextual support, but also with substantial textual evidence.

From the first depictions of the theatregoers, the male narrator exaggerates and criticises everything around him. He then extends this perspective to the performers, and eventually, to Miss Vampire, lending her representation an air of incredulity. If he perceives everything to be distorted and perverse, how is the reader supposed to accept his perceptions about a woman whom he himself acknowledges pursuing, not the other way around? He admits to 'my besieging of the dangerous beauty', as if she were his target, which problematises his earlier assumption: 'my gut was telling me that, for this woman, men were just that: targets of her pleasure-seeking and greed, something that she would destroy, annihilate, and then abandon in a miser-

INTRODUCTION

able wreck.' (p. 24) In this same scene, which is his first up-close encounter with her, he tellingly notes how she resonated 'a powerful life force, such an intense joy, a reflection of passion, will, and power that I found both *fascinating and frightening* at the same time' (pp. 23–24; original emphasis). On the surface, this depiction seems to support a more traditional reading of Miss Vampire, one that aligns with fears spurred by the heightened presence of the New Woman in the public sphere nearing the end of the nineteenth century. A closer reading, however, reveals a mockery of those same fears. Here, de Hoyos is directly highlighting how the more alive, joyous, sexual and powerful a woman is, the more frightening she becomes, for she is a direct threat to the moral code and public/private distinction inherent to bourgeois patriarchal society.

The tale's denouement also challenges the European literary female vampire model. When the narrator first begins to awaken, he is caught somewhere between dream and reality, in a state of 'odd happiness' that becomes more painful the more he feels it (p. 24). He forces himself fully awake, and then feelings of heaviness, immense fatigue and confusion overcome him. This initial description relies on the gothic strategies of cultivating suspense, mystery and the Sublime, and harks back to even the earliest depictions of female vampires. As Nancy Schumann posits, Lilith left men exhausted by not only draining them of their blood, but also their semen.[112] The specific *fin-de-siècle* context is also significant, as this was a period when female sexual desire was increasingly regarded by physicians and psychologists as a problematic behaviour that required treatment.[113] The tale appears to align with these earlier models as well as medical discourses circulating at the time, for he determines: 'I was Mr Cadaver and lying beside me on the wide bed of a banal hotel room was Miss Vampire!' (p. 24) He has come to the conclusion that he is but another in a long line of victims, and yet, as he contemplates her body, she is the one who appears sick, even cadaver-like: laying cold and stiff, she has lost her 'principal charm', her face is alabaster-white, she has bags under her eyes, and there is a 'strange rotting smell emanat[ing] from her scarlet lips' (p. 25). Lee Six suggests that this description hints at disease, and more specifically, at the fear of sexually transmitted diseases (ALS, 177), but it can also encourage an against-the-grain reading wherein she is the victim of not only this one man, but society at large. Quite tellingly, the narrator states she has lost her 'principal charm', echoing the misogynistic, even predatory, pretence that women lose their 'charm' once men's sexual curiosities have been satisfied. This description is also suggestive of the incredibly high expectations placed on women's appearance in patriarchal society: a 'beautiful creature' at night and from afar, but up close and under scrutiny she is simply not as appealing. The tale therefore points to the superficiality and arbitrariness of double standards, contributing to Miss Vampire's sympathetic portrayal.

The narrator's resulting actions further support this reading. Not only is he able to get out of bed, presumably unscathed both physically and

THE TALES IN THIS COLLECTION

monetarily,[114] but he also comes to embody the character trait that had supposedly frightened him so much about Miss Vampire: identify a target to then 'abandon in a miserable wreck' (p. 24). Supposedly thrown into a 'panic' by her 'repulsive iciness', he abandons her sleeping body, and the tale ends with the line, 'I set out for Constantinople that same night' (p. 25). While her sudden and silent abandonment speaks to the disposability of women in patriarchal society, the fact that the tale ends with a reference to the site of his next jaunt suggests that it is the narrator who moves from one urban setting to the next to satisfy his own desires and evade the consequences. Indeed, he is the one who pursued her, the one who abandoned her, and the one who views the world through an erotic and distorted lens, lending weight to a reading where Miss Vampire is the real victim, and not a vampire at all. At the same time, the text also seems to suggest that men's fears concerning sex and female sexual desire are outdated in a secular and decadent society. As he contemplates her cold body, the narrator 'thought of the tragic mystic legends of the Middle Ages, in which, by a miracle of God, beautiful women would become cold statues in the arms of sacrilegious monks tempted by Satan' (p. 25). Reading the tale as a satire of earlier female vampire models, this particular intertextual reference can also be argued to satirise the religious and didactic literature that warned men of the dangers of lust.

In addition to the more obvious gothic tropes that are relevant to this study and its aim of establishing a trend of sympathetic female vampire characters in the first decades of the twentieth century, this tale, like the others in this collection, highlights the many (at times seemingly conflicting) literary currents and artistic trends circulating at the time: from the fantastic to Decadence to *modernismo*.[115] Whether or not *modernismo* influenced the Spanish literary landscape to a significant degree is a thorny subject, arguably a result of Spanish authors—and even contemporary Spanish scholars—having propagated the false claim that Rubén Darío was Spanish and not Nicaraguan.[116] Yet the influence Darío and other Latin American *modernistas* had on de Hoyos are especially evident in this tale. One of the more obvious examples is de Hoyos's adorned language and lyrical tone. As Cuban author, revolutionary and early *modernista* José Martí once stated: 'Words must be resplendent like gold, light like wings, solid like marble' (cited in AG, 9). De Hoyos takes this sentiment earnestly, even conjuring images of gold and marble in his representation of Miss Vampire: golden hair, golden eyelashes, an alabaster-white complexion and marble statue body.

Olivio Jiménez contends that *modernistas* decorated their carefully curated visual imagery with brilliant colors, clearly defined lines and luxurious materials such as gold, marble, silk and gems (JOJ, 29). De Hoyos's visual imagery adheres to this model from the very first scene:

> The women were striking, curvaceous and dressed to the nines, adorned with shimmering combs in their hair and big fat diamonds in their ears.

xli

INTRODUCTION

Equally ostentatious moneylenders fluttered their sausage fingers so their rings—the spoils of some disaster—would sparkle as they caught the light. (p. 19)

The narrator's description of the theatregoers focuses on their ostentatious displays of elegance in an ironic way, conveying his amused disapproval of both materialism and the mingling of social classes. However, he is more admiring of Miss Vampire's appearance: 'her face [was] a perfect harmony of lines haloed by golden locks of hair. Her red lips were a display of voluptuousness, and two amethysts glittered beneath her golden eyelashes.' (p. 20) Gems appear again, this time in the description of the dancer interpreting Salome's Dance of the Seven Veils:

Her undulating body, unwholesome in its grace, swayed in a dizzying shimmer of gems. Between the tremble of the enigmatic emeralds, the tragic glow of the rubies—the Persian red, the colour of love, joy and life—and the pale aurora of the pearls, her nubile erect breasts were on sinful display. (p. 21)

Important to note here is the emphasis on the ruby, a likely homage to Darío's short story 'El rubí', which appeared in the collection *Azúl* [Blue] (1888).[117]

In addition to experimental lyrical prose adorned with luxurious materials and precious stones, 'Mr Cadaver and Miss Vampire' also displays a *modernista* penchant for fashion and exoticism. González notes how *modernistas* were not only concerned with language and literary technique, but also cultural cosmopolitanism, novelty and fashion (AG, 1). This is evident in the narrator's description of the female theatregoers: 'Sprinkled throughout and adding a touch of the exotic to the box seats were giant French hats worn by either a tart or a lady that was up to no good.' (p. 20) Later, the focus on clothing extends to the performers, one of which was dressed like a 'Parisian miscreant', as well as to the first Mr Cadaver, whom the narrator describes as 'reminiscent of a dandy from 1830', despite his dishevelled hair that was 'defiant to British fashions' (p. 20). These descriptions add to the setting's blending of cultural styles that speaks to *modernista* syncretism and the proclivity for recreating exotic and cosmopolitan worlds. This is most evident, however, in the performance itself:

The show was something of a history of dance over the centuries, from Salome's Dance of the Seven Veils to the dance of the *chulos* and the *apaches* [...] The evocation of the ancient world was followed by the ceremonial dances of the medieval liturgy, then the pompous genuflexions of frivolous eighteenth-century elegance, and now, finally, the perverse lasciviousness of the common people's dances. (p. 21)

As González observes, in many *modernista* short stories, 'the setting is frequently an artificial (specifically, philological) recreation of environments previously encoded in literature' (AG, 68). De Hoyos cleverly adapts this model by transposing it to a theatrical performance, drawing explicit attention to the performative elements of both literature and social status. He also clearly draws on gothic strategies as his gaze turns back to the theatregoers, whom he now sees as one distorted monstrosity: 'terri-

xlii

THE TALES IN THIS COLLECTION

fying monsters and grotesque rodents; shapeless beings and chameleons; absurd flora and fauna gathered in unlikely company, breeding other irregular beings, which, in turn, linked together in a shocking synthesis of horror.' (p. 22) In these intricate and striking representations of spectacle, cosmopolitanism meets a dark, sublime scene that weaves in erotic notes to seemingly both unsettle and engage the reader.

There is thus highly suggestive textual evidence that de Hoyos deliberately engaged both the gothic and *modernista* traditions. It is also important to note the similarities between 'Mr Cadaver and Miss Vampire' and the two tales that appear before it in this anthology: Lugones's 'The Female Vampire' (1899) and Palma's 'The White Farmhouse' (1904). Lugones was widely read and published in Spain,[118] and while there is no evidence of 'The Female Vampire' having been published on that side of the Atlantic, there is textual evidence suggesting de Hoyos was familiar with the tale. The most significant is the male narrator who tries to impose his negative view of the titular character onto the reader, even when there is evidence to the contrary. With regards to Palma's tale, it is strikingly similar in its coalescence of sex and vampirism. Palma's reads:

> It was madness, an insatiable thirst that progressed in a strange and alarming way. It was a divine and diabolical delirium, an ideal and carnal vampirism composed of both the kind and prodigal piety of a goddess and the diabolical ardor of an infernal alchemy . . . (p. 13)

And de Hoyos's reads:

> I recalled the fierce fits of insatiable desire, the erotic brutalities, the demonic whirlwind that had carried us away like a Dantean curse. The cruel, endless, life-sucking kisses, and the deep, intense, knowing caresses that destroyed the bone marrow in spasms of painful voluptuousness that felt like dying. (pp. 24–25)

The similarities in lexical arrangement and the resulting analogous images they conjure are difficult to deny.[119] As are their implications. In both tales, sex is depicted as equally brutal and pleasurable, equally desirable and diabolical, and its procreative purpose is disregarded, thus posing a direct challenge to patriarchal conservativism. Yet even more importantly, these scenes ascribe vampiric agency to both the male and female characters: note the lack of subject distinction in the first passage and the 'us' in the second. Now, as is the case with Lugones, it is unclear whether de Hoyos had read Palma, but given his adoration of Miguel de Unamuno, who wrote a prologue for one of de Hoyos's novels as well as for the collection in which 'The White Farmhouse' appears, it is extremely likely. Accordingly, it can be suggested that de Hoyos's tale takes up the gauntlet thrown down by his Latin American literary peers, delivering a sympathetic female vampire narrative thick with social criticism and literary ingenuity.

xliii

INTRODUCTION

The Cold Woman (1922)

Carmen de Burgos y Seguí (1867–1932) was a Spanish author, feminist and public figure who until the last few decades was all but erased from literary history.[120] At sixteen, de Burgos married against her family's wishes to a man twelve years her senior.[121] They had four children together, only one of whom survived infancy, and, later, as a means of gaining financial independence from her abusive husband, she decided to study teaching.[122] After she was accepted at La Escuela Normal de Maestras de Guadalajara, she separated from her husband.[123] Yet she could not obtain a legal divorce, a personal dilemma that became a social mission. As Judith Kirkpatrick notes, 'she became an outspoken advocate of legalizing divorce and of revising the penal code that was so prejudicial to women in Spain.'[124] Under the penname 'Colombine', she became a prolific author of twelve novels, over one hundred novellas and short stories, and a variety of essays on topics ranging from politics to women's etiquette and beauty.[125] In addition to contributing to several literary journals of the time, she founded her own, *Revista Crítica* [Critical review],[126] and went on to become Spain's first female journalist and war correspondent.[127] Kirkpatrick asks how it was possible for de Burgos to have been forgotten, suggesting that after the fall of the Republic, her feminist agenda had to be censored.[128] The fact that she was a woman, of course, did not help matters, as she was not considered part of the Generations of 1898 or 1927, literary categories created by and consisting of her male contemporaries.[129]

'La mujer fría' ['The Cold Woman'], a novella originally published in 1922 in the magazine *Flirt: Revista Frívola* [Flirt: frivolous review], traces the evolution of a woman from sexualised object to a subject capable of making her own sexual choices. As an inclusion for this volume, 'The Cold Woman' offers a unique take on the female vampire trope through its complex and sympathetic portrayal.[130] Moreover, it serves as a vital point of comparison to the male-authored stories, as the tale offers a significant example of how vampire literature written by women in the early twentieth century can not only question patriarchal norms and male discursive practices but go as far as acknowledging female subjectivity and supporting female autonomy. From a historical and feminist perspective, the story yields many questions. Does the fact that the author employs an already exhausted trope (the female vampire) entail that women authors are incapable of writing their own images? Does the author solely invert images to challenge the status quo, or does her reappropriation have greater implications, both within and outside the text? And finally, what is the purpose of giving Blanca a voice, a gaze and sexual agency if she just ends up broken-hearted?

Like the other tales in this anthology, Blanca's portrayal conforms—at least on the surface—to *fin-de-siècle* representations of women in cultural production. Robin Ragan argues that Blanca aligns with the Decadent movement and Pre-Raphaelite artistic images of women, while also stressing the dangerous nature of these images in the formation of beauty stand-

xliv

THE TALES IN THIS COLLECTION

ards.[131] In a similar vein, Kirkpatrick suggests that the text 'is a commentary on the dangerous images of women created by men in art and literature at the beginning of the century.'[132] Blanca is clearly a response to Decadent aesthetics, but she is also much more than that: she challenges binary oppositions, the one-dimensionality of female characters and the ways in which patriarchal society has defined Woman. From Eve and the 'angel of the house' to Lilith and the nineteenth-century *femme fatale*,[133] men have constructed different notions of Woman throughout history. Yet, as Carol Smart observes:

> Not only have there always been contradictory discursive constructs of Woman at any one time, thus allowing Woman herself to be contradictory, but the subject, Woman, is not merely subjugated; she has practised the agency of constructing her subjectivity as well.[134]

The principal way in which the tale communicates the rupture of the strict categories of Woman—thus, by extension, male discursive practices— is through the overlapping archetypes in Blanca's character. At the beginning of the novella, the omniscient narrator describes Blanca as beautiful, statue-like, passive and the object of someone else's gaze, clearly aligning with Decadent conventions. As the novella advances, however, other characteristics are introduced that complicate her categorisation: 'Those hands were frozen stiff. It wasn't the coldness of marble or of snow, but that of frozen flesh. The cold hand of death itself.' (p. 37) Here, Blanca's character has notes of vampirism, but her coldness, in addition to her having lost two husbands and two children, likens her to the snake-woman as well, another type of *femme fatale*. At one point, Don Marcelo, her longtime friend, even tells Fernando, her love interest: '"There have been men of science who have thought that a strange, cold-blooded, reptilian organism took on the form of a female human"' (p. 42). Yet as Ragan observes, 'instead of the perverse satanic being the snake woman has always represented, Blanca is a harmless, kind, loving woman,'[135] a representation at odds with typical *femmes fatales*. In her relationship with Fernando, Blanca also steps out of the confines of the archetypes that have been laid out for her by beginning to question how society views her actions. In one scene, she tells Fernando: '"It's that they don't understand that a woman who has been a wife and a mother can love with even more fervour than a girl who still doesn't know a thing about love."' (p. 36) In saying this, Blanca distinguishes between love born of desire and love born of the construction of the nuclear family and motherhood. Fernando replies that if she had not professed her love first, he would not have been able to profess his, thereby identifying her as the more active agent in their relationship. In this way, Blanca's character defies male-authored literary constructions of women by manipulating already existing tropes.

Another way the text confronts male constructs of Woman is by challenging the juxtaposition between 'the good girl' and 'the bad girl'. Fernando thinks of Edma, the young woman he abandons for Blanca, and Blanca

xlv

INTRODUCTION

as opposites: as the 'angel of the house' and the seductress, respectively. But are they really that extreme or different from one another? When Blanca enquires about the seriousness of his relationship with Edma, Fernando tells her that he loved her like a sister, like something very familiar. Later, however, when he tells Don Marcelo about his at-times combative feelings towards Blanca, he declares that he may still love Edma:

'It's that even I don't know what I want. I've managed to conquer Blanca's love, and I adore her, despite still loving Edma. Yet when Blanca fell in love and into my arms, I was overcome with an inexplicable repulsion and rejected her.' (p. 41)

Fernando admits that he cannot interpret his own feelings, as he is torn between two conflicting ideals of Woman. Consequently, he cannot be content with one or the other ideal because his stance towards love and marriage is shaped by social constructions that impose limits and unrealistic expectations. In this way, the text makes it clear that these ideals are not representative of actual women (or either character). As Ragan observes, '[Fernando's] contradictory stance reveals the impossible double standard for women's sexuality that rests at the heart of this story.'[136] Blanca does not fit neatly into the category of a seductress or a *femme fatale*, given that Fernando leaves apparently unscathed. Meanwhile, Edma is not as 'familiar' or innocent as Fernando would like to think. During a conversation with her uncle, Edma asks him to find out the brand of Blanca's perfume. Don Marcelo dismisses this by insisting that she has the scent of youth, to which Edma retorts: '"There's much talk of natural beauty, goodness and innocence, but I can tell that what men really want is a woman with experience. They leave their virtuous women for the 'perverse' ones, or isn't that what you call them?"' (p. 31) Whether through her actions or merely through the perception of experience, Edma expresses her duality, making her a more complex character than she might at first seem. Therefore, in a departure from the literary female vampire tradition up until this point, the virgin/seductress dichotomy is presented ironically, which by way of revealing the deficiencies of female archetypes, subverts male discursive practices.

As is the case with the other tales in this collection, several facets of Blanca's depiction align her with the literary female vampire tradition. Like many of her predecessors, Blanca is beautiful, cold to the touch, has a slew of dead bodies in her mysterious past, fosters abjection and 'infects' others with her coldness/illness, including her own children, her husbands, Fernando and possibly her mother at birth. The fact that she was raised in the wild after the deaths of her parents is also significant given the strong connection between vampires and animals. In fact, as Juan Carlos Rodríguez argues, if vampires can so easily morph into animals, it is because they *are* animals.[137] Vampires' human characteristics, however, and the fact that humans are their prey, made them all the more terrifying in the first two centuries of their literary representations because they showcased the connection between Human and Nature, evoking a fear of the savage and the

xlvi

THE TALES IN THIS COLLECTION

bestiality within. Blanca, however polished she may be on the surface, was nurtured far from civilisation, an interesting thought when considering how she is at times viewed by Fernando (with horror) and treated by society (unjustly). This connection to both nature and vampires is strengthened by the fact that Blanca is never seen outside during the day, likening her to the nocturnal creatures that populate vampire narratives. She is either at the theatre, inside her hotel or in the hotel garden at night; at one point, she even tells Fernando to leave as daybreak approaches. In addition to her apparent aversion to daylight, Blanca has also been the cause of both animal and human suffering, a typical vampire trait.

Like the vampire, Blanca is always on the move—from the Basque country to India, Egypt, Vienna and Madrid—yet her movement has implications that speak more so to her freedom (and to women's liberties more broadly) than to simply being on the hunt. For example, as Lee Six points out, 'the fact that Blanca felt constrained to marry two men, neither of whom she loved, reflects the difficulties for women to survive economically without a man, difficulties the author overcame against the odds, but of which she was acutely aware.'[138] The first man she marries is described as 'somewhat degenerate and sadistic' (p. 43), which not only inverts the victim/villain dichotomy, but also speaks to the very real fears plaguing economically impoverished young women that marry out of pure necessity. Thus, Blanca's move from the countryside to international destinations can be understood as a recourse to which girls and women turned for the sake of survival. Her movements thereafter also seem to be prompted by external factors: 'Don't say how little you know about me. Curiosity follows me wherever I go, never letting me feel at ease in any place, and I don't want that to happen here.' (p. 29) Here, she implies that it is others' perceptions and probing that prompted her many moves, not an intrinsically motivated or perturbed reason more in line with the female vampire tradition.

Now settled in Madrid, she lives in a beautiful, modern-day space that symbolises transience and luxury, which is significant for two major reasons. First, its selection appears to play on male anxieties related to women's spending habits. In the bourgeois conception of the private sphere, women's governing of the home typically included the management of household income, and its mismanagement could precipitate a fall from the middle to the lower classes. According to Ragan: 'The cultural fear of women's activities—as consumers of products or consumers of men—also spur the literary and artistic portrayals of beautiful, passive and passionless women who are themselves consumed rather than consumers.'[139] While Blanca originally adheres to the Decadent image of a passive woman, her living arrangements—as well as her reversal of the gaze as she watches Fernando leave through her own binoculars[140]—promote the idea that she is a consumer. The hotel is also significant because, as Ricardo Krauel observes, it is detached from the traditional feminine space of the home.[141] For DeWees, this became a trend in female-authored vampire fiction:

xlvii

INTRODUCTION

Ironically, while male writers portrayed women as the natural geniuses of the domestic sphere, women's writing is far less concerned with the domestic world that men were so eager to protect. Appropriately, as the roles of living women moved beyond the sphere of the home, so too did vampire fiction, as practiced by women writers.[142]

Blanca's international and domestic movements, while typical of vampire fiction, thus speak more to women's freedoms (or lack thereof) at the time, further advancing her sympathetic portrayal.

It can be suggested that Blanca is associated with vampirism because she is a sexually experienced woman who dares to gaze and desire. According to Schumann: 'The vampire motif is clearly used to suggest a sexually aggressive woman in the very traditional sense of the Gothic novel', even in contemporary representations.[143] During the *fin de siècle*, sexually experienced women were not considered 'marriage material', and they were typically not capable of being truly loved by the men that tried to conquer them. This is evident in 'The Cold Woman': not only is Blanca twice widowed and has twice borne children, but she has also had other suitors, which clearly bothers Fernando, even though she assures him that these were merely 'flirtations that didn't mean anything' (p. 48). This could help explain his disgusted reaction towards both her body and her sexual advances, given that his knowledge of her past in addition to her current behaviour makes her undesirable, monstrous even. Accordingly, Fernando's quick departure shortly thereafter could be attributed to his uneasiness towards Blanca's past sexual experience, as well as her current sexual desire outside marriage.[144] The text never reveals the precise reason(s) behind Fernando's departure, but it does allow the reader access to Blanca's thoughts. Lee Six argues that this reveals 'the magnitude of her suffering' and encourages the reader to 'realise she is a victim herself'.[145]

In addition to Blanca's sexual desire, the text further challenges the victim/villain dichotomy inherent to vampire fiction in its treatment of motherhood. Vampires impede the reproduction of humans through sickness, murder and the propagation of vampires like themselves, furthering a chaotic and terrifying alternative to the natural order of things. The female vampire, however, is doubly stigmatised because she is not only a vampire, but also a body that cannot perform its natural and primary function as a woman. According to Warwick, '[w]hat the female vampire is threatening to draw out of the man is not blood but semen [...] and to no reproductive end.'[146] As a mother of deceased children and a potential vampire who is most likely unable to provide Fernando with a family, it would make sense that Fernando not only be terrified of Blanca, but that he also leave her after he gets what he wants from her. As the reader learns through the narrator's focalisation of Fernando, this is for an unattainable woman to love him: 'there would be such glory in procuring the love of one of those exceptional women supposedly incapable of it' (p. 38). From Fernando's perspective, Blanca is there to fulfill his expectations and desires, and once she has ful-

xlviii

THE TALES IN THIS COLLECTION

filled the ones that she is capable of, he has no use for her, indicative of how women's roles and worth are unjustly determined by men in patriarchal society.

Blanca is not a female vampire in the traditional sense. She is not Carmilla, Lilith, Lucy or one of the female vampires living in Dracula's castle. At the same time, she does not align with the other extreme: Mina, Laura or the other victims who find their way back on a course set out for them by the patriarchy. In her complex representation that questions customary female archetypes, Blanca shatters superficial images of the 'angel of the house' and the *femme fatale*. Additionally, she is a product of many literary currents, styles and modes: Romanticism, melodrama, the gothic, the fantastic, Decadence, the *avant-garde* and *modernismo*.[147] This reappropriation and blending of styles to serve progressive concerns could be a factor in how the text moves away from horror and towards parody. Here, the reader is not persuaded to fear Blanca, but fear *for* her in such a way that calls attention to the oppressive systems that determine both her worth and that of female authorship. In this way, the text serves as a precursor to what Elton Honores Vásquez has argued to be a shift from gothic horror to gothic parody in the representation of the vampire figure during the mid-twentieth century.[148] It is also a significant contribution to the vampire theme in Hispanic literature and beyond, and showcases how female authors can dialogue with the male-dominated literary canon while writing their own images of women.

The Vampire (1927)

Horacio Quiroga was born on 31 December 1878, in Salto, Uruguay, to a well-off and well-known family.[149] His father died the following year from an accidental self-inflicted gunshot wound; after his mother remarried, his beloved stepfather died by a self-inflicted gunshot wound to the head after suffering a cerebral hemorrhage.[150] Quiroga was an avid reader who ingrained himself in literary circles, collaborating in literary journalism under the pseudonym Guillermo Eynhardt.[151] He later became a photographer with his own laboratory and accompanied his friend and mentor Leopoldo Lugones to Misiones, Argentina in the capacity of his photographer.[152] Still, Quiroga continued to experience tragedy after tragedy in his adult life: two of his siblings died from illnesses, he accidentally shot the brother of a friend, killing him instantly, and his first wife and mother to his children, Ana María, died by suicide with poison.[153] After years of writing and serving as a consul himself, he was diagnosed with stomach cancer, and in response, died by self-induced cyanide poisoning on 19 February 1937.[154]

Quiroga published articles, novels, plays and short stories, all of which tend to be marked by death, and according to Noè Jitrik, by isolation and exile.[155] In life, he was supposedly a difficult man who preferred isolation to company, and a simple and rural environment to a luxurious and modern one. Yet, he was also taken with modern innovations and found new modes

xlix

INTRODUCTION

of artistic representation to be incredibly important.[156] According to Beatriz Sarlo, well before film became a topic of the intellectual elites, Quiroga felt the pull of cinema from two domains, technology and the imagination: 'Motion pictures offered a new setting for the literature of the fantastic; where Quiroga's poetics was concerned, cinema allowed still unknown creative possibilities to be grounded in technological developments.'[157] Although the characters in his later literary works continued to be affected by death and isolation, his fascination with film gave way to new possibilities, forms and recurring motifs in these works, as is the case with 'The Vampire'.

'El vampiro' ['The Vampire'] is a fascinating and suspenseful tale that relies on tropes and narrative elements from various currents and modes; from *modernismo*, Decadence and science fiction to the gothic and the fantastic. Like the other tales in this anthology, it portrays the female vampire character sympathetically, with even the title suggesting that the source of vampirism lies elsewhere.[158] Yet, this tale departs from the more glaring ideological concerns of the previous tales in that its vampire logic expresses anxieties toward a shifting global economy where greater capitalist and colonial systems of exploitation are at work. Specifically, it manifests anxieties at the expansion of American economic and cultural hegemony through its two vampire characters: a mysterious man of foreign origin named Rosales and the spectre of an American actress that he created through pseudo-scientific processes. By displacing the locus and meanings of horror, 'The Vampire' is thus an interesting case study of the female vampire figure in both the Latin American and global gothic literary traditions.

The literary vampire has political and economic connotations dating back to early eighteenth-century territorial disputes between the Ottoman and Habsburg Empires.[159] As the century progressed, yielding more reports of vampire sightings, stakings and burnings, the vampire became not only a popular topic to debate among intellectual circles, but also a useful trope for writers, philosophers and artists when criticising political and economic institutions. This happened for the first time in 1764, when Voltaire (1694–1778) dedicated an entry to vampires in *Dictionnaire philosophique*, ridiculing the superstition and claiming that true vampires were in fact real men, from 'stock-jobbers, brokers, and men of business, who sucked the blood of the people in broad daylight'[160] to 'the monks, who eat at the expense of both kings and people'.[161] In Spain, artist Francisco de Goya (1746–1828) tended to employ the vampire as a means of communicating the anxieties and concerns of Spanish society, and the institutions and processes that exploited, turned their backs on and violated the lower classes and society's most vulnerable: *Sueño 16: crecer después de morir* [Dream 16: rising after death] (1797–1798) and his later collection of etchings, *Desastres de la guerra* [Disasters of war] (1810–1820), are prime examples. A few decades later, Karl Marx famously employed the vampire to convey the economic and political tensions of the era, specifically criticising capitalist modes of production: 'Capital is dead labour, that, vampire-like,

THE TALES IN THIS COLLECTION

only lives by sucking living labour, and lives the more, the more labour it sucks.'[162] As a result, by the nineteenth century: 'The image of this parasitic being that feeds off the blood and life of its victims became a metaphor for exploitation.'[163] Gail Turley Houston examines this connection in her work, *From Dickens to Dracula: Gothic, Economics, and Victorian Fiction* (2005), suggesting that the novel *Dracula* conveys public and private fears generated by the London banking crisis at the turn of the nineteenth century.

While Quiroga's 'The Vampire' does not express fiscal fears with the same frankness as *Dracula*, its vampire logic does suggest fears concerning postcolonial and imperial realities. Latin America has never quite been able to escape its colonial status because after the revolutionary wars its nations were dependent on non-Spanish foreign capital and investments to enter the global economy.[164] The US government's imperialistic tactics throughout the nineteenth and twentieth centuries created a somewhat dependent, and oftentimes exploitative, relationship with its northern neighbor. According to Alan Knight, 'U.S. economic hegemony in Latin America has, despite fluctuations, remained relatively secure; like British hegemony in the nineteenth century, it is largely voluntaristic and noncoercive, and this makes it more durable, though no less unequal.'[165] Several Latin American intellectuals at the turn of the twentieth century denounced American imperialism for the way it was shaping the political, economic and cultural landscapes. *Modernista* writers such as José Martí (Cuba, 1853–1895), José Enrique Rodó (Uruguay, 1871–1917), Rubén Darío (Nicaragua, 1867–1916) and Quiroga criticised American culture and imperialism through various forms of narrative. According to Todd S. Garth, a compendium of articles titled *Los heroismos* [Heroism], originally published in 1927—curiously, the same year 'The Vampire' appeared—draws attention to Quiroga's plight for a national, transcendental heroism in the face of imperialist powers and bourgeois society. He argues that, as was the case throughout Latin America, 'the preponderance of Argentina's cultural voices were far more concerned with the consolidation of national character in the face of an opposing imperialism, that of the United States.'[166] In 'The Vampire', American cultural hegemony presents itself in the image of the American actress/spectre/vampire who represents Hollywood, and thus American culture. Rosales obsesses over this, which ultimately leaves him without 'a drop of blood' in his veins. Meanwhile, economic hegemony is presented through Rosales, representative of foreign interests in Latin America: he exploits other nations' peoples and resources, such as technology and scientific knowledge, to expand his own knowledge and power.

As critics have observed, the male narrator–protagonist's impression encourages a reading of the spectre of the actress as a vampire.[167] But, besides her allure and the account of Rosales' death given by the narrator, Guillermo Grant, she does not fit into the typical mould of the late nineteenth- and early twentieth-century female vampire. She is not mysterious, but rather a version of a well-known actress. She is not a widow or cold to the touch. Moreover,

li

INTRODUCTION

she is not likened to the overlapping images of female monstrosity of the time, such as the serpent-woman. She is instead a spectre created by a Victor Frankenstein-type figure to both satisfy his own ego and entertain himself and his friend. As a film star, she was an exotic and glamourous Other, but as a spectre in his home she suffers in a constant state of dependence, compliance and anguish. As Grant tells Rosales: 'All your pain and suffering wouldn't be enough to make up for even one of that young lady's blistering moans.' (p. 62) Such a depiction is more typical of the suffering heroine trope than the female vampire trope. Indeed, it is not until Rosales attempts to extract her with love, and not simply curiosity, as his motivator, that she reveals any kind of sexual (and therefore subversive) desire. Moreover, unlike the typical spendthrift *femme fatale*, she is not interested in material comforts; she had them with Rosales, and she burned them down.

Although the spectre of the actress is the character Grant associates with vampirism, Rosales is arguably the true vampire of the story. Some critics have explored this interpretation of the story, citing his likeness to Count Dracula or the male vampire in general,[168] but the implications of this association have yet to be explored. The association between Rosales and Dracula begins implicitly, upon Grant's first perceptions of him: 'He parted his black hair neatly to the side. His calm, almost cold, gaze expressed the same collected self-confidence and refinement as his demeanour.' (p. 55) Grant is surprised by his lack of a Spanish or Latin American accent given his name, so asks him whether he is Spanish, to which Rosales replies that he is not. Yet Grant observes that when Rosales speaks, he 'endeavoured to sound like a Spanish nobleman' (p. 59). His lack of an accent and use of old Castilian is interesting when considering Dracula as a symbol of a bygone feudal era. As Rodríguez argues, Dracula's castle lacks servants because it is 'fantasmal';[169] he has no servants because what he represents (feudalism) no longer exists. The association between Rosales and Dracula is therefore consolidated when he makes several allusions to his service, or lack thereof. When he extends a dinner invitation to Grant for the first time, he warns, '"I had an excellent chef, but he's fallen ill . . . Some of my servants may also be missing"'. A few days later, he explains why he had stood Grant up: '"Do you recall what I told you about my serving staff? Well, this time I was the sick one"'. This does not go unnoticed by Grant: 'Again with the servants' (p. 58), he says to himself, sounding both irritated and curious.

Rosales may be mysterious and, like Dracula, a relic of feudalism in a capitalist era, but the ways he spends his wealth is likened to the bourgeoisie of the time, and what Quiroga and various other *modernistas* despised about them. According to Garth: 'As Martul Tobío and March point out, in his fiction, Quiroga consistently equates bourgeois ease, wealth and pragmatism with the abandonment of "spiritual ideals," "sincerity" and "original purity".'[170] In 'The Vampire', Rosales is described in French as *vieux-riche* (old money), but his materialism and frivolous spending habits equate him more with the bourgeoisie than the aristocracy. He confesses, for exam-

lii

THE TALES IN THIS COLLECTION

ple, that his fortune allowed him to build a top-of-the-line laboratory, one which far exceeded his scientific capabilities. Likewise, he is excessive in his decor and his cuisine: 'The second thing I noticed was the size of the incredibly opulent dining room. It was so big that it swallowed up the table, upon which laid a feast but only three place settings.' (p. 59) While Rosales is therefore likened to Dracula, strengthening the argument that he is a vampire, he is also equated with the Latin American elite that was buying into American cultural values, such as materialism.[171] According to Mejías López:

> In the battle of racial discourses, the Iberian-American countries were considered backward, lacking in material resources and economic development; as we will see, Spanish American *modernistas* retorted by writing of their northern neighbors as overtly materialistic, a culture of consumers rather than thinkers, and ultimately the antithesis of the true modern spirit.[172]

Rosales is the ultimate consumer, a vampire that uses the capital at his disposal to exploit foreign resources: most notably, a foreign body, but also a domestic one, Grant, whom he makes complicit in his ill-fated pursuits.

The effects Rosales has on both Grant and the spectre of the actress also suggest he is a vampire. Anna Reid proposes that it is Rosales who falls under the spectre's spell,[173] but it can alternatively be suggested that both she and Grant fall under his. She, for one, is under his control until her emotions drive her to excess (or perhaps revenge?). In Grant's case, he begins to understand that he is living a double life, one in which he has no control.[174] During the day, he believes he goes about his previous life's activities, but at night he finds himself at Rosales's door, keeping company with him and the spectre till sunrise. In the beginning, Rosales would invite Grant over for dinner, but later it seems that an invitation is no longer required, as he is programmed to arrive at his home at the same time every night. Another way in which both Grant and the spectre seem to be under Rosales's spell is their ability to 'see' where he is and what he is doing when he travels to Hollywood to kill the actress. She, for example, says to Grant, '"He has already left San Diego"', and later, '"He's in Santa Monica"' (p. 63). Grant's character seems even more connected to Rosales: 'I closed my eyes and the image of a man flashed before me. He held a dagger over a sleeping woman.' In being under Rosales's control and having his gaze dominate their own, both characters thus seem to be under his spell, not vice versa.

The inspiration behind this murder is a combination of curiosity and divine destiny. Rosales's curiosity lead him to manipulate film through processes he did not quite understand, but once faced with the fact that he had only partially realised his goal, his curiosity prompts him to cross more significant ethical (and national) borders. In justifying the crime, he says to Grant that his experiment '"has an almost divine purpose"' (p. 63), echoing the United States' nineteenth-century expansionist attitude, Manifest Destiny. As Knight explains:

Even aggressive ambitions were justified in moral terms. A U.S. takeover of

INTRODUCTION

Central America, it was stated in 1859, would lead to immigration and development; war, ignorance, superstition, and anarchy would be replaced by 'peace, knowledge, Christianity, and our heaven-born institutions'.[175]

Now, even though the tale makes no explicit connections between Rosales and the United States, it is implied through his crossing of national borders, his foreignness, his wealth and materialism, and the justification of his actions as divine. This is only further encouraged when taking the author's contemporary views of American imperialism into account.

The treatment of exploitation through vampire logic therefore invites a political reading of the tale wherein Grant is suggestive of an imperial power exercising political and economic dominance, and the spectre–vampire an occupied territory. So, while the tale superficially engages fears over female autonomy and sexual predation, it challenges the victim/vampire dichotomy by implying that the vampiric *femme fatale* is more so a victim of greater systemic forms of hegemony and oppression than a vampire herself. While the tale portrays the female vampire sympathetically, it thus diverts from the others in this volume through its combined expression of political and ideological anxieties. By extension, the treatment of vampirism suggests a shift in the female body as the locus of horror, and in doing so, the tale ushers in a more modern iteration of the female vampire that serves as a segue to the politically and ideologically layered representations of the late twentieth and early twenty-first centuries.

NOTES

1. Barbara Creed, 'Horror and the Monstrous Feminine: An Imaginary Abjection', in *The Dread of Difference*, ed. by Barry Keith Grant (Austin: University of Texas Press, 1996), pp. 35–65 (p. 44).
2. See e.g. Kathy S. Davis, 'Sympathy for the Devil: Female Authorship and the Literary Vampire' (unpublished doctoral thesis, Ohio State University, 1999), p. 7; Nancy Schumann, 'Women with Bite: Tracing Vampire Women from Lilith to Twilight', in *The Universal Vampire: Origins and Evolution of a Legend*, ed. by Barbara Brodman and James E. Doan (Lanham, MD and Plymouth: Fairleigh Dickinson University Press and Rowman & Littlefield Publishing, 2013), pp. 109–20 (p. 115); and Gina Wisker, 'Female Vampirism', in *Women and the Gothic: An Edinburgh Companion*, ed. by Avril Horner and Sue Zlosnik (Edinburgh: Edinburgh University Press, 2016), pp. 150–65 (pp. 157–58).
3. Abigail Lee Six cites the publication date of de Hoyos's tale as 1919 (ALS, 173–88), but the first edition of the collection in which it appears was published in 1910.
4. Sandra Casanova-Vizcaíno and Inés Ordiz, 'Introduction: Latin America, the Caribbean, and the Persistence of the Gothic', in *Latin American Gothic in Literature and Culture*, ed. by Sandra Casanova-Vizcaíno and Inés Ordiz (New York: Routledge, 2018), pp. 1–12 (p. 3).
5. Xavier Aldana Reyes, *Spanish Gothic: National Identity, Collaboration and Cultural Adaptation* (London: Palgrave Macmillan, 2017), p. 10.

liv

NOTES

6. For more on the Enlightenment as the age of both reason and counter-rational reason, see Paul Ilie, *The Age of Minerva: Goya and the Paradigm of Unreason in Western Europe, Volume I* (Philadelphia: University of Pennsylvania Press, 1995), pp. 12–16.

7. José B. Monleón, 'Vampiros y donjuanes: sobre la figura del seductor en el siglo XIX', *Revista Hispánica Moderna*, 48.1 (1995), 19–30 (p. 24).

8. Juan Carlos Rodríguez, *Theory and History of Ideological Production: The First Bourgeois Literatures (The 16th Century)*, trans. by Malcolm K. Read (Newark: University of Delaware Press, 2002), p. 54.

9. Miriám López Santos, *La novela gótica en España (1788–1833)* (Vigo: Academia del Hispanismo, 2010), pp. 145–205.

10. Ibid., pp. 205–80.

11. Abigail Lee Six, *Gothic Terrors: Incarceration, Duplication, and Bloodlust in Spanish Narrative* (Lewisburg: Bucknell University Press, 2010), pp. 14–15.

12. Ann Davies, *Contemporary Spanish Gothic* (Edinburgh: Edinburgh University Press, 2017); Aldana Reyes, *passim*.

13. *Encomiendas* were grants of forced native labour and tribute given to settlers in the Americas by the Spanish crown.

14. K. Steenland, 'Notes on Feudalism and Capitalism in Chile and Latin America', *Latin American Perspectives*, 2.1 (1975), 49–58.

15. Johann Wolfgang von Goethe, 'The Bride of Corinth', in *The Essential Goethe*, ed. by M. Bell (Princeton: Princeton University Press, 2016), pp. 21–26.

16. José María Heredia, 'La novia de Corinto', in *Poesías completas de José María Heredia* (Madrid: Iberoamericana Editorial Vervuert, 2020), pp. 396–400 (my translation).

17. A. Owen Aldridge, 'The Vampire Theme in Latin America', in *Otros mundos otros fuegos: fantasía y realismo mágico en Iberamérica*, ed. by Donald A. Yates (Pittsburgh: K&S Enterprises, 1975), pp. 145–52 (p. 148).

18. Reading nation-building literature through a gothic lens is a nascent trend that has already yielded compelling insights. See e.g. Ana Consuelo Mitlich Osuna, 'El gótico en la novela histórica mexicana del siglo XIX', *Hispanet Journal*, 4 (2011), 1–17; R. Terezinha Schmidt, 'Difference and Subversion: Gothic Migrations in Nineteenth-Century Latin American Novels', in *Tropical Gothic in Literature and Culture: The Americas*, ed. by Justin Edwards and Sandra Guardini Vasconcelos (New York: Routledge, 2016), pp. 218–39; Carlos Ferrer Plaza, 'Imaginario gótico e intencionalidad política en *Amalia*, de José Mármol', *Itinerários*, 47 (2018), 83–99.

19. Edwards and Guardini Vasconcelos, eds, *Tropical Gothic*; Casanova-Vizcaíno and Ordiz, eds, *Latin American Gothic*; Antonio Alcalá González and Ilse Bussing López, eds, *Doubles and Hybrids in Latin American Gothic* (New York: Routledge, 2020); Carmen A. Serrano, *The Gothic Imagination in Latin American Fiction and Film* (Albuquerque: University of Mexico Press, 2019); Gabriel Eljaiek-Rodríguez, *Selva de fantasmas: el gótico en la literatura y el cine latinoamericano* (Bogotá: Pontificia Universidad Javeriana, 2017); Gabriel Eljaiek-Rodríguez, *The Migration and Politics of Monsters in Latin American Cinema* (Cham: Palgrave Macmillan, 2018).

20. 'Introduction', in *Doubles and Hybrids in Latin American Gothic*, ed. by Alcalá González and Bussing López, p. 14.

21. Davies, *Contemporary Spanish Gothic*, p. 171.

INTRODUCTION

22. Edgar Allan Poe, 'The Philosophy of Composition' (1846), in *Edgar Allan Poe, Critical Theory: The Major Documents*, ed. by Stuart Levine and Susan F. Levine (Champaign: University of Illinois Press, 2010), pp. 55–76.

23. Hannah Thompson, 'Decadence', in *The Cambridge History of French Literature*, ed. by William Burgwinkle, Nicholas Hammond and Emma Wilson (Cambridge: Cambridge University Press, 2011), pp. 541–48 (p. 548).

24. Ibid., p. 546.

25. Matei Calinescu, *Five Faces of Modernity: Modernism, Avant-Garde, Decadence, Kitsch, Postmodernism* (Durham, NC: Duke University Press, 1987), p. 156 (original emphasis).

26. Gabriela Mora, *Clemente Palma: el modernismo en su versión decadente y gótica* (Lima: IEP, 2000).

27. See e.g. Margo Glantz, 'Poe en Quiroga', in *Aproximaciones a Horacio Quiroga*, ed. by Angel Flores (Caracas: Monte Avila, 1976), pp. 93–118.

28. In her introduction to a special issue of *Horror Studies*, Ann Davies coalesces Latin American and Spanish horror traditions under the term 'Hispanic' but does not go as far as suggesting that this grouping entails a 'cross-pollination', borrowing the term she herself uses to describe how the gothic functions transnationally and transdisciplinarily—see Ann Davies, 'Hispanic Horror: An Introduction', *Horror Studies*, 10.2 (October 2019), 145–53.

29. Alejandro Mejías-López, 'Modernismo's Inverted Conquest and the Ruins of Imperial Nostalgia: Rethinking Transatlantic Relations in Contemporary Critical Discourse', *Arizona Journal of Hispanic Cultural Studies*, 12 (2008), 7–29 (p. 8). Mejías-López is not the first scholar to note the impact of *modernismo* on Spanish letters (see e.g. AG, 1), but his broader focus on authors besides Darío, as well as his extensive research on publication history, make his study a particularly crucial one for the purposes of this edition.

30. See Miguel Ángel Lizaso Tirapu, 'Datos para una biografía del Duende Crítico de Madrid', *Príncipe de Viana*, 75.259 (2014), 185–237 (pp. 207 and 234).

31. Carlos Abraham, *La literatura fantástica argentina en el siglo XIX* (Buenos Aires: Fundación CICCUS, 2015), p. 108.

32. Ibid., p. 109 (my translation).

33. Ibid., p. 129.

34. Voltaire, *Philosophical Dictionary*, trans. by H. I. Woolf (New York: Knopf, 1924).

35. Roberto Alcalá Flecha, 'El vampirismo en la obra de Goya', *Goya: Revista de Arte*, 233 (1993), 258–67 (p. 264).

36. Marie Elise Escalante, 'La subversion fantástica del discurso histórico: fantasmas, memoria e historia en los cuentos de Juana Manuela Gorriti', *Revista Iberoamericana*, 79.244–45 (2013), 1069–85 (p. 1070).

37. Mejías-López, p. 15.

38. With *Gothic Terrors*, Lee Six is possibly the first Hispanist to draw attention to gothic trends in writers such as Pardo Bazán, Galdós and Unamuno, prompting numerous articles, book chapters and dissertations by various scholars.

39. For example, Pardo Bazán's tale 'El balcón de la princesa' was published in the Chilean literary magazine *Prism* on 18 May 1907. Many thanks to Sandra García Gutiérrez for bringing this to my attention.

40. Ana Peluffo, 'Rizomas, redes y lazos transatlánticos: América Latina y España (1890–1920)', in *No hay nación para este sexo: la re(d)pública transatlántica*

NOTES

de las letras: escritoras españolas y latinoamericanas, ed. by Pura Fernández (Madrid and Frankfurt: Iberoamericana Editorial Vervuert, 2015), pp. 207–24 (p. 220).

41. Abraham, p. 19.

42. Horacio Quiroga's collection, *Más allá [Beyond]*, which includes the tale 'The Vampire', was translated by Elisa Taber (Seattle: Sublunary Editions, 2022), and Clemente Palma's *Cuentos malévolos [Malevolent Tales]* was first translated by Guillermo I. Castillo-Feliú (New York: Irvington, 1983), and later by Shawn M. Garrett (Middletown, DE: Strange Ports Press, 2023). Garrett translates Palma's tale 'La granja blanca' as 'The White Farm', but it appears in the present anthology as 'The White Farmhouse'.

43. For more on the dynamics of supply and demand in vampire fiction and women's role in the print economy, see Lana L. Dalley and Jill Rappoport, eds, *Economic Women: Essays on Desire and Dispossession in Nineteenth-Century British Culture* (Columbus: Ohio State University Press, 2013).

44. Jennifer Smith, 'Women and the Deployment of Sexuality in Nineteenth-Century Spain', *Revista de Estudios Hispánicos*, 40 (2006), 145–170 (p. 166).

45. Christine Arkinstall, *Spanish Female Writers and the Freethinking Press: 1879–1926* (Toronto: University of Toronto Press, 2014), p. 17.

46. Ibid., p. 221, n. 110.

47. Nancy LaGreca, *Rewriting Womanhood: Feminism, Subjectivity, and the Angel of the House in the Latin American Novel, 1887–1903* (University Park: Penn State University Press, 2009), p. 171.

48. Ibid., pp. 88–89.

49. Maxine Molyneux, *Women's Movements in International Perspective: Latin America and Beyond* (London: Palgrave Macmillan, 2001), p. 17.

50. Ibid., pp. 18–21.

51. Ibid., p. 36.

52. Leopoldo Lugones, 'La educación de la mujer: lo que es y lo que debe ser', in *Las primeras letras de Leopoldo Lugones: reproducción facsimilar de sus primeros trabajos*, ed. by Leopoldo 'Polo' Lugones (Buenos Aires: Centurion, 1963), n. pag. (my translation).

53. Cynthia Jeffress Little, 'Education, Philanthropy, and Feminism: Components of Argentine Womanhood, 1860-1926', in *Latin American Women: Historical Perspectives*, ed. by Asunción Lavrin (Westport, CT: Greenwood Press, 1978), pp. 235–53 (p. 240).

54. Ibid., p. 235.

55. Ibid, p. 239.

56. Francine Masiello, 'Women, State, and Family in Latin American Literature of the 1920s', in *Women, Culture, and Politics in Latin America: Seminar on Feminism and Culture in Latin America*, ed. by Emilie Bergmann, et al. (Berkeley, Los Angeles, Oxford: University of California Press, 1990), pp. 27–47 (p. 29).

57. Carol A. Senf, *The Vampire in Nineteenth-Century English Literature* (Bowling Green: Bowling Green State University Press, 1988), p. 154.

58. Heather Braun, *The Rise and Fall of the Femme Fatale in British Literature, 1790–1910* (Lanham, MD and Plymouth: Fairleigh Dickinson University Press and Rowman & Littlefield Publishing, 2012), p. 141.

lvii

INTRODUCTION

59. Francine Masiello, *Between Civilization and Barbarism: Women, Nation, and Literary Culture in Modern Argentina* (Lincoln, NE: University of Nebraska Press, 1992), p. 7.

60. Julia Kristeva, *Powers of Horror: An Essay on Abjection* (New York: Columbia University Press, 1982).

61. Gabriela Mora, 'Decadencia y vampirismo en el modernism hispanoamericano: un cuento de Clemente Palma', *Revista de Crítica Literaria Latinoamericana*, 23.46 (1997), 191–98 (p. 195).

62. William J. Robinson, 'Excessive Sensuality or the Woman Vampire', in *Married Life and Happiness: Or, Love and Comfort in Marriage* (New York: Eugenics, 1922), pp. 89–93 (p. 90).

63. Alexandra Warwick, 'Vampires and the Empire: Fears and Fictions of the 1890s', in *Cultural Politics at the Fin de Siècle*, ed. by Sally Ledger and Scott McCracken (Cambridge: Cambridge University Press, 1995), pp. 202–20.

64. Part of the content of this section is developed from Megan DeVirgilis, 'Lugones and the Woman Question: Reconsidering the Status Quo and Reimagining the *Femme Fatale* in His Early Works', *Bulletin of Hispanic Studies*, 96.3 (2019), 307–21.

65. Jorge Luis Borges, *Leopoldo Lugones* (Buenos Aires: Troquel, 1955), p. 10.

66. Martín Artagaveytia, 'Nota biográfica', in *Los cuentos de Leopoldo Lugones*, ed. by Martín Artagaveytia (Buenos Aires: Díada, 2011), pp. 5–13 (p. 5).

67. Ibid., p. 6.

68. Alfredo Canedo, *Aspectos del pensamiento político de Leopoldo Lugones* (Buenos Aires: Marcos, 1974), p. 10.

69. David Rock, *Authoritarian Argentina: The Nationalist Movement, Its History and Its Impact* (Berkeley: University of California Press, 1993), pp. xxii and 95.

70. See *Las primeras letras*, ed. by Polo Lugones, n. pag.

71. Diego Labra, '¿Vivió Buenos Aires una "periódico-manía" hacia 1870? Una reflexión sobre los periódicos para "niñas", la prensa ilustrada y la ampliación del público lector porteño', *Estudios de Teoría Literaria*, 9.20 (2020), 309–21 (p. 311).

72. Lugones, 'La cuestión feminista', in *Las primeras letras*, ed. by Polo Lugones, n. pag.

73. For more on Pre-Raphaelite images of women in art, see Karen Z. Sproles, 'D. H. Lawrence and the Pre-Raphaelites: Love among the Ruins', *D. H. Lawrence Review*, 22.3 (1990), 299–305.

74. All remaining quotations from this tale are my translations: see pp. 3–6 in the present edition.

75. Francisco Sánchez-Verdejo Pérez, 'El vampiro femenino de Poe: metáfora maldita de la femme fatale y ejemplificación edificante de la mujer sin sombra', in *Edgar Allan Poe (1809–2009): doscientos años después*, ed. by Beatriz González Moreno and Rigal Aragón (Cuenca: Universidad Castilla-La Mancha, 2010), pp. 87–96 (p. 93).

76. Brian Frost, *The Monster with a Thousand Faces: Guises of the Vampire in Myth and Literature* (Bowling Green: Bowling Green University Popular Press, 1989), p. 6.

77. For more on this, see e.g. David Melville Wingrove, '"La Belle Dame": Lilith and the Romantic Vampire Tradition', in *Rethinking George MacDonald: Contexts and Contemporaries*, ed. by Christopher MacLachlan, John Patrick

lviii

NOTES

Pazdziora and Ginger Stelle (Glasgow: Association for Scottish Literary Studies, 2013), pp. 175–97 (p. 184).

78. As Olivio Jiménez observes, gemstones and luxurious materials were common in *modernistas'* ornamental language (JOJ, 29).

79. Sánchez-Verdejo Pérez, p. 94 (my translation).

80. José Ricardo Chaves, 'Romanticism, Occultism and the Fantastic Genre in Spain and Latin America', in *Romantic Prose Fiction*, ed. by Gerald Gillespie, Manfred Engel and Bernard Dieterie (Amsterdam: Benjamins, 2008), pp. 622–42 (p. 626).

81. Soledad Quereilhac, 'Shadows of Science in the Río de la Plata Turn-of-the-Century Gothic', in *Latin American Gothic*, ed. by Casanova-Vizcaíno and Ordiz, pp. 155–71 (p. 159).

82. José Miguel Oviedo, *Antología crítica del cuento hispanoamericano: del romanticismo al criollismo (1830–1920)* (Madrid: Alianza, 1989), p. 338.

83. Leopoldo Lugones, 'Ensayo de una cosmogonía en diez lecciones', in *Las fuerzas extrañas* (Buenos Aires: Agebe, 2009), pp. 107–40.

84. Beth Pollack, 'The Supernatural and the Occult as Literary Elements in Selected *modernista* Short Stories' (unpublished doctoral thesis, University of California, Santa Barbara, 1988), p. 101.

85. As the text states: 'Drop by drop, his soul transfused into his loved one, abandoning the poor vessel that was his body for the magnificent vessel that was his wife. To adore her better, *he gave her* his life' (see p. 4; emphasis mine).

86. Pollack, p. 146.

87. The essay from 1897 is Lugones's 'La educación de la mujer'.

88. Dalley and Rappoport, p. 12.

89. Deanna K. Kreisel, 'Demand and Desire in *Dracula*', in *Economic Women*, ed. by Dalley and Rappoport, pp. 110–23 (p. 119).

90. For more on this, see Susan Leigh Rogers, 'Vampire Vixens: The Female Undead and the Lacanian Sybolic Order in Tales by Gautier, James, and Le Fanu' (unpublished doctoral thesis, University of California, Irvine, 1993).

91. Typically, whether they be male or female, vampires die at the end of the story. For example, *Dracula*'s Lucy has a stake driven through the heart; Carmilla is staked, decapitated and burned; and Clarimonde crumbles into a pile of dust and bones after being doused with holy water. Yet, Lugones's vampire lives on, albeit in a state of epilepsy from which she does not recover, only furthering her sympathetic portrayal.

92. Elisabeth Bronfen, *Over Her Dead Body: Death, Femininity and the Aesthetic* (Manchester: Manchester University Press, 1991), p. 181.

93. Part of the content of this section is developed from Megan DeVirgilis, 'Hearth and Home and Horror: Gothic Trappings in Early C20th Latin American Literature', *Gothic Studies*, 23.2 (2021), 201–16.

94. José Miguel Oviedo, *Historia de la literatura hispanoamericana vol. 3: postmodernismo, vanguardia, regionalismo* (Madrid: Alianza, 2001), pp. 325–26.

95. Ibid., p. 21.

96. Gabriela Mora, 'La sexualidad femenina en el modernismo decadente: la narrativa de Clemente Palma', in *Delmira Agustini y el modernismo: nuevas propuestas de género*, ed. by Tina Escaja (Buenos Aires: Viterbo, 2000), p. 26 (my translation).

INTRODUCTION

97. See e.g. Pollack, p. 165; Oscar Hahn, *Antología del cuento hispanoamericano: Siglo XX*, 8th edn (Santiago de Chile: Editorial Universitaria, 1990), p. 29.
98. Curiously, Palma dedicates another vampire tale in his collection *Cuentos malévolos*, 'La leyenda de hachisch' [The legend of hashish], to Benito Pérez Galdós, a Spanish writer of the time that scholars have also read through a gothic lens. See e.g. Sylvia López, 'The Gothic Tradition in Galdós' *La sombra*', *Hispania*, 81.3 (1998), 509–18.
99. In Oviedo, p. 326.
100. See Mora, *Clemente Palma*.
101. Mora, '"La granja blanca" de Clemente Palma: relaciones con el decadentismo y Edgar Allan Poe', *Casa de las Américas*, 38.205 (1996), 62–69.
102. Ibid., p. 65.
103. Like Lugones's 'The Female Vampire', Palma's 'The White Farmhouse' is another tale of 'metempsychosis' (the substition of one soul for another in the same body), possibly influenced by Poe's 'Morella' (1835). In Poe's tale, the learned but dying Morella gives birth to a daughter, who grows to resemble her mother uncannily. She remains unnamed by her father until her tenth birthday, when he decides to have her baptised. After he names her 'Morella', his daughter cries out 'I am here!' before dying. Bearing her body to the tomb in which her mother was interred, the narrator finds no trace of the original Morella's remains, taking this to indicate that the mother's soul has possessed her daughter's body.
104. According to e.g. Kason: 'This painting is a repeated leitmotif with symbolic importance, for it foreshadows the resurrection of Cordelia' (NMK, 94).
105. In e.g. *Dracula*, this dichotomy is clearly delineated in the juxtaposition between Lucy and Mina: while the sweet but flirtatious Lucy questions why she may only have one male suitor, thereby threatening the moral code and leaving her vulnerable to Dracula's attacks, Mina is the morally superior ideal wife, thereby awarded survival, a happy marriage and motherhood.
106. Amanda Raye DeWees, 'Blood Lines: Domestic and Family Anxieties in Nineteenth-Century Vampire Literature' (unpublished doctoral thesis, University of Georgia, 1998), p. 87.
107. José Miguel Sardiñas, 'El vampirismo en relatos modernistas', *Fuentes Humanísticas*, 19.35 (July–December 2007), 34–44 (p. 39; my translation).
108. Juan Carlos Rodríguez, *Tras la muerte del aura: en contra y a favor de la Ilustración* (Granada: Universidad de Granada, 2011), p. 62.
109. Gabriela Mora, '*Los cuentos malévolos* de Clemente Palma: integración más allá del bien y del mal', in *Ojo en el caleidoscopio: las colecciones de textos integrados en la literatura latinoamericana*, ed. by P. Brescia and E. Romano (Mexico City: National Autonomous University of Mexico, 2006), p. 386.
110. Given the discrepancies in scholarly sources and de Hoyos himself supplying contradictory dates, his exact date of birth is uncertain (see JASR, 23).
111. María del Carmen Alfonso García, 'D'Annunzio, Hoyos y Martirio de San Sebastián: sobre androginia, hermafroditismo y homosexualidad en el fin de siglo', *Antipodas: Journal of Hispanic Studies of the University of Auckland*, 11/12 (1999), 187–220 (p. 211).
112. Schumann, p. 112.
113. Examples include *Psychopathia Sexualis* (1886) by Richard von Krafft-Ebing (1840–1902), *Studies in the Psychology of Sex* (1897) by Havelock Ellis (1859–

lx

NOTES

1939) and works by Sigmund Freud (1856–1939) on dreams, hysteria and sexual theory from 1893 to 1905. See Mora, 'Decadencia y vampirismo', p. 195.

114. As Lee Six notes, they spend the night in a 'banal' hotel room, 'with no details suggesting luxury or pressure on him to spend money on her' (ALS, 180).

115. As Lee Six observes, the question as to whether Miss Vampire is a supernatural *femme fatale* is never resolved, allowing the story to sit in 'undecidable territory' and thus meets the parameters set forth in Todorov's structuralist approach to the fantastic genre (ALS, 176–78).

116. According to Olivio Jiménez, 'Spanish America and Spain reunited during the *modernista* period, and Darío's impact is of such magnitude on Spanish poetry that, as a result, they have always considered him one of their own' (JOJ, 25; my translation). A relevant example in this case is JASR, who categorises Darío as a Spanish Modernist (and not *modernista*) throughout his dissertation.

117. This is further supported when considering the plethora of other similar representations of gems, materials, luxury and women's bodies in both stories.

118. Mejías-López, p. 15.

119. Since this is a comparison between words and their resulting images, it is important to include the original Spanish text: 'Fué una demencia, una sed insaciable, que crecía en progresión alarmante y extraña. Fué un delirio divino y satánico, fué un vampirismo ideal y carnal, que tenía de la amable y pródiga piedad de una diosa y de los diabólicos ardores de una alquimia infernal [...]'— Clemente Palma, 'La granja blanca', in *Cuentos malévolos*, 2nd edn (1904; Paris: Ollendorff, 1912), pp. 122–23 (archaic use of accents in original). '[L]os feroces arrebatos de un deseo insaciable, las eróticas brutalidades, el demoníaco torbellino que nos había arrebatado como en dantesca maldición. Y los besos crueles, inacabables, absorbedores de vida, y las caricias sabias, intensas, profundas, que destrozaban la medula en espasmos de voluptuosidad dolorosa en que se sentía acabar la vida'—Antonio de Hoyos y Vinent, 'El señor Cadáver y la señorita Vampiro', in *Del huerto del pecado* (Madrid: Primitivo Fernández, 1910), pp. 99–100.

120. The first critic to 'rescue' Carmen de Burgos from oblivion (from a feminist perspective) was Elizabeth Starcevic in her dissertation, *Carmen de Burgos: defensora de la mujer* [Carmen de Burgos: defender of women] (Almería: Cajal, 1976).

121. Michael Ugarte, 'Carmen de Burgos ("Colombine"): Feminist *Avant la Lettre*', in *Spanish Women Writers and the Essay: Gender, Politics, and the Self*, ed. by Kathleen Glenn and Mercedes Mazquiarán de Rodríguez (Columbia, MO: University of Missouri Press, 1998), pp. 55–74 (p. 57).

122. Rita Catrina Imboden, *Carmen de Burgos ('Colombine') y la novela corta* (Zurich: Peter Lang, 1999), p. 16.

123. Ibid., pp. 16–17.

124. Judith Kirkpatrick, 'Skeletons in the Closet: Carmen de Burgos Confronts the Literary Patriarchy', *Letras Peninsulares*, 8 (Winter 1995), 389–400 (p. 389).

125. Ugarte, p. 57.

126. Imboden, p. 20.

127. Robin Ragan, 'Carmen de Burgos's "La mujer fría": A Response to Necrophilic Aesthetics in Decadentist Spain', in *Disciplines on the Line: Feminist Research on Spanish, Latin American, and U.S. Latina Women*, ed. by Anne J. Cruz, et al. (Newark: Cuesta, 2003), pp. 235–55 (p. 235).

lxi

INTRODUCTION

128. Kirkpatrick, 'Skeletons in the Closet', p. 390.
129. Kirkpatrick's study discusses the problems that arise when an entire period of literature is created and based on the works of a few writers, especially when the categorisation applies exclusively to male authors. See Judith Kirkpatrick, *Redefining Male Tradition: Novels by Early Twentieth-Century Spanish Women Writers* (Bloomington: Indiana University Press, 1993), p. 6.
130. In several of her publications on 'The Cold Woman', Lee Six has noted Blanca's sympathetic portrayal. In her introduction to de Burgos's *Three Novellas*, she posits that Blanca is 'if not the very first, at least among the first vampires we can pity, a stage in the figure's evolution often credited to Anne Rice decades later.' See Carmen de Burgos y Seguí, *Three Novellas: 'Confidencias', 'La mujer fría' and 'Puñal de claveles'*, ed. by Abigail Lee Six (Manchester: Manchester University Press, 2016), p. 16. As this anthology has proposed, this appears to be the case in Spanish literature, while examples of pitiable female vampires appear even earlier in Latin American literature.
131. Ragan, p. 253.
132. Kirkpatrick, *Redefining Male Tradition*, pp. 14–15.
133. For clarification purposes, '[o]f course, the femme fatale was not the invention of the Decadents, or even the Romantics—cruel, sensuous women with a penchant for destroying their lovers are to be found throughout the literature of Antiquity and the Renaissance—but it was the Decadents, and later the Symbolists, who made her into an established type. So much so that by the turn of the century the "vamp" had become a cliché'—see Frost, pp. 44–45.
134. Carol Smart, 'Disruptive Bodies and Unruly Sex: The Regulation of Reproduction and Sexuality in the Nineteenth Century', in *Regulating Womanhood: Historical Essays on Marriage, Motherhood, and Sexuality*, ed. by Carol Smart (New York: Routledge, 1992), pp. 7–32 (p. 7).
135. Ragan, p. 244.
136. Ibid., p. 248.
137. Juan Carlos Rodríguez, *Tras la muerte del aura: en contra y a favor de la Ilustración* (Granada: Universidad de Granada, 2011), p. 84.
138. Lee Six, 'Introduction', in De Burgos, *Three Novellas*, p. 14.
139. Ragan, p. 242.
140. While the opening scene portrays Blanca as the object being 'consumed through the audience's opera glasses, this is reversed during the course of her relationship with Fernando, who becomes the subject she watches leave her hotel through the same glasses' (Ragan, p. 247).
141. Ricardo Krauel, 'Hacia una redefinición de la sensualidad femenina en la modernidad: *La mujer fría* de Carmen de Burgos', *Bulletin of Hispanic Studies*, 80.4 (2003), 525–36.
142. DeWees, pp. 207–8.
143. Schumann, p. 117.
144. Fernando's repulsion can also be attributed to Blanca's Basque 'race': before he leaves her at the end of the novella, he tries to convince himself that her smell is nothing more than 'the scent of her race' (p. 50). According to Lee Six, this implies that Fernando sees Basques as alien, a long-standing perspective within dominant Spanish culture—see 'Introduction', in De Burgos, *Three Novellas*, p. 42. Blanca's possible racial Otherness is interesting given vampire fiction's penchant for linking foreignness and disease. According to Warwick, the fears

NOTES

at the turn of the century were race, gender and disease, thus the foreignness of female vampirism expressed fears surrounding degeneration (p. 211). So, while the text does not directly imply that Blanca is non-native or non-white (her name insists that she is), it does engage with the racial politics of the time.

145. Lee Six, 'Introduction', in De Burgos, *Three Novellas*, p. 11.

146. Warwick, p. 212.

147. If 'The Cold Woman' is indeed directly influenced by Antonio de Hoyos y Vinent's 'Mr Cadaver and Miss Vampire', as ALS convincingly suggests, and the influence of Rubén Darío and *modernismo* is so prevalent in that tale, then it can certainly be sustained that 'The Cold Woman' engages *modernista* aesthetics, whether or not this was de Burgos's intention. Examples include the plasticity of the images, the adorned and lyrical language, references to precious stones and materials ('emerald eyes' and 'marble body'), an overwhelming sense of alienation or nihilism, and even the blending of literary styles and currents themselves. Each of these characteristics are noted in JOJ.

148. Elton Honores Vásquez, *Los que moran en las sombras* (Lima: El Lamparero Alucinado, 2010).

149. Oscar Masotta and Jorge Lafforgue, 'Cronología', in *Horacio Quiroga: una obra de experiencia y riesgo*, ed. by N. Jitrick (Montevideo: ARCA, 1967), pp. 13–49 (p. 13).

150. Ibid.

151. Ibid., pp. 14–15.

152. Beatriz Sarlo, 'Horacio Quiroga and Technoscientific Theory', in *The Technical Imagination: Argentine Culture's Modern Dreams*, trans. by Xavier Callahan (Stanford: Stanford University Press, 2008), pp. 13–36 (p. 22).

153. Masotta and Lafforgue, pp. 19–29.

154. Ibid., pp. 44–45.

155. Noè Jitrik, *Horacio Quiroga: una obra de experiencia y riesgo* (Montevideo: ARCA, 1967), p. 112.

156. Masotta and Lafforgue, p. 33.

157. Sarlo, p. 18.

158. In English, 'the vampire' could refer to either a male or female vampire, but in Spanish, the title 'El vampiro' is less ambiguous, implying that the vampire is male.

159. Erik Butler, *Metamorphosis of the Vampire in Literature and Film: Cultural Transformations in Europe, 1732–1933* (Rochester: Camden House, 2010), pp. 38–39.

160. William F. Fleming, *The Works of Voltaire: A Contemporary Version* (New York: DuMont, 1901), p. 268.

161. Ibid., p. 270.

162. Karl Marx, 'The Working Day' (1867), in *Capital: A Critique of Political Economy*, ed. by Friedrich Engels, vol. 1 (Moscow: Foreign Language Publishing House, 1959), p. 233.

163. Monleón, p. 20 (my translation).

164. Alejandro Mejías López, *The Inverted Conquest: The Myth of Modernity and the Transatlantic Onset of Modernism* (Nashville: Vanderbilt University Press, 2009), p. 7.

INTRODUCTION

165. Alan Knight, 'U.S. Imperialism/Hegemony and Latin American Resistance', in *Empire and Dissent: The United States and Latin America*, ed. by Fred Rosen (Durham, NC: Duke University Press, 2008), pp. 23–52 (p. 37).
166. Todd S. Garth, 'Horacio Quiroga's Heroic Paradigm', *Revista de Estudios Hispánicos*, 29.3 (2005), 453–68 (p. 465).
167. See e.g. Sardiñas, p. 42; and Anna Reid, 'El vampiro sudamericano: parásitos y espectros en los cuentos de Quiroga', *Espéculo*, 44 (2010), n. pag.
168. For example, in 'La metamorphosis del vampiro', *Revista de Bellas Artes*, 28 (1976), 2–12, Margo Glantz acknowledges that Rosales is also a vampire; in E. S. Speratti-Piñero, 'Horacio Quiroga, precursor de la relación cine-literatura en la América Hispánica', *Nueva Revista de Filología Hispánica*, 36.2 (1988), 1239–49 (p. 1246), Speratti-Piñero argues that there are clear suggestions to F. W. Murnau's 1921 film, *Nosferatu*. Likewise, Persephone Braham mentions Rosales's likeness to Dracula in 'Los vampiros, el cine y el simulacro del dictador', in *Nuevas aproximaciones al cine hispánico: migraciones temporales, textuales y étnicas en el bicentenario de las independencies iberoamericanas (1810–2010)*, ed. by Santiago Juan-Navarro and Joan Torres-Pou (Barcelona: PPU, 2011), pp. 123–40 (p. 132).
169. Rodríguez, *Tras la muerte del aura*, p. 70.
170. Garth, p. 457.
171. Despite Quiroga's disdain for particular aspects of American culture, his views on American cinema were ambivalent; he adored Hollywood starlets, for example, but had a distaste for America's commercial and mediocre films—see Carlos Dámaso Martínez, *Horacio Quiroga: cine y literatura* (Buenos Aires: Losada, 2007), p. 16.
172. Mejías López, *Inverted Conquest*, p. 48.
173. Reid, p. 3.
174. Reid (ibid.) has already noted the similarity between Grant and the priest seduced by the titular character in Gautier's 'Clarimonde', who lives one life during the day and another at night.
175. Knight, p. 40.

lxiv

SELECT BIBLIOGRAPHY

Abraham, Carlos, *La literatura fantástica Argentina en el siglo XIX* (Buenos Aires: Fundación CICCUS, 2015).

Alcalá Flecha, Roberto, 'El vampirismo en la obra de Goya', *Goya: Revista de Arte*, 233 (1993), 258–67.

Alcalá González, Antonio, and Ilse Bussing López, eds, *Doubles and Hybrids in Latin American Gothic* (New York: Routledge, 2020).

Aldana Reyes, Xavier, *Spanish Gothic: National Identity, Collaboration and Cultural Adaptation* (London: Palgrave Macmillan, 2017).

Aldridge, A. Owen, 'The Vampire Theme in Latin America', in *Otros mundos otros fuegos: fantasía y realismo mágico en Iberamérica*, ed. by Donald A. Yates (Pittsburg: K&S Enterprises, 1975), pp. 145–52.

Alfonso García, María del Carmen, 'D'Annunzio, Hoyos y Martirio de San Sebastián: sobre androginia, hermafroditismo y homosexualidad en el fin de siglo', *Antipodas: Journal of Hispanic Studies of the University of Auckland*, 11/12 (1999), 187–220.

Arkinstall, Christine, *Spanish Female Writers and the Freethinking Press: 1879–1926* (Toronto: University of Toronto Press, 2014).

Artagaveytia, Martín, 'Nota biográfica', in *Los cuentos de Leopoldo Lugones*, ed. by Martín Artagaveytia (Buenos Aires: Díada, 2011), pp. 5–13.

Braham, Persephone, 'Los vampiros, el cine y el simulacro del dictador', in *Nuevas aproximaciones al cine hispánico: migraciones temporales, textuales y étnicas en el bicentenario de las independencies iberoamericanas (1810–2010)*, ed. by Santiago Juan-Navarro and Joan Torres-Pou (Barcelona: PPU, 2011), pp. 123–40.

Braun, Heather, *The Rise and Fall of the Femme Fatale in British Literature, 1790–1910* (Lanham, MD and Plymouth: Fairleigh Dickinson University Press and Rowman & Littlefield Publishing, 2013).

Bronfen, Elisabeth, *Over Her Dead Body: Death, Femininity and the Aesthetic* (Manchester: Manchester University Press, 1991).

Butler, Erik, *Metamorphosis of the Vampire in Literature and Film: Cultural Transformations in Europe, 1732–1933* (Rochester: Camden House, 2010).

Calinescu, Matei, *Five Faces of Modernity: Modernism, Avant-Garde, Decadence, Kitsch, Postmodernism* (Durham, NC: Duke University Press, 1987).

Canedo, Alfredo, *Aspectos del pensamiento político de Leopoldo Lugones* (Buenos Aires: Marcos, 1974).

Casanova-Vizcaíno, Sandra, and Inés Ordiz, eds, *Latin American Gothic in Literature and Culture* (New York: Routledge, 2018).

INTRODUCTION

Chaves, José Ricardo, 'Romanticism, Occultism and the Fantastic Genre in Spain and Latin America', in *Romantic Prose Fiction*, ed. by Gerald Gillespie, Manfred Engel and Bernard Dieterie (Amsterdam: Benjamins, 2008), pp. 622–42.

Creed, Barbara, 'Horror and the Monstrous Feminine: An Imaginary Abjection', in *The Dread of Difference*, ed. by Barry Keith Grant (Austin: University of Texas Press, 1996), pp. 35–65.

Cruz Casado, Antonio, 'La novela erótica de Antonio de Hoyos y Vinent', *Cuadernos hispanoamericanos*, 426 (1985), 101–16.

Dalley, Lana L., and Jill Rappoport, eds, *Economic Women: Essays on Desire and Dispossession in Nineteenth-Century British Culture* (Columbus: Ohio State University Press, 2013).

Dámaso Martínez, Carlos, *Horacio Quiroga: cine y literatura* (Buenos Aires: Losada, 2007).

Davies, Ann, *Contemporary Spanish Gothic* (Edinburgh: Edinburgh University Press, 2017).

————, 'Hispanic Horror: An Introduction', Horror Studies, 10.2 (October 2019), pp. 145–53

Davis, Kathy S. 'Sympathy for the Devil: Female Authorship and the Literary Vampire' (unpublished doctoral thesis, Ohio State University, 1999).

De Burgos y Seguí, Carmen, *Three Novellas: 'Confidencias', 'La mujer fría' and 'Puñal de claveles'*, ed. by Abigail Lee Six (Manchester: Manchester University Press, 2016).

De Hoyos y Vinent, Antonio, *Del huerto del pecado* (Madrid: Primitivo Fernández, 1910).

Del Aguila, Jesús Miguel Delgado, 'Recepción cronológica de la crítica literaria sobre *Cuentos malévolos* (1904)', *Actio Nova: Revista de Teoría de la Literatura y Literatura Comparada*, 3 (December 2019), 367–83.

De Unamuno, Miguel, 'Prologue', in Clemente Palma, *Cuentos malévolos* (Barcelona: Salvat, 1904), pp. v–xvi.

DeVirgilis, Megan, 'Hearth and Home and Horror: Gothic Trappings in Early C20th Latin American Literature', *Gothic Studies*, 23.2 (2021), 201–16.

————, 'Lugones and the Woman Question: Reconsidering the Status Quo and Reimagining the *Femme Fatale* in his Early Works', *Bulletin of Hispanic Studies*, 96.3 (2019), 307–21.

DeWees, Amanda Raye, 'Blood Lines: Domestic and Family Anxieties in Nineteenth-Century Vampire Literature' (unpublished doctoral thesis, University of Georgia, 1998).

Edwards, Justin, and Sandra Guardini Vasconcelos, eds, Tropical Gothic in Literature and Culture: The Americas (New York: Routledge, 2016).

SELECT BIBLIOGRAPHY

El Ateneo: Revista Mensual de Ciencias y Bellas Artes, 2.11 (May 1900).

Eljaiek-Rodríguez, Gabriel, *Selva de fantasmas: el gótico en la literatura y el cine latinoamericano* (Bogotá: Pontificia Universidad Javeriana, 2017).

——, *The Migration and Politics of Monsters in Latin American Cinema* (Cham: Palgrave Macmillan, 2018).

Englekirk, John E., 'Unamuno: crítico de la literatura hispanoamericana', *Revista Iberamericana*, 3.5 (February 1941), 19–37.

Escalante, Marie Elise, 'La subversion fantástica del discurso histórico: fantasmas, memoria e historia en los cuentos de Juana Manuela Gorriti', *Revista Iberoamericana*, 79.244–45 (2013), 1069–85.

Ferrer Plaza, Carlos, 'Imaginario gótico e intencionalidad política en *Amalia*, de José Mármol', *Itinerários*, 47 (2018), 83–99

Flirt: Revista Frívola, 25 March 1922.

Frost, Brian, *The Monster with a Thousand Faces: Guises of the Vampire in Myth and Literature* (Bowling Green: Bowling Green University Popular Press, 1989).

Garth, Todd S., 'Horacio Quiroga's Heroic, 'Poe en Quiroga', in *Aproximaciones a Horacio Quiroga*, ed. by Angel Flores (Caracas: Monte Avila, 1976), pp. 93–118.

Goethe, Johann Wolfgang von, 'The Bride of Corinth' (1797), in *The Essential Goethe*, trans. by Matthew Bell (Princeton: Princeton University Press, 2016), pp. 21–26.

González, Aníbal, *A Companion to Spanish American* modernismo (Woodbridge and Rochester, NY: Tamesis, 2007).

Hahn, Oscar, *Antología del cuento hispanoamericano: Siglo XX*, 8th edn (Santiago de Chile: Editorial Universitaria, 1990).

Heredia, José María, 'La novia de Corinto', in *Poesías completas de José María Heredia* (Madrid: Iberoamericana Editorial Vervuert, 2020), pp. 396–400.

Honores Vásquez, Elton, *Los que moran en las sombras* (Lima: El Lamparero Alucinado, 2010).

Ilie, Paul, *The Age of Minerva: Goya and The Paradigm of Unreason in Western Europe*, vol. 1 (Philadelphia: University of Pennsylvania Press, 1995).

Imboden, Rita Catrina, *Carmen de Burgos ('Colombine') y la novela corta* (Zürich: Peter Lang, 1999).

Jeffress Little, Cynthia, 'Education, Philanthropy, and Feminism: Components of Argentine Womanhood, 1860–1926', in *Latin American Women: Historical Perspectives*, ed. by Asunción Lavrin (Westport, CT: Greenwood Press, 1978), pp. 235–53.

INTRODUCTION

Jitrik, Noè, *Horacio Quiroga: una obra de experiencia y riesgo* (Montevideo: ARCA, 1967).

Kason, Nancy M., *Breaking Traditions: The Fiction of Clemente Palma* (Lewisburg: Bucknell University Press, 1988).

Kirkpatrick, Judith, *Redefining Male Tradition: Novels by Early Twentieth-Century Spanish Women Writers* (Bloomington: Indiana University Press, 1993).

——, 'Skeletons in the Closet: Carmen de Burgos Confronts the Literary Patriarchy', *Letras Peninsulares*, 8 (Winter 1995), 389–400.

Knight, Alan, 'U.S. Imperialism/Hegemony and Latin American Resistance', in *Empire and Dissent: The United States and Latin America*, ed. by Fred Rosen (Durham, NC: Duke University Press, 2008), pp. 23–52.

Krauel, Ricardo, 'Hacia una redefinición de la sensualidad femenina en la modernidad: *La mujer fría* de Carmen de Burgos', *Bulletin of Hispanic Studies*, 80.4 (2003), 525–36.

Kreisel, Deanna K., 'Demand and Desire in *Dracula*' in *Economic Women*, ed. by Dalley and Rappoport, pp. 110–23.

Kristeva, Julia, *Powers of Horror: An Essay on Abjection* (New York: Columbia University Press, 1982).

Labra, Diego, '¿Vivió Buenos Aires una "periódico-manía" hacia 1870? Una reflexión sobre los periódicos para "niñas", la prensa ilustrada y la ampliación del público lector porteño', *Estudios de Teoría Literaria*, 9.20 (2020), 309–21.

LaGreca, Nancy, *Rewriting Womanhood: Feminism, Subjectivity, and the Angel of the House in the Latin American Novel, 1887–1903* (University Park: Penn State University Press, 2009).

Lee Six, Abigail, *Gothic Terrors: Incarceration, Duplication, and Bloodlust in Spanish Narrative* (Lewisburg: Bucknell University Press, 2010).

——, *Spanish Vampire Fiction since 1900: Blood Relations* (New York and London: Routledge, 2019).

——, 'The Last of the Vamp(ire)s: Two Spanish Stories at a Semantic Fork in the Road', *Horror Studies*, 10.2 (2019), 173–88.

Linton, Anne E., 'Redeeming the *Femme Fatale*: Aesthetics and Religion in Théophile Gautier's *La morte amoureuse*', *French Review*, 89.1 (2015), 145–56.

López, Sylvia, 'The Gothic Tradition in Galdós' *La sombra*', *Hispania*, 81.3 (1998), 509–18.

López Santos, Miriám, *La novela gótica en España (1788–1833)* (Vigo: Academia del Hispanismo, 2010).

Lugones, Leopoldo, 'Ensayo de una cosmogonía en diez lecciones', in *Las fuerzas extrañas* (Buenos Aires: Agebe, 2009), 107–40.

SELECT BIBLIOGRAPHY

Lugones, Leopoldo 'Polo', ed., *Las primeras letras de Leopoldo Lugones: reproducción facsimilar de sus primeros trabajos* (Buenos Aires: Centurion, 1963).

Marx, Karl, 'The Working Day', in *Capital: A Critique of Political Economy*, ed. by Friedrich Engels, vol. 1 (Moscow: Foreign Language Publishing House, 1959).

Masiello, Francine, *Between Civilization and Barbarism: Women, Nation, and Literary Culture in Modern Argentina* (Lincoln, NE: University of Nebraska Press, 1992).

————, 'Women, State, and Family in Latin American Literature of the 1920s', in *Women, Culture, and Politics in Latin America: Seminar on Feminism and Culture in Latin America*, ed. by Emilie Bergmann, et al. (Berkeley, Los Angeles, Oxford: University of California Press, 1990), pp. 27–47.

Masotta, Oscar, and Jorge Lafforgue, 'Cronología', in *Horacio Quiroga*, ed. by Jitrik, pp. 13–49.

Mejías López, Alejandro, 'Modernismo's Inverted Conquest and the Ruins of Imperial Nostalgia: Rethinking Transatlantic Relations in Contemporary Critical Discourse', *Arizona Journal of Hispanic Cultural Studies*, 12 (2008), 7–29.

————, *The Inverted Conquest: The Myth of Modernity and the Transatlantic Onset of Modernism* (Nashville: Vanderbilt University Press, 2009).

Mitlich Osuna, Ana Consuelo, 'El gótico en la novela histórica mexicana del siglo XIX', *Hispanet Journal*, 4 (2011), 1–17.

Molyneux, Maxine, *Women's Movements in International Perspective: Latin America and Beyond* (London: Palgrave Macmillan, 2001).

Monleón, José B., 'Vampiros y donjuanes: sobre la figura del seductor en el siglo XIX', *Revista Hispánica Moderna*, 48.1 (1995), 19–30.

Mora, Gabriela, *Clemente Palma: el modernismo en su versión decadente y gótica* (Lima: IEP Ediciones, 2000).

————, 'Decadencia y vampirismo en el modernism hispanoamericano: un cuento de ClementePalma', *Revista de Crítica Literaria Latinoamericana*, 23.46 (1997), 191–98.

————, '"La granja blanca" de Clemente Palma: relaciones con el decadentismo y Edgar Allan Poe', *Casa de las Américas*, 38.205 (1996), 62–69.

————, 'La sexualidad femenina en el modernismo decadente: la narrativa de Clemente Palma', in *Delmira Agustini y el modernismo: nuevas propuestas de género*, ed. by Tina Escaja (Buenos Aires: Viterbo, 2000), pp. 23–37.

—————, 'Los *Cuentos malévolos* de Clemente Palma: integración más allá del bien y del mal', in *Ojo en el caleidoscopio: las colecciones de textos integrados en la literatura latinoamericana*, ed. by P. Brescia and E. Romano (Mexico City: National Autonomous University of Mexico, 2006), pp. 371–88.

O'Brien, Mac Gregor, 'Bibliografía de las revistas literarias peruanas', *Hispania*, 71.1 (March 1988), 61–74.

Olivio Jiménez, José, *Antología crítica de la poesía modernista hispanoamericana* (Madrid: Hiperión, 2011).

Oviedo, José Miguel, *Antología crítica del cuento hispanoamericano: del romanticismo al criollismo (1830–1920)* (Madrid: Alianza, 1989).

—————, *Historia de la literatura hispanoamericana, vol. 3: postmodernismo, vanguardia, regionalismo* (Madrid: Alianza, 2001).

Palma, Clemente, *Cuentos malévolos*, 2nd edn (1904; Paris: Ollendorff, 1912).

Peluffo, Ana, 'Rizomas, redes y lazos transatlánticos: América Latina y España (1890–1920)', in *No hay nación para este sexo: La re(d)pública transatlántica de las letras: escritoras españolas y latinoamericanas*, ed. by Pura Fernández (Madrid and Frankfurt: Iberoamericana Editorial Vervuert, 2015), pp. 207–24.

Poe, Edgar Allan, 'The Philosophy of Composition' (1846), in *Edgar Allan Poe, Critical Theory: The Major Documents*, ed. by Stuart Levine and Susan F. Levine (Champaign: University of Illinois Press, 2010), pp. 55–76.

Pollack, Beth, 'The Supernatural and the Occult as Literary Elements in Selected *modernista* Short Stories' (unpublished doctoral thesis, University of California, Santa Barbara, 1988).

Quereilhac, Soledad, 'Shadows of Science in the Río de la Plata Turn-of-the-Century Gothic', in *Latin American Gothic*, ed. by Casanova-Vizcaíno and Ordiz, pp. 155–71.

Ragan, Robin, 'Carmen de Burgos's 'La mujer fría': A Response to Necrophilic Aesthetics in Decadentist Spain', in *Disciplines on the Line: Feminist Research on Spanish, Latin American, and U.S. Latina Women*, ed. by Anne J. Cruz, et al. (Newark: Cuesta, 2003), pp. 235–55.

Reid, Anna, 'El vampiro sudamericano: parásitos y espectros en los cuentos de Quiroga', *Espéculo*, 44 (2010), n. pag.

Robinson, William J., 'Excessive Sensuality or the Woman Vampire', *Married Life and Happiness: Or, Love and Comfort in Marriage* (New York: Eugenics, 1922), pp. 89–93.

Rock, David, *Authoritarian Argentina: The Nationalist Movement, Its History and Its Impact* (Berkeley: University of California Press, 1993).

SELECT BIBLIOGRAPHY

Rodríguez, Juan Carlos, *Theory and History of Ideological Production: The First Bourgeois Literatures (The 16th Century)*, trans. by M. K. Read (Newark: University of Delaware Press, 2002).

———, *Tras la muerte del aura: en contra y a favor de la Ilustración* (Granada: Universidad de Granada, 2011).

Rogers, Susan Leigh, 'Vampire Vixens: The Female Undead and the Lacanian Sybolic Order in Tales by Gautier, James, and Le Fanu' (unpublished doctoral thesis, University of California, Irvine, 1993).

Sánchez Franco, Moisés Samuel Ysmael, 'La representación del sujeto aristócrata y del sujeto juvenil drogado en *Historietas malignas* de Clemente Palma' (unpublished doctoral thesis, Universidad Nacional Mayor de San Marcos, Lima, 2007).

Sánchez-Verdejo Pérez, Francisco, 'El vampiro femenino de Poe: metáfora maldita de la femme fatale y ejemplificación edificante de la mujer sin sombra', in *Edgar Allan Poe (1809–2009): doscientos años después*, ed. by Beatriz González Moreno and Rigal Aragón (Cuenca: University Castilla-La Mancha, 2010), pp. 87–96.

Sanz Ramírez, José Antonio, 'Antonio de Hoyos y Vinent: genealogía y elogio de una pasión' (unpublished doctoral thesis, Universidad Complutense de Madrid, 2010).

Sardiñas, José Miguel, 'El vampirismo en relatos modernistas', *Fuentes Humanísticas*, 19.35 (July–December 2007), 33–44.

Sarlo, Beatriz, 'Horacio Quiroga and Technoscientific Theory', in *The Technical Imagination: Argentine Culture's Modern Dreams*, trans. by Xavier Callahan (Stanford: Stanford University Press, 2008), pp. 13–36.

Schumann, Nancy, 'Women with Bite: Tracing Vampire Women from Lilith to *Twilight*', in *The Universal Vampire: Origins and Evolution of a Legend*, ed. by Barbara Brodman and James E. Doan (Lanham, MD and Plymouth: Fairleigh Dickinson University Press and Rowman & Littlefield Publishing, 2013), pp. 109–20.

Senf, Carol A., *The Vampire in Nineteenth-Century English Literature* (Bowling Green: Bowling Green State University Press, 1988).

Serrano, Carmen A., *Gothic Imagination in Latin American Fiction and Film* (Albuquerque: University of Mexico Press, 2019).

Smart, Carol, 'Disruptive Bodies and Unruly Sex: The Regulation of Reproduction and Sexuality in the Nineteenth Century', in *Regulating Womanhood: Historical Essays on Marriage, Motherhood, and Sexuality*, ed. by Carol Smart (New York: Routledge, 1992), pp. 7–32.

Smith, Jennifer, 'Women and the Deployment of Sexuality in Nineteenth-Century Spain', *Revista de Estudios Hispánicos*, 40 (2006), 145–70.

INTRODUCTION

Speratti-Piñero, Emma Susan, 'Horacio Quiroga, precursor de la relación cine-literatura en la América Hispánica', *Nueva Revista de Filología Hispánica*, 36.2 (1988), 1239–49.

Sproles, Karen Z., 'D. H. Lawrence and the Pre-Raphaelites: Love among the Ruins', *D. H. Lawrence Review*, 22.3 (1990), 299–305.

Starcevic, Elizabeth, *Carmen de Burgos: defensora de la mujer* (Almería: Cajal, 1976).

Steenland, Kyle, 'Notes on Feudalism and Capitalism in Chile and Latin America', *Latin American Perspectives*, 2.1 (1975), 49–58.

Terezinha Schmidt, Rita, 'Difference and Subversion: Gothic Migrations in Nineteenth-Century Latin American Novels', in *Tropical Gothic in Literature and Culture: The Americas*, ed. by Justin Edwards and Sandra Guardini Vasconcelos (New York: Routledge, 2016), pp. 218–39.

Thompson, Hannah, 'Decadence', in *The Cambridge History of French Literature*, ed. by William Burgwinkle, Nicholas Hammond and Emma Wilson (Cambridge: Cambridge University Press, 2011), pp. 541–48.

Ugarte, Michael, 'Carmen de Burgos ("Colombine"): Feminist *Avant la Lettre*', in *Spanish Women Writers and the Essay: Gender, Politics, and the Self*, ed. by Kathleen Glenn and Mercedes Mazquiarán de Rodríguez (Columbia, MO: University of Missouri Press, 1998), pp. 55–74.

Voltaire, *Philosophical Dictionary*, trans. by H. I. Woolf (New York: Knopf, 1924).

Warwick, Alexandra, 'Vampires and the Empire: Fears and Fictions of the 1890s', in *Cultural Politics at the Fin de Siècle*, ed. by Sally Ledger and Scott McCracken (Cambridge: Cambridge University Press, 1995), pp. 202–20.

Wingrove, David Melville, '"La Belle Dame": *Lilith* and the Romantic Vampire Tradition', in *Rethinking George MacDonald: Contexts and Contemporaries*, ed. by Christopher MacLachlan, John Patrick Pazdziora and Ginger Stelle (Glasgow: Association for Scottish Literary Studies, 2013), pp. 175–97.

Wisker, Gina, 'Female Vampirism', in *Women and the Gothic: An Edinburgh Companion*, ed. by Avril Horner and Sue Zlosnik (Edinburgh: Edinburgh University Press, 2016), pp. 150–65.

Note on the Texts

OF THE TALES INCLUDED IN THIS ANTHOLOGY, three have never before been translated into English, while two were previously translated by independent publishers. This is the first instance, however, where all five tales originally written in Spanish have been translated into English with extensive annotations and critical notes for the purposes of introducing the stories to a scholarly audience.

TEXTUAL HISTORY OF THE TALES

The Female Vampire (1899)

While Leopoldo Lugones (Argentina, 1874–1938) is one of the most influential and recognised Latin American authors, his tale 'La vampira' ['The Female Vampire'] (1899) has been all but neglected. This is arguably owing to the fact that, unlike many of the other tales that he published in newspapers around that time, 'La vampira' did not reappear in the canonised collection, *Las fuerzas extrañas* [*Strange Forces*] (Buenos Aires: Moen, 1906).

In fact, it was not until Lugones's son, Polo (1897–1971), published the 1963 collection, *Las primeras letras de Leopoldo Lugones: reproducción facsimilar de sus primeros trabajos literarios escritos entre sus dieciocho y veinticinco años* [Leopoldo Lugones's early writings: a facsimile reproduction of his first literary works written between the ages of eighteen and twenty-five], that the tale came to light.[1] Organised chronologically, this rare collection—according to WorldCat, there are fifty-nine copies in existence—is made up of approximately 150 of Lugones's writings, including book reviews, essays, poems and numerous short stories. They are photoreproductions of the original periodical publications, and as a result many of the works have imperfections, such as illegible words, as well as lines or entire sections that have been manually scratched out, while others include handwritten notes in the margins by Lugones himself.

In some cases, publication information does not appear in the original clipping, and so it seems that journal titles and dates have been stamped onto the copies at the end of those texts. In the case of 'La vampira', 'Tribuna—enero 25 de 1899' appears in bold under the author's name at the end of the tale, but a newspaper with 'Tribuna' in the title does not seem to have been in circulation in Buenos Aires in 1899. *La tribuna* was a major Argentine periodical in the mid- to late nineteenth century,[2] although it ceased to operate in 1880.[3] There were periodicals with the same or a similar title in circulation in other Latin American countries at the time, but it is unclear

lxxiii

NOTE ON THE TEXTS

whether Lugones published in these venues, and some appear to have not been operating in 1899. More archival work will hopefully clear up this mystery one day.

The present translation thus uses as its copy text the facsimile provided in Polo Lugones's 1963 collection, and is the first time the tale appears in print outside of the original '1899' newspaper clipped into the 1963 facsimile.

The White Farmhouse (1904)

Clemente Palma (Peru, 1872–1946) was the son of the canonical writer Ricardo Palma (1833–1919), and an author in his own right. He is widely considered the founder of the fantastic short story in Peru, but his tales and novels also demonstrate a *fin-de-siglo* affinity for the gothic and the occult: see, for example, his two short story collections, *Cuentos malévolos* [*Malevolent Tales*] (Barcelona: Salvat, 1904) and *Historietas malignas* [Evil vignettes] (Lima: Garcilaso, 1925).

While 'La granja blanca' ['The White Farmhouse'] was included in both the first (Barcelona: Salvat, 1904) and second (Paris: Ollendorff, 1912) editions of *Cuentos malévolos*,[4] it was originally published under the title '¿Ensueño o realidad?' [Daydream or reality?] in *El Ateneo: Revista Mensual de Ciencias y Bellas Artes* [The Athenaeum: monthly journal of science and the fine arts] for May 1900.[5] *El Ateneo* was a Lima-based publication in operation from 1899 to 1908.[6] As detailed in the Introduction (pp. xxviii–xxix), this was a time in Latin America that experienced tremendous periodical expansion. *El Ateneo* was subscription-based and catered to both domestic and international audiences.[7] It is curious to note that Palma served as secretary of the journal at the time the story was published. Moreover, the tale appears in the section 'Artículos varios' [Various articles] alongside essays titled 'El tipo criminal' [The criminal type] and 'Estudios filológicos' [Philological studies], granting the story an air of scientific credibility.

Cuentos malévolos has received much critical attention in the last few decades as a *modernista*, Decadent and gothic collection, with its unsettling images relayed through swift and often gripping storytelling. Yet at the time of publication, according to Gabriela Mora, it did not receive the same level of attention as collections by Palma's contemporaries. She attributes this to the text's treatment of sexuality; for instance, the declaration in his gothic parody, 'Vampiras', that female sexual desire is a natural occurrence, not deviant behaviour. She writes: 'One does not need to be reminded of the audacity, at that time, of making such a declaration, and I would not be surprised if that audacity were one of the reasons behind the critical silence of the Peruvian's work'.[8]

Indeed, only a few reviews of the first edition of the collection have been unearthed. One is a 1904 letter from celebrated Spanish author Miguel de Unamuno (1864–1936), which Palma included as the prologue to the first book edition. In it, Unamuno thanks Palma for the 'favour' of having sent

lxxiv

TEXTUAL HISTORY OF THE TALES

him the collection to read.[9] Yet, Unamuno reserves most of the review's space to criticise the anti-Christian sentiment of two of the collection's tales: 'El quinto Evangelio' [The fifth gospel] and 'El hijo pródigo' [The prodigal son].[10]

Later in 1904, two reviews were published in Lima-based literary journals. One, written by Octavio Espinoza and published in *Actualidades* [Current affairs],[11] closes the review with words of praise, but first criticises Palma's work for imitating Hoffmann, Poe, Mendes and Maupassant, as well as for not taking an interest in 'the issues of the nation'.[12] In July of that year, an anonymous review was published in *La Prensa* [The press] under the title '*Cuentos malévolos*, opiniones con respecto a su prólogo y temas generales' [*Malevolent Tales*: opinions regarding its prologue and general themes],[13] which notes how one story in particular reveals 'moral deformities and the psychology of vulgar souls'.[14] It appears, then, that the collection did receive some critical attention upon its original publication, but any positive reviews were eclipsed by criticism of the tale's treatment of subversive themes.

In recent years, the collection has been reprinted by small publishers and on independent publishing platforms. Spanish editions appeared under the title *Cuentos malévolos*, edited by Augusto Tamayou Vargas (Lima: Piesa, 1974) and edited by Marcelo Morión (Mexico City: La Casa de las Palabras, 2020). Two separate English translations of the collection appeared, the first translated by Guillermo I. Castillo-Feliú (New York: Irvington, 1983) and the second by by Shawn M. Garrett (Middletown, DE: Strange Ports Press, 2023).

The present translation uses as its copy text a version of the tale that appears in the second edition (1912) of *Cuentos malévolos*, as this was the last edition to which Palma made revisions during his lifetime. Both the 1904 and 1912 versions differ slightly in wording and structure from the tale's original May 1900 publication in *El Ateneo*. An example of a sentence-level modification is 'Faltaba próximamente un mes para que se realizara nuestro enlace', where it appears in the original as 'Faltaba próximamente un mes para nuestro enlace.' There are various sentence-level modifications beteen the two versions, in addition to the retitling of the story as 'The White Farmhouse'. It is likely that the original title 'Dream or Reality?' was perceived to be a little too on the nose.

Mr Cadaver and Miss Vampire (1910)

Antonio de Hoyos y Vinent (Spain, *c.* 1884–1940) was an author and openly gay man who was jailed after the conservative Nationalist party won the Spanish Civil War (1936–1939). He died shortly thereafter in prison, abruptly ending a flourishing literary career and careening his legacy into obscurity until recently.

His tale, 'El señor Cadáver y la señorita Vampiro' ['Mr Cadaver and Miss Vampire'], appears to have first been published in the collection *Del huerto*

lxxv

NOTE ON THE TEXTS

del pecado [From the garden of sin] (Madrid: Primitivo Fernández, 1910), and not previously in a literary magazine.[15] As the collection was widely read and well received, a second edition was published in 1919 by the Madrid firm Renacimiento.[16] Both editions are identical, apart from the first edition's use of accents on the single-letter words *a* and *o*, which is not the case for the second. It is likely that during the 1910s accenting of one-letter forms fell out of favour.

The tale does not appear to have been reprinted since the second edition of 1919 or translated into another language. As Abigail Lee Six observes, 'Mr Cadaver and Miss Vampire' may have heavily influenced Carmen de Burgos's 1922 tale 'The Cold Woman' (ALS, 181), also included in this anthology. For a fuller consideration of the context of these details and the tale's own influences—from Baudelaire's *Les Fleurs du mal* (1857) and Darío's *Azúl* (1888)—please see the Introduction, p. xxxviii.

The present volume uses the first edition of the tale, given the near-identical state of both the 1910 and 1919 editions.

The Cold Woman (1922)

Carmen de Burgos y Seguí (Spain, 1867–1932) was an author, feminist and public figure who, like her contemporary de Hoyos y Vinent, was all but erased from literary history, most likely owing to censorship during the Franco Regime (1939–1975). Indeed, it was Elizabeth Starcevic's 1976 study that appears to have put de Burgos's literary works back on the map.[17]

Her novella 'La mujer fría' ['The Cold Woman'] was first published in the literary magazine *Flirt: Revista Frívola* [Flirt: frivolous review] in 1922.[18] As its title suggests, *Flirt* catered to early twentieth-century interests such as frivolity, sensuality and other topics pertaining to the private sphere, thus making it the ideal medium for de Burgos's story. Released every Thursday in Madrid, the literary magazine 'was to Spain what "La Vie Parisienne" was to France'.[19] As Judith Kirkpatrick observes, de Burgos took advantage of a 'new arena of print culture that took off like wildfire in the first decades of the twentieth century—the highly profitable paperback short novel series pitched both in price and style toward a mass audience'.[20] While the publication, like its French inspiration, was geared towards a male audience, female readership in Spain was widening, and de Burgos's audience was predominantly middle-class women.[21] De Burgos later included 'The Cold Woman' in the collection *Mis mejores cuentos* [My best stories] (Madrid: Prensa Popular, *c.* 1925), which was reprinted in 1986 by Editoriales Andaluzas Unidas, Seville.

Abigail Lee Six makes a convincing case that 'The Cold Woman' was deeply influenced by de Hoyos y Vinent's 'Mr Cadaver and Miss Vampire' (1910), if not a direct response to it. De Burgos and de Hoyos travelled in similar circles in Madrid and admired each other, and those readers familiar with de Hoyos's tale, 'which would have been numerous', would surely have noticed the similarities between the tales (ALS, 180–81).

lxxvi

TEXTUAL HISTORY OF THE TALES

'La mujer fría' was republished in 2003 by El Cid Editor (Santa Fe, Argentina); in 2012 by Torremozas (Madrid); and in 2023 by Libros Mablaz (Madrid). The tale also appeared in *La mujer fría y otros relatos* [The Cold Woman and other stories] (Barcelona: Plaza & Janes, 1968); in *La mujer fría y otros cuentos* [The Cold Woman and other stories] (Madrid: Torremozas, 2019) and in *Three Novellas: 'Confidencias', 'La mujer fría' and 'Puñal de claveles'* (Manchester: Manchester University Press, 2016). While this last collection, edited by Abigail Lee Six, is in Spanish, it does include English translations of some phrases and sentences in the footnotes.

The present volume contains the first full translation of 'The Cold Woman', and uses as its copy text the *Flirt* magazine version, in order to remain as close to the original text as it first appeared.

Horacio Quiroga, The Vampire (1927)
Horacio Quiroga (1878–1937) was a Uruguayan author who left an indelible mark on Latin American literature. He published articles, novels, plays and short stories, and his collection *Cuentos de amor, de locura y de muerte* [Tales of Love, Madness and Death] (Salta: Sociedad Cooperativa, 1917) is a staple of the early twentieth-century literary canon. His works are often marked by death, with forces such as nature and technology tending to doom his human protagonists.

Such is the case with 'El vampiro' ['The Vampire'], published in 1927 in *La Nación*.[22] In 1935, the story appeared in the collection *Más allá [Beyond]* (Buenos Aires: Sociedad Amigos del Libro Rioplatense, 1935), and is not to be confused with a different, shorter story of the same title that appeared in Quiroga's originally undated collection, *El vampiro*.[23] The collection was republished in Buenos Aires in 1952 by Editorial Lautaro, and has also been republished as *Más allá y otros cuentos* [Beyond and other stories], edited by Alberto Zum Felde (Montevideo: García, 1945); and as *Él más allá* [The beyond] (Buenos Aires: Pingüino, 1952 and Buenos Aires: Losada, 1954). Various independent publishers in Latin America have republished the collection using these different titles.

The present volume uses the 1952 edition published by Lautaro as its copy text, owing to issues of access caused by the COVID-19 pandemic during the time of preparation.

THE PRESENT EDITION

My methodology is grounded in maintaining a faithful translation that also recognises the reading practices and needs of an English-speaking, twenty-first-century readership. I have therefore attempted to maintain the lyrical tone of the tales—expressed through elaborate, even labyrinthine sentences and an abundance of descriptors—when possible, but adjusted accordingly to facilitate a smoother, more enjoyable read in English. All of the tales experiment with language and form in ways that can make for a challenging

lxxvii

NOTE ON THE TEXTS

read, and while it was important to maintain the integrity of the tales, it was equally important to meet readers' expectations of the English language.

Where secondary sources written in Spanish have been referenced and quoted directly, I have included my own English translations. I have also elected to follow some but not all referenced titles, such as those of literary journals or scholarly books, with their English translations in parenthesis. My rationale for doing so is that some titles in Spanish are easily understood by readers of English while others are not, so I opted for not overwhelming the reader when possible.

Lastly, I have elected to keep French words or expressions that appeared in the original Spanish tales in French. My reason for this is that the marked influence of French literature, language and culture on both Latin American and Spanish authors is an important element to consider when reading turn-of-the-twentieth-century Hispanic literature, and losing that connection would have done these tales a disservice.

A number of editorial decisions were made in preparing the present edition. This volume makes use of UK English spelling for the translated texts. Obvious errors in the spelling and presentation of proper nouns have been corrected. Any italicisation that appears in the original copy texts is retained, and foreign words are italicised as standard throughout to emphasise their non-hispanophone qualities. In keeping with the house style of the Gothic Originals series, double quotations have been replaced by single quotations throughout the text, and full stops at the end of titles and abbreviations have been omitted as appropriate.

NOTES

1. Leopoldo 'Polo' Lugones, ed., *Las primeras letras de Leopoldo Lugones: reproducción facsimilar de sus primeros trabajos literarios escritos entre sus dieciocho y veinticinco años* (Buenos Aires: Centurion, 1963).
2. See Marcelo Garabedian, 'Lectores y periódicos españoles en la Ciudad de Buenos Aires (1870–1910)', in *Los españoles en Buenos Aires: activismo politico e inserción sociocultural (1870–1960)*, ed. by N. De Cristóforis (Buenos Aires: Teseo, 2020).
3. See Amelia Aguado de Costa, 'Newspapers in the Public Library of the Universidad Nacional de La Plata', *Información, Cultura y Sociedad*, 17 (2007), 13–38 (p. 17).
4. 'La granja blanca' appears in *Cuentos malévolos* (1904), pp. 115–44 and (1912), pp. 107–34.
5. Clemente Palma, '¿Ensueño o realidad?', *El Ateneo: Revista Mensual de Ciencias y Bellas Artes*, 2.11 (May 1900), 427–44.
6. See NKM, 122, and Mac Gregor O'Brien, 'Bibliografía de las revistas literarias peruanas', *Hispania*, 71.1 (March 1988), 61–74 (p. 62).
7. See e.g. 'En el extranjero rejirán los mismos precios con solo el recargo postal', *El Ateneo*, 2.11 (May 1900), inside front cover.

lxxviii

NOTES

8. Gabriela Mora, 'La sexualidad femenina en el modernismo decadente: la narrativa de Clemente Palma', in *Delmira Agustini y el modernismo: nuevas propuestas de género*, ed. by Tina Escaja (Buenos Aires: Viterbo, 2000), pp. 23–37 (p. 32; my translation).

9. See Miguel de Unamuno, 'Prologue', in Palma, *Cuentos malévolos* (1904), pp. v–xvi (p. xvi).

10. Ibid., pp. viii–xiv.

11. Octavio Espinoza, 'Clemente Palma', *Actualidades*, 2.70 (1904), 8.

12. See Moisés Samuel Ysmael Sánchez Franco, 'La representación del sujeto aristócrata y del sujeto juvenil drogado en *Historietas malignas* de Clemente Palma' (unpublished doctoral thesis, Universidad Nacional Mayor de San Marcos, Lima, 2007), p. 12.

13. '*Cuentos malévolos*, opiniones con respect a su prólogo y temas generals', *La Prensa*, 24 July 1904.

14. See Jesús Miguel Delgado del Aguila, 'Recepción cronológica de la crítica literaria sobre *Cuentos malévolos* (1904)', *Actio Nova: Revista de Teoría de la Literatura y Literatura Comparada*, 3 (December 2019), 367–83 (p. 370; my translation)

15. Antonio de Hoyos y Vinent, *Del huerto del pecado* (Madrid: Primitivo Fernández, 1910).

16. Antonio de Hoyos y Vinent, *Del huerto del pecado* (Madrid: Renacimiento, 1919).

17. Elizabeth Starcevic, *Carmen de Burgos: defensora de la mujer* (Almería: Cajal, 1976).

18. Carmen de Burgos, 'La mujér fría', *Flirt: Revista Frívola*, 25 March 1922, n.p.

19. As quoted on the cover of the magazine, no. 328, 25 March 1922 (my translation).

20. Judith Kirkpatrick, 'Women as Cultural Agents in Spanish Modernity', in *A Companion to Spanish Women's Studies*, ed. by Xon de Ros and Geraldine Hazbun (Woodbridge: Tamesis, 2011), pp. 227–41 (pp. 239–40).

21. Michelle M. Sharp, 'The Narrative of Carmen de Burgos: An Innovative Portrayal of Family and Gender Roles in Spain' (unpublished doctoral thesis, University of Wisconsin, Madison, 2009), p. 29.

22. See José Miguel Saridiñas, 'El vampirismo en relatos modernistas', *Fuentes Humanísticas*, 19.35 (2007), 33–44 (p. 41).

23. While details of its original publication is unknown, the other short story titled 'El vampiro' can be found in a recent edition as Horacio Quiroga, *El Vampiro* (Buenos Aires: Rei Argentina, 1990).

lxxix

The Female Vampire in Hispanic Literature

The Female Vampire

LEOPOLDO LUGONES

TEARY-EYED AND EARNESTLY IN LOVE, Adolfo told me of his pain and sorrow, of his doubts more awful than the certainty of disaster.

I had only seen her two or three times, but that strange woman of majestic stature, profound eyes, and splendid pallor had me worried. The widow of an immensely wealthy colonel,[1] she enjoyed an outrageously lavish lifestyle with his fortune. Her behaviour was fodder for gossip in certain circles, but she remained untouchable as spurned lovers crowded her, envy chased her and false accusations were thrown at her. It was as if something majestic were protecting her. She possessed the smile and spirit of a sphinx,[2] provoking a fright-filled affection in those around her.[3] She couldn't be reached through mere ambition or fame. The only road to her was love, and like I said, love found her indifferent.

Adolfo was her favourite, or so I thought until his sudden confession made me think otherwise. The good lad and I had suddenly stopped speaking about a year prior, which I thought to be the end of our long-time friendship. Now he had come to me to explain that she was to blame for it all. To see her and to be possessed by her wicked love were one and the same. Indeed, her love was a demon that consumed both his mind and his soul. He had battled it for a year to no avail. He was unsure of whether the enigmatic beauty was even taking his efforts seriously. A victim of the terrible persuasions of flirtation, all the bitterness of Calvary[4] came rushing over him with every passing minute. She showed him slightly more affection than one would a lovely doll but treated him worse. Her lips were exquisitely worn out and passion would flash across her green eyes like golden lightning. Adolfo kissed her cheeks and hands, his promises awakening her wild fervour, yet he only received restrained, almost maternal affection, which shamed his masculine pride and crushed his sick spirit. This only fanned the flames of his passion, and instead of becoming enraged, he deteriorated into a state of lachrymose[5] enslavement. He was truly possessed, and it would surely be difficult to extinguish the fateful fervour that was devouring him.

He was lovesick, which was made worse by a new complication. Two days prior, the terrible woman had confided in him.

They were in the garden, and as always, Adolfo was softly pleading with her. She would listen without really hearing him, as she always did, her eyes fixed on the horizon, forever cold and inexpressive. The groves' shadows

THE FEMALE VAMPIRE IN HISPANIC LITERATURE

were getting darker and silent birds flew over the sky's crepuscular opal.[6] Adolfo whined. His pleas were as trivial and monotonous as the recitation of a street beggar, as impertinent as the complaints of a child. He felt infinitely detached from the world, from any sense of comfort or formula. Staggering over an abyss, he felt faint-hearted and pitiful,[7] as if sentenced to death. He would have given his life, his desires, everything for just one glimmer of requited love. Like a sick and insolent child, he could not help but repeat the same painful phrase: 'Madam ... Why is it so hard for you? ... Just be good to me!'

For the first time, a flicker of life seemed to revive that magnificent marble statue. The awful woman turned to look at the poor man that adored her.

In a maternal tone that revealed her unsparing coldness, she told him, 'Adolfo, calm down and listen, then judge me as you wish.'

She went on to tell him the story of her marriage.

Irresistible desires that she had tried in vain to control had propelled her towards the colonel. Like a true lioness, she loved him furiously and violently, and was terribly jealous. Four years passed in a continuous state of delirium. The solitude they found in the countryside protected them from the hustle and bustle of society, so bothersome with its pressing needs.

Their endless happiness could have filled firmament upon firmament.[8] But one day the colonel became melancholy, and even he did not know why. It was a kind of fatigue that, filled with infinite sweetness, could not temper the intensity of his love. As he tenderly began to wither away, she blossomed. She soaked up his life force, swigging deliriously from that fruitful cup, multiplying her graces and her love to battle her husband's inexplicable deterioration. Once she realised that it was her love that was killing him, it was too late. She tried to stop herself, to stave off his caresses and extinguish the mutual fire, but it was useless! Just one plea from the dying man would best her most valiant attempts. So, little by little, she could feel more of him within her. Their thoughts would coincide, and the same word would frequently reach each of their lips at the exact same time.

The strange woman in love was transformed. Two years prior, she was of few words, slight frame, and small bust. Now, in a cruel twist of fate, her fragile beauty had become splendid, almost terrible, on account of her husband's demise. Her flesh had grown visibly more opulent. Her voice had taken on a commanding timbre, her speech a vibrant abundance. All the irreparable catastrophe did was multiply her charm. In his final days, the sick man could only speak through her words and see through her eyes. Drop by drop, his soul transfused into his loved one, abandoning the poor vessel that was his body for the magnificent vessel that was his wife. To adore her better, he gave her his life. And then one night, at the peak of his listlessness and pain, his heart gave way, and he died.[9]

She lived the strangest life from that point on. Despite the protests of her old conscience, which grew weaker every day, a powerful joy—a fresh vigour of triumphant convalescence—floated over her initial stupor. All that male energy mixed with hers, delicate and refined until then, thumping intensely in her breast. Her pulse beat more rapidly. Her kindheartedness dissolved in copious amounts, hurling her with epic bursts towards the horizon of her dreams. She felt invaded by the soul she had absorbed, aroused by the delicious confusion of her emotions and ideas with those of her beloved dead husband, at times still her double. They oscillated between their wavering old love and the still-hazy ecstasy of their new one, babbling phrases that would culminate in an immense and victorious cry of love as two became one.

Next began her desperate attempt to conceal her incredible secret. Her friends noticed she was different upon her return to the city, but they kept quiet because they found her more beautiful. With just a glance she understood that their silence masked hostility, so she became inaccessible and arrogant. Her consciousness, now stable, abridged her disturbing dualism into a scornful mightiness. When she noticed a calumnious smile or envious look, she would often undergo strange aggressive impulses that, rather than being manifested into action, were restrained by an anguished hesitation that expressed her female side. The delightful rapport of their old love was replaced by a frightful agony. For a year now she had been suffering. She both loved and detested Adolfo. Her soul was at war with itself.[10]

Gifted as she was with a wicked power that turned her lovers into fools, she knew she could never love a man without absorbing him. Her life was frightfully complete, and therefore isolated, lacking all form of social dealings besides women's envy and hatred and men's degrading servility. She was dying of love for Adolfo, but at the same time hated him with every fibre of her being. She was jealous of her own love—a wild jealousy that conflicted with her fierce passion. The lover she once was arose from her overwhelming sense of yearning, but it was at odds with the other that was now her. For her excessive pleasures she suffered the hellish torment of her sexual energy being neutralised by a jealous rage.

The tone of her voice, which fluctuated sharply from a masculine vibration to a feminine sweetness, dropped suddenly. In a hushed plea, she asked that Adolfo leave the garden so she could privately let out the tremendous pain she had confessed earlier in a bizarre fit of madness.

Always obedient to her, and finding her influence more powerful than ever, he left in silence. His hands were soaking wet with tears from eyes that did not look like they were made to cry.[11]

I advised my friend at length, practically commanding that he distance himself. Naturally, I did not believe one word of her fantastic tale, but he was unfortunately blinded by the ravings of a madwoman. Although I was wary of my own logic, I was resolute and zealous in my convictions, and he seemed reassured when he left.

But as I had feared, he went back to her.

The visit was a page right out of the final scene of a tragedy, although it's difficult to say exactly what happened between the two lovers. Having suffered an epileptic fit from which she has yet to recover, she could barely articulate the following:

After their usual conversation in the garden, her love for Adolfo briefly overpowered her. The freshness of the foliage, the rustling of the wind, and the serenity of the evening momentarily soothed her spirit. My poor friend had been wanting a kiss that she had refused, despite herself. That moment's peace overcame her repugnance. They leaned forward and touched tips, and she felt fireworks go off in her soul.[12]

Then the hostility she harboured within suddenly overcame her with the force of a hurricane. Her eyes filmed over. Her lips drank in the ecstasy as her fingers, cat-like in their viciousness, slowly made their way to her lover's neck, and in one uncontrollable impulse, they strangled him.

The White Farmhouse

CLEMENTE PALMA

to Lady Emilia Pardo Bazán[1]

I

*I*S LIFE REALLY LIVED, or is it just a prolonged illusion? Are we autonomous and independent beings, travellers in the journey of life, or just characters in *someone else's daydream*? Are we mere forms, tragic or grotesque shadows that illustrate the nightmares and sweet dreams of *some eternal sleeper*? If so, why are we the ones experiencing life's joys and suffering? We should be indifferent and insensitive; suffering and pleasure should fall to the eternal dreamer in whose imagination we play these shadows, these fantastic creations.

I would always present these types of cynical ideas to my old philosophy teacher, who would laugh and affectionately denounce my constant tendency to skew philosophical theories and lead them down purely imaginative paths. More than once, he would go on to explain the real meaning behind Hegel's principle: *what is real is ideal, and what is ideal is real;*[2] a principle which, according to my teacher, I interpreted iniquitously to apply to my ultra-Kantian views.[3] The philosopher from Könisberg[4] affirmed that our representation of the world was a twisted vision, an inexact reflection, a *noumenon*,[5] an ill-defined shadow of reality. I maintained my view that Kant was wrong because he accepted that within us was an erroneous representation of reality. But there is no such real world. The world is an intermediate state where humans are situated between the void (which does not exist) and reality (which doesn't exist either). It is a simple act of imagination, a mere daydream in which humans float around giving the appearance of having individual personalities. This is necessary for the eternal dreamer, that insatiable sleeper in whose imagination we all live, to amuse himself and feel more intensely. In any case, He is the only possible reality . . .

The good old man and I would spend long hours debating the most arduous and intricate ontological problems.[6] Our debates would end with my teacher more or less stating that I would end up a madman, never a philosopher. He said that I twisted every philosophical theory, however clear it was, as if they were balls of wax exposed to the heat of an extravagant sun; that I did not possess the necessary serenity to steadily follow a system or

THE FEMALE VAMPIRE IN HISPANIC LITERATURE

theory, and that quite to the contrary, I preferred fantasy, transforming the most transparent ideas, even axioms,[7] into complex matters; that I made gigantic rocks of pebbles by virtue of absurd and intolerable subtleties. He would add that I gave the impression of one of those ornamental flowers that become silvan- or bestial-headed gryphons,[8] or a blind feral horse that gallops woefully through a jungle on fire. He never wanted to admit that his philosophers were the insatiable feral horses, the ones whose imaginations had run wild, while I was the calm and astute one. However, I think that *my case*, in which he was but a mere actor, made him reassess his philosophical ideas . . .

II

From the time I was eight years old, I had become accustomed to thinking of my cousin Cordelia[9] as the woman I would marry. My father and her parents had arranged the union, supported by the affection we had for each other, which would later become a wild and passionate love. Cordelia, who was a few months younger than I, was my childhood companion. It was with my cousin that I grieved the loss of my parents, and once we were adolescents, we became each other's teachers. As a result, our souls began to blend in such a way that we experienced the same impressions of the same readings and objects. I was her mathematics and philosophy teacher, while she taught me music and drawing. Naturally, what I taught Cordelia was a despicable distortion of my own teacher's area of expertise.

On summer nights, Cordelia and I would go up to the terrace to talk by moonlight.

Cordelia was tall, slender, and pale. Her plentiful blonde hair, the colour of dried sprigs, was in stark contrast to her red lips and the feverish sparkle of her brown eyes. There was something strange in her remarkable beauty that was hard to pin down, but it would leave me pensive and melancholy. In the city's cathedral there was a painting, *The Resurrection of Jairus's Daughter*, by a Flemish painter.[10] The protagonist was a girl with dull hair whose face was very similar to that of Cordelia's; like that of surprise at having just awoken from the heavy sleep of death. Her eyes held traces of the dark depths of the mysteries of the grave . . . Every time I was with Cordelia, I would firmly recall the painting of the maiden who had returned to life.

Cordelia would calmly debate with me, her head a pallid archangel resting on my shoulder. The ideas in her mind followed the same mental process as mine, overflowing in a pure and delicate torrent of idealism. Our souls, slightly separated at the beginning of our discussion, would join again like old friends meeting at a crossroads and continuing the journey together. At this point in the conjunction, we would abandon our conversation on the philosophical and artistic to talk solely about our love.

Love is life. Why then, in my blind love for Cordelia, did I perceive an impalpable waft of death? Cordelia's luminous smile was life; her gazes,

THE WHITE FARMHOUSE (PALMA)

damp and passionate, were life; the intimate happiness in which we were both carried away, filling our souls with joy and faith, was life. Yet I had the impression that Cordelia was dead, that she was incorporeal. In winter, as the snow fell outside, we would stay up late playing Beethoven's beautiful sonatas[11] and Chopin's passionate nocturnes.[12] The music flowed, imbued by the feelings that united us. Yet as I experienced that ineffable happiness, I felt as though that same snow falling outside were infiltrating my soul; as if in that admirable weaving of harmonies, a thread were coming undone, already cut off from our entangled fate. I could feel the sad and indefinable weight of a tombstone . . .

III

Cordelia and I still had a year before turning twenty-three, the age we were to be married.

My entailed estate[13] provided me with substantial income. One of my rustic possessions was the *white farmhouse*, an old chapel that one of my ancestors had converted into a palace. It was in the depths of a vast forest, away from human foot traffic. No one had lived there for two centuries, and while it looked nothing like a farmhouse, family records referred to it as such. This was where we decided to live our life together, to enjoy our love, without any witnesses, in the freedom that nature provided. Every three or four months, Cordelia, my teacher, and I would venture out to the *white farmhouse*. It was a difficult task, but I managed to replace the outdated furniture with new pieces, and my bride oversaw the rooms' decor with the impeccable taste she was known for. How beautiful she looked in her white tunic and wide-brimmed hat folded over her cheeks, framing her pale face in a shadow that made her large and mysterious pupils sparkle! Having just descended from the covered wagon, Cordelia ran through the forest like a joyful child, gathering wild lilies, carnations, and roses. Butterflies and dragonflies circled exuberantly around her head as if waiting for the right moment to fall on her lips, as tempting as fresh red strawberries. She would sneakily try to get lost in the woods so that I would have to look for her. I would find her under the lemon trees, at the bottom of a stream, or hiding in a rose bush, then take her in my arms and give her a long kiss on her lips or her smooth pale cheeks . . . And despite my happiness, after those pure and passionate kisses I would get the slight impression of having just kissed the silky petals of a great fleur-de-lis[14] that blossomed from a tombstone.

IV

It was one month until the wedding, and Cordelia and I had agreed to take our last trip out to the *white farmhouse*. One morning, my teacher and I went off in the carriage to collect her, but she was sick and could not come out. I went in to see her and found that the poor thing was still in bed. As

I entered her room, she appeased me with a smile and stretched out her hand for a kiss. Oh, how her hand burned and how much she resembled Jairus's daughter! Her fever worsened in the coming days, and we came to find that she had malaria![15] Her hands were so hot to the touch, and my lips would burn when they came to rest on her forehead. My God, what to do! Cordelia was dying on me. She could feel it. She knew she would soon be taken out in a white box to spend eternity far, far away from me; far from the *farmhouse* that she had arranged to be our mysterious love nest; far from the forest that, dressed in white, she would traverse like a grand lily among the roses and carnations. Why such injustice? Why would she be snatched from my side? Could my little virgin really be happy in heaven without my kisses? Could she find a hand there that would caress her pale and vaporous hair with more tenderness than mine? . . . I was overcome with the most awful anguish upon hearing her hallucinate about the *white farmhouse*. My lips formed curses and blessings, blasphemy and prayer, demanding Cordelia's return to health. It didn't matter whether it was God or the Devil who granted it. All I wanted was Cordelia healthy. I would have bought it with my soul, my life, my fortune. I would have committed the most foul and criminal acts, incited the universe's outrage and God's eternal damnation, thrown all of humanity's blood into a cauldron, from Adam[16] to the last living man, and prepared a decoction in Hell with the fire destined for my damnation if it meant I could obtain a drug that would return Cordelia to good health. I would have withstood not one but *a thousand eternal damnations in succession* to experience the joy that nature was snatching from me with relentless malignance. Oh, what suffering!

One morning, Cordelia awoke feeling better. I had not rested in four nights, so I returned home to sleep. I awoke the next afternoon, and what a horrible afternoon it was! As I approached the house, I saw a crowd gathered and her front door closed. Pallid with anxiety and mad with anguish, I inquired about the crowd and an imbecile responded: Miss Cordelia has died!

I felt a sharp pain in my head and fell to the floor . . . I don't know who helped me, nor how much time—hours, years, or centuries—I was unconscious. When I came to, I found myself at my teacher's home, a short distance from Cordelia's. I flew to the window and opened it wide to find that Cordelia's house appeared as though nothing had happened. I ran off like a madman and barged into my fiancée's home . . .

V

The first person I saw was Cordelia's mother. Riddled with anxiety, I took her hand.

'My dear mother, how is Cordelia?'

'You can find her in the garden, my son . . . she should be there, watering her violets and heliotropes.'[17]

THE WHITE FARMHOUSE (PALMA)

Thrilled, I went to the garden and indeed found her there, seated at a marble bench, watering her flowers. I kissed her feverishly on the forehead. Later, overcome with emotion, I laid my head on her lap and began to cry like a child. I was there for quite a while as Cordelia's hands caressed my hair and her sweet voice whispered words of comfort: 'You thought I was dying, did you not?'

'Yes . . . I thought you had died. Even worse, my angel, I thought I had watched your burial. Oh, how horribly wicked to have been robbed of the only light in my life!'

'How mad you are! To have died before experiencing our happy life together! They say that no one is spared from malaria, but you see, it has spared me because of our love. It settled for having robbed me of just a little blood.'

Cordelia's lips were truly pale, as was her skin. Her hands and face were so pale they were almost transparent. Yet despite the toll malaria had taken, she was somehow more beautiful than before.

Cordelia and I were married in great splendour one month later, and on the very same day as our nuptials, I shut myself away in the secluded *white farmhouse* with my treasure.

VI

Our first year of happiness passed by with the swiftness of a shooting star. I doubt another mortal were as fortunate as I during that first year with my Cordelia in the peaceful and secluded dwelling we had chosen. Now and again, a lost hunter or curious villager would pass by. Our entire serving staff consisted of an old lady as deaf as a post. And I can't forget about my loyal dog, Ariel. Once, at the end of the year, I drove to the city to collect a midwife and bring her back to the *white farmhouse*, where Cordelia gave birth to a beautiful baby girl that filled our new home with joy.

I believe I mentioned that Cordelia was skilled at drawing. In those momentary breaks between caring for our daughter she set out to paint a portrait of me. What lovely mornings we would spend in my study! I would read aloud while she reproduced my likeness on canvas. It took longer than expected because we would pause our work to surrender ourselves to the wild fantasies of our love. It took three months to complete, but I must admit that while it was irreproachable in execution, it looked nothing like me. What I desperately longed for was that Cordelia paint me a portrait of herself. After several months of refusal, she finally gave in one morning. I was surprised by the strange and melancholic tone of her voice; *the voice that Jairus's daughter must have had.* She begged that I *do not enter my study while she was painting, nor try to catch a peek of the canvas before its completion.*

'It is cruel, my love, to not see you for two or three hours a day! Look, I take back what I asked of you. I would rather be without the painting than to deprive myself of your presence. After all, why would I need a copy when I possess the original forever?'

'Listen to me,' she responded, her arms draped around my neck, 'I'll paint only one day a week, and I know how to compensate you for my time away. Do you accept?'

'I suppose I grudgingly accept, if only because I'm curious to find out how I'll be repaid.'

From that week forward, Cordelia would shut herself away in my study every Saturday morning for two hours. Afterwards, she would emerge agitated, her cheeks paler than usual, her eyes red as though she had been crying. Cordelia explained that this was because of the extreme focus and attention she paid to extracting her image from the mirror and reproducing it accurately on canvas.

'Oh, my love, that will harm you! . . . I want you to abandon the painting.'

'That's impossible!' she murmured, as if speaking to herself. 'If only I had one more year to complete it! The deadline is unavoidable!'

She immediately began to shower me ardently with affection. She clung to me and our daughter for the rest of the day, as though she were trying to make up for the hours she had spent away from us with an abundance of love.

VII

We were coming up on the end of our second year at the *white farmhouse*. Cordelia was finishing up her portrait. One morning, I had the reckless idea to watch her through the keyhole, and what I saw made me tremble in anguish: Cordelia crying bitterly, her hands covering her face, her chest heaving from her muffled sobs . . . I would occasionally hear her murmur a plea. To whom? I don't know. I moved away from the door, full of anxiety. I consoled our crying daughter and waited for Cordelia to emerge. When she did, she bore a profound secret sadness on her face, an expression I had come to know on Saturdays. Then, as if coming back to herself, she was once again caring, cheerful and passionate, showering us with love. I sat her on my lap, took her face in my hands, and looked her in the eye: 'My heart and soul, why were you crying in my study?'

Cordelia appeared shaken and rested her head on my shoulder.

'Oh, you saw me! You promised you wouldn't spy on me while I worked. You can't be trusted! Today, I awoke a nervous wreck, and it very much pained me to see you break your word. I began to cry when I sensed you approaching the door.'

I could tell by Cordelia's trembling and distraught voice that she was lying, but since I had in fact broken my word, I could not insist further.

'Forgive me, Cordelia!'

'Of course I forgive you. My king, I forgive you with all my heart.'

She took my head in her hands and kissed my eyelids.

THE WHITE FARMHOUSE (PALMA)

The following Saturday was our two-year anniversary. It was customary for Cordelia to wake me as soon as she got out of bed, but that day I was already awake. When she leaned over my forehead, I grabbed her by the waist.

'Do you know what day it is today? . . . It's our anniversary.'

Cordelia shuddered, and through her clothing it was as if I could feel a current of ice-cold blood pass through her veins.

At ten that morning, Cordelia cheerfully called me from my study. I ran to her. With childlike joy she opened the doors and led me by the hand to where, positioned on an easel, was a frame draped in a red cloth. When she removed it, I gasped. The likeness was marvellous. It would have been impossible to more meticulously capture the expression of love and melancholy that made Cordelia so adorable. There was her supernatural paleness, her shining dark eyes, like black diamonds, her remarkable mouth . . . A mirror would have reproduced her face with the same accuracy, but it would not have suggested the presence of her soul, that sultry and tragic something, that spark of love and sadness, of infinite passion, mystery, strange idealism, and extra-human affection. It would not have copied that indefinable likeness between Jairus's daughter's and Cordelia's souls which I could detect without quite being able to put my finger on which exact facial feature or expression conjured the idea of a woman brought back to life from evangelical legend.[18]

We were madly in love in that day, as if under a spell. It was as though Cordelia wanted to absorb my entire body and soul. Our love was a voluptuous and bitter desperation, as if we were attempting to use up the wealth of our eternal love in a single day; as if an acidic force were corroding our insides. It was madness, an insatiable thirst that progressed in a strange and alarming way. It was a divine and diabolical delirium, an ideal and carnal vampirism composed of both the kind and prodigal piety of a goddess and the diabolical ardour of an infernal alchemy . . .

VIII

It must have been around one in the morning when I was startled awake. I had dreamt that a cold, marble-like mouth had kissed my lips, that a frozen hand had snatched my wedding band from my finger, and that a sad, muffled voice had murmured a heartbreaking goodbye in my ear. A few seconds later I heard a kiss, followed by little Cordelia's piercing cry for her mother.

In a weak voice, I called out 'Cordelia!' as I tried to make out my wife's bed and listen for the faintest sound in the darkness. Nothing.

'Cordelia!' I repeated loudly, sitting up. The same silence. My temples were bathed in a cold sweat, and I felt my body shudder in terror. I turned on a light and looked over at my wife's bed. It was empty. Mad with fear and surprise, I jumped out of bed.

'Cordelia! Cordelia!'

I opened the doors and called out for my wife, my voice hoarse with pain.

'Cordelia!'

I searched for her in every room and in every corner of the *white farmhouse*. In the hallway, with his tail between his legs and his hair standing on end, Ariel howled. The wolves[19] in the surrounding forest replied lugubriously.[20]

'Cordelia!'

I guided Ariel to the bedroom, calmed him down, and entrusted him with little Cordelia. I immediately grabbed the first horse I could find in the stable. I jumped on the black foal, and we galloped off into the thick darkness of the forest.

'Cordelia! Cordelia!'

My cries were met with the furious howls of the wolves, their eyes shining on both sides of the trail like phosphoric splatter along the grass. Blinded and out of my mind from pain, I didn't think about the danger I was in. Emboldened by my horse's dramatic gallop, the wolves and their deafening howls launched in pursuit: a black moving stain scattered with luminous dots stretched out behind us.

'Cordelia! Cordelia!'

All that responded was the air buzzing between the leaves, the frightened nocturnal birds flying overhead, the sharp thud of my horse's foot on the grass, and the hungry rabid howls of the savage beasts. I don't know how far I rode from the *white farmhouse*. Guided by instinct, my foal took a detour, and we arrived back at the desolate *farmhouse* as the dawn dusted the eastern sky with nacre.[21] I felt defeated by my own anguish and the inexorable cruelty of my destiny. I laid across the steps for a long time while the birds welcomed the dawn with their stupid, beautiful prayer.

IX

I once again searched for Cordelia throughout the house. Her bed was empty, but her pillow still held the scent of her hair and the impression of her head. Little Cordelia slept in her crib while Ariel kept watch. The poor thing! I went to my study so as not to wake her, and when I lifted the cloth that draped over Cordelia's portrait, my hair stood on end with fright. The canvas was blank! Where Cordelia's eyes had once been, there now stood two imperceptible stains that looked like tears! My brain wavered, and it seemed that my intelligence was walking a tightrope on the edge of a road overlooking an abyss; the slightest force would have plunged it into the void. I was within the grips of death and madness. I needed to cry so that one of them would not triumph over me, and in that moment, I heard my daughter cry, and I was saved. I cried as well.

A strange phenomenon overcame me: an invasion of indifference and stoicism,[22] a lapse of memory that rose like a wave of apathy. It seemed

THE WHITE FARMHOUSE (PALMA)

that someone new was rising up inside me; that my sense of self had been ruptured by the superposition or invasion of a new personality. I knew with absolute certainty that I would never again see Cordelia. Just a few hours had passed since a mysterious and supernatural tragedy had occurred, but I was no longer shocked by it. It was as if centuries had been interposed between the past and the present. As if an immense dull crystal was between the current moment and the previous night, leaving me unable to make out the contours of the events or of my emotions. The portrait Cordelia had painted of me was on my desk. In the other room was our daughter and my wife's bed. All around the house were objects that she had used, flowers she had picked, everything that had permeated our daily lives. It was just Cordelia who was no longer there. Yet the mental state I found myself in gave me the impression that *nothing had changed and that nothing had ever existed.*

Upon hearing the gallop of a horse, I peered out the window and recognised my old teacher. He was dressed in black and heading for the *white farmhouse.*

X

He brought me a letter from Cordelia's mother:

'Two years have passed since the death of the light of my life, my adored daughter, my Cordelia, your fiancée whom you loved so much. Minutes before she expired, she requested that on the day that would have been your two-year anniversary, I send you her engagement ring, the ivory carved Christ that should have been placed on her coffin, and the miniature that Stein[23] painted for her. I am fulfilling my poor daughter's wishes. I know you have experienced immense pain, and that to this day you have lived alone, like a hermit, in the refuge of your white farmhouse, accompanied by the memory of your fiancée. Weep for her, my son, because Cordelia was worthy of your love. This poor old woman, whose only solace is the hope that she will soon be reunited with her daughter, sends you a maternal kiss.'

By pure coincidence, the small box containing the objects was wrapped in paper from the *Gazette* that was dated the day of my Cordelia's burial. Her funeral announcement was placed below a black cross. I calmly read it, along with the letter. I then opened the little box and thoroughly examined the objects it contained. I had kissed Cordelia's magnificent portrait by Stein's skilful hand so many times! I recalled the night Cordelia and I exchanged rings. How beautiful she looked dressed in white with her profuse, muted blonde curls falling on her shoulders! I didn't recognise the ivory Christ; the conventional pain in his cold expression annoyed me . . .

My teacher watched as I contemplated the objects, surprised by my lack of emotion. We remained silent for a long time.

'Teacher, do you insist on believing that life and death are real? Bah! I'll have you know that don't believe in either one. They are both illusory episodic daydreams that can only be told apart in the mind of that great

THE FEMALE VAMPIRE IN HISPANIC LITERATURE

sleeper imagining us ... My beloved teacher, you must think me the same madman of yesteryear, entertaining philosophical fantasies ... '

'No. All I can say is that I don't understand your love for Cordelia or your respect for her memory. You talk about philosophical needs but all your thoughts, guided by the sacred memories I have brought you, should be focused on that poor beautiful girl that loved you, and who died two years ago.'

'She died last night,' I interjected coldly.

'She died fifty years ago to you!' he rectified with bitter irony.

'Oh, teacher! Your sixty-five-year-old self is going to give me lessons on love? Seriously? I'll tell you what Hamlet told Laertes at Ophelia's funeral: "I loved Ophelia. Forty thousand brothers could not with all their quantity of love make up my sum. What wilt thou do for her?"[24] Don't get angry, my teacher. I was going to talk about Cordelia. You, the letter from my mother-in-law, and the *Gazette* would all have me believe the ridiculous notion that Cordelia died two years ago. Well, had you arrived yesterday, Cordelia and I would have received you with joyful laughter. Had you arrived last night, you and I would have run into each other in the forest you just crossed, had the wolves not devoured you first. You happen to arrive today, and I am simply telling you that Cordelia did not die two years ago. Cordelia, my adored wife, has lived here until last ... I find it curious the way you're now looking at me. You just expressed indignation at my indifference to the memory of that poor beautiful girl, but now your face shows just the opposite: fear that I have gone mad from suffering. Oh, beloved teacher, please don't make that face! I'm not insane. Listen. Even if you don't believe me, accept the hypothesis I'll later verify: Cordelia—body and soul—has lived at the *white farmhouse*. If, as you're suggesting, Cordelia died two years ago, then life and death are for me one and the same, and as a result, your positivist philosophy[25] collapses.'

'My poor child! You're talking nonsense ... what you are saying is absurd.'

'Well then, teacher, reality itself is absurd.'

'Prove it!'

'Do you recall Cordelia's handwriting?'

'Yes. I would recognise it instantly.'

I went to my desk for one of my notebooks filled with correspondence. Cordelia had written many of the letters I later signed. I showed them to my teacher.

'Yes, yes ... it's a very good imitation of her handwriting ... Forgive me, I'm not suggesting that you wish to fool me ... but you could have unconsciously taken on her script, replacing yours with hers. Furthermore, your transcriber ... '

'I don't have one. I already knew you wouldn't believe me. Do you remember Cordelia's style of drawing? Just look at this portrait that my wife painted of me earlier this year.'

16

THE WHITE FARMHOUSE (PALMA)

The teacher shuddered at the sight of Cordelia's work. Yet in the end, I could tell that he thought this was all a trick. I begged him to wait. A moment later I returned with the little girl in my arms, followed by Ariel.

'Here you have the most convincing proof: our daughter!'

'Cordelia!' exclaimed the old man. He was pale with fright. His eyes bulged out of their sockets and his hands trembled.

'That's right, teacher . . . young Cordelia.'

'It's her face . . . her expression.'

'Yes, the same expression as Cordelia and Jairus's daughter.'

The good old man appeared to be hypnotised by her curious, intelligent, sweet gaze. Little Cordelia smiled at him and extended her arms, as though someone had whispered to her that he was an old friend. Trembling, he took her in his arms.

'It's Cordelia! It's Cordelia!' he murmured as I relentlessly continued my line of reasoning.

'Ergo, teacher, I have been married to the dead woman for two years. Ergo, despite what you, her doctor, and her gravedigger witnessed, Cordelia's death was an incident that occurred in *someone's daydream*, outside the scope of positivist reality. All lives, yours and mine included, are aerial illusions; unformed, illogical shadows that are not beholden to reason. Our lives are ghost ships that aimlessly wander a choppy and absurd ocean whose waves have never met the shores of reality, no matter how much we imagine extensive beaches and steep cliffs on the horizon. The truth, my teacher, is that reality doesn't exist. Or in other words, that reality is nothingness with forms.'

'Silence! This absurd mystery, alive in my very arms, is making me question reason itself. Don't lie to me . . . This little girl is one-year-old Cordelia. . . She looked at me and extended her arms in the same way . . . This is Cordelia back from the dead . . . It's Cordelia reborn! My God! I've gone mad, and so have you! But it's her! It's her!'

His frightened ramblings and the phrase 'It's Cordelia reborn!' opened an immense and terrible horizon before my eyes: If the illusion of life can be repeated, then one can return to the illusion of happiness.

'It's Cordelia reborn!' I exclaimed. My entire soul was transported to the future, where I saw mother and daughter become one.

'It's Cordelia reborn!' I repeated, my voice so hoarse and disturbed that my teacher looked over at me. What did he see in my face? I don't know.

'What do you plan to do? You can't stay here in the *white farmhouse*. You need to educate your daughter . . .'

'I'm staying put,' I responded, as if talking to myself. 'Cordelia's soul lives on in the soul of this child, and both are inseparable from the *farmhouse*. We'll all die here, but we'll also be happy here. My dear Cordelia, why can't we continue these daydreams filled with life, happiness, and death? Oh, Cordelia! The illusion of your life begins again . . .'

THE FEMALE VAMPIRE IN HISPANIC LITERATURE

'You wretched man!' my teacher interrupted, gazing at me in horror. 'Do you wish to make your daughter your wife?'

'Yes,' I answered tersely.

Then, without my being able to stop him, the old man abruptly approached the window with Cordelia, gave her a quick kiss on her forehead, and threw her headfirst over the stone staircase. I heard a thud when her little skull hit the ground.

Do you think I sought vengeance in my despair? That I grabbed my teacher by the neck and beat him mercilessly? No, nothing of the kind. I watched him ride off on horseback until he was lost in the fateful shadow of the forest, then continued to lean against the window. I felt *empty*, devoid of any elements that would indicate the presence of a human personality. Our old servant beckoned me several times. I let her know through gestures that Cordelia and our daughter had left and that I did not want to eat. Little Cordelia was dead, just ten feet below the window where I stood. What would have later reproduced the happiness I had lost was now laying in a pool of her own blood. There she was, and I felt nothing. I couldn't feel suffering or pleasure; I was empty, my brain devoid of any activity at all.

The afternoon and evening went on like this. Ariel stood guarding little Cordelia's body in the darkness for a long time. The poor animal howled and barked. The wolves could smell the blood and began moving in little by little. They snuck through the gate and from then until dawn, all I could hear were muffled grunts and the sound of bone crushing between the ferocious beasts' sharp and formidable teeth.

At the crack of dawn, I began to mindlessly saturate the furniture and walls of the *white farmhouse* with combustible substances, and before the sun's rays had touched the treetops, I set fire to it on all four sides. I climbed onto my horse and cruelly spurred his flanks as we set off in an unbridled gallop from that cursed region, never to return.

I forgot to mention that when I set fire to the *farmhouse*, the poor old deaf woman was still inside.

𝕸𝖗 𝕮𝖆𝖉𝖆𝖛𝖊𝖗 𝖆𝖓𝖉 𝕸𝖎𝖘𝖘 𝖁𝖆𝖒𝖕𝖎𝖗𝖊

ANTONIO DE HOYOS Y VINENT

Imbecil ! —de son empire
Si nos efforts te délivraient,
Tes baisers ressusciteraient
Le cadavre de ton vampire!
— Charles Baudelaire
Le Vampire[1]

N ACRID SMELL, A MIX OF FILTH AND CHEAP PERFUMES, filled the establishment. Clouds of smoke and dust spread through the oppressive atmosphere and intensified the opacity of the diminished electric bulbs, contributing to the sad and hostile appearance of the large hall. In the public theatre, a buzzing sound—dwarfed from time to time by high-pitched laughter that, interspersed with shameless exclamations, chanted off-colour jokes—rose without interruption but for the culmination of some sensational number.

Crammed into the stalls was a horrid crowd that roared with laughter, applauded furiously, chanted *couplets* and shouted obscenities at the performers, who were content with the scandalous display that guaranteed their contracts. It was a cross section, a fine sample of lower-class misfits: pimps, domineering women, vendors from the nearby Plaza de la Cebada,[2] greengrocers, bricklayers and soldiers. They all pressed against each other, becoming aroused or indignant in unison, the shudders of pleasure or disgust running over them with the same strangeness as water ruffled by the wind. Figures typical of wayward Madrid[3] looked on and showed off from their box seats. Bullfighters in light-coloured suits, wearing watch chains as thick as cables, lavish diamond rings, and white cordovan hats[4] gracing the napes of their neck, were speaking with their jaunty-aired wives or lovers. The women were striking, curvaceous and dressed to the nines,[5] adorned with shimmering combs in their hair and big fat diamonds in their ears. Equally ostentatious moneylenders fluttered their sausage fingers so their rings—the spoils of some disaster—would sparkle as they caught the light. Pretentious madams chatted with the less garish-looking men accompanying them. Paying the women little mind and unconcerned with looking refined, the men kept their caps on as they talked amongst themselves and smoked fine cigars. A flabby, hideous female butcher, decked out in jewels, laughed at the jokes of the handsome young man flirting with her, mak-

THE FEMALE VAMPIRE IN HISPANIC LITERATURE

ing her breasts tremble. Sprinkled throughout and adding a touch of the exotic to the box seats were giant French hats[6] worn by either a tart[7] or a lady that was up to no good. Their class was difficult to discern since the prostitutes did their best to look like ladies and the ladies didn't shun the resemblance, giving them all a certain air of agreeable family. That night, they were united in a single impulse of unhealthy curiosity to contemplate the publicised performance.

I was settled into my box next to Prince Atilio, a tireless seeker of eccentricities, curiously contemplating the colourful scene when my companion called my attention to a couple who had just taken their seats in the stalls.

It really was worth a look, and if the audience had not looked over en masse, it was because the daubed curtain had been drawn and the anticipated *début*[8] was about to begin.

Never in my life of unusual adventures had I encountered such an odd and disturbing couple who so swiftly effused the chilling sensation of tragedy. Not of vulgar tragedy, but rather of one of those mysterious, macabre, haunting tragedies that we can divine in Poe[9] and Hoffman.[10] He was, at first glimpse, just a very thin, overdressed man. His innate refinement stood out most in his somewhat romantic attire, reminiscent of a dandy[11] from 1830. His tailored blue tailcoat had very tight sleeves and opened over a grey waistcoat with diamond buttons. The front of his shirt was buttoned with thick pink pearls and adorned with ruffles, while his hair, defiant to British fashions,[12] was dishevelled. But if you looked at him closely, you could sense a touch of something broken or tired, something that made one think of skeletons, marionettes, lugubrious[13] and grotesque things. Moreover, his movements had a soft undulation to them, as if by one of those terrible diseases that afflict humans, his bones had been liquidated. The slightest movement, the most insignificant change in posture, gave the impression of having taken immense, superhuman effort. And his face . . . . Oh! I'll never forget the horror of that pallid, emaciated face with protruding cheekbones, very red lips parted over the black abyss of his mouth, and violet eyelids that fell heavily over lackluster pupils.

In striking contrast to him, the woman sitting at his side was one of the most beautiful creatures I had ever seen. And not a dreamy, fragile beauty, but a splendid beauty, brimming with life. Her black velvet dress moulded the opulent curves of her body, while the small square neckline exposed the prodigious shape of her milk-white throat. The great Rembrandt,[14] overwhelmed by feathers, served as a background to her face, a perfect harmony of lines haloed by golden locks of hair. Her red lips were a display of voluptuousness, and two amethysts glittered beneath her golden eyelashes.

'Do you know them?' I asked my friend.

'Know who? *Monsieur la Cadavre et á madame Vampire?*'

After he finished laughing, he explained: 'Yes, I know them. I saw them one winter in Nice,[15] one summer in Ostend,[16] one autumn in Venice[17] . . .'

'So, are they French, Russian, Italian?'

20

MR CADAVER AND MISS VAMPIRE (HOYOS)

'I don't know; they're . . . citizens of the world.'

'And you're sure it's them?'

'Yes, it's them . . . ' He hesitated. 'At least, it's her. I think it's him as well, but I couldn't swear by it. This one time I saw him he seemed older. Another time, younger. What I am sure of is that he's always the same in his theatrical, exaggerated elegance, in his lax air, in that immensely tired appearance, and in that pallor of a dying man.'

The curtain had risen while we were talking, and against the sad and ugly background of the unfortunate set, a couple had begun their dance. The show was something of a history of dance over the centuries, from Salome's Dance of the Seven Veils[18] to the dance of the *chulos*[19] and the *apaches*.[20] First, she, a slender and pale young woman—a true bundle of nerves, or so the saying goes—had in her dark and naked body, under the luminous iris of the precious stones, embodied Herodias's[21] daughter's perverse charm while dancing before the melancholic and lascivious Herod,[22] imprisoned by the curse of his incestuous desires. Her undulating body, unwholesome in its grace, swayed in a dizzying shimmer of gems. Between the tremble of the enigmatic emeralds, the tragic glow of the rubies—the Persian red,[23] the colour of love, joy and life—and the pale aurora of the pearls, her nubile, erect breasts were on sinful display. Meanwhile, her hips, as harmonious as the sides of an amphora,[24] oscillated in a considerable lustful rhythm. The evocation of the ancient world was followed by the ceremonial dances of the medieval liturgy,[25] then the pompous genuflexions of frivolous eighteenth-century elegance, and now, finally, the perverse lasciviousness of the common people's dances.

Her hair was tied back, forming a tall metal helmet, and around her neck, made visible by the opening of her blouse, was a narrow, black velvet ribbon. Her breasts were squeezed into a red bodice, and her legs stuffed into a tight, black and white checkered skirt. He was dressed in the classic attire of a Parisian miscreant: wide, black velvet pants, a blue denim jacket and a silk cap tilted to the side. They both danced. It was a dance of slow cadence, of an exasperated and silent lasciviousness; a dance in which their bodies clung to each other, merging in an absurd embrace, oscillating slowly, very slowly, in a voluptuous, spastic rhythm. The feminine curves moulded themselves to the sturdy musculature of the male, fusing their bodies together. With their eyes locked and their lips so close that their breaths became one, they danced slowly to the monotonous whine of the violins, which either dragged their languid notes, whispering desires, or would leap, separate and come together again in a strange fever that was something of a passionate embrace and something of an acrobatic exercise. This was all underscored by the stormy drumming of the orchestra, which erupted into a tempest of furious melody.

The atmosphere of the hall was thick with morbid sensuality: desires, restrained passions, sensuality, perversity, the filth of bedrooms and hospitals, the lustfulness that was lying in wait like nocturnal birds that need

THE FEMALE VAMPIRE IN HISPANIC LITERATURE

darkness and silence to live. In their eyes you could see the eagerness to take part in that feast of carnal desire. As in one of those absurd miracles that enrich the lives of holy ascetics,[26] I thought I saw strange monsters, like the astonishing ones in Bosch's paintings,[27] dancing in the bluish clouds of smoke to the chords of the diabolical melody. And the monsters came and went, jumping from lips to lips, from eyes to eyes, from ears to ears, weaving chimerical[28] garlands. Lava, reptiles, human foetuses, strange beings that were the things of nightmares, female torsos with serpent heads; the sexless bodies of children, gelatinous and repulsive in their flaccidity; men of strange physiques, both Herculean[29] and frail at once; flowers, which had long tentacles for stalking prey in the place of leaves; roses, among whose leaves worms of death germinated in a stench of rot; orchids of a repulsive sexuality; water lilies blooming in glutinous rot; unclassifiable hybrid animals; terrifying monsters and grotesque rodents; shapeless beings and chameleons; absurd flora and fauna gathered in unlikely company, breeding other irregular beings, which, in turn, linked together in a shocking synthesis of horror.

My eyes fell on the box where the enigmatic couple were sitting. The haughty and unapproachable Miss Vampire smiled as she fixed her gaze on the scene. But there was something cruel and voluptuous, something chilling, in those bright violet-tinged eyes and those red, dewy, parted lips. Now awake from his strange and seemingly agonising slumber, he leaned over the box's guardrail and, instead of contemplating the stage, he contemplated her, galvanised in a strange fever of desire.

* * *

The second time that I saw them also happened to be in a theatre: L'Olympia in Paris.[30] The splendid locale was bathed in glowing light, putting the sumptuous magnificence of its blue, white, and gold scenery on elegant display. Creatures of love and luxury revelled in the box seats, and adventurous women of every type walked along the *promenoir*[31] in search of unsuspecting men upon which to cast their nets. Meanwhile, the luckier ones sat at the bar tables drinking champagne with the likes of scrawny, ill-tempered Englishmen or South Americans; Brazilians and Chileans with bold eyes and an adventurous demeanour, their fingers loaded with diamonds.

I contemplated the show from my seat as I waited for the actual stage show to begin. At last, the velvet curtains slowly opened, revealing a glorious tropical garden. Enormous palm trees and tree ferns formed a jungle in the background; in the foreground, acrobats appeared on a thick red velvet carpet. They were two adolescents, or rather, two children. Their slim, petite bodies had a disturbing and perverse androgynous grace; thin, muscular, prepubescent. Their faces, pale with finely defined profiles, were disturbingly similar. The only differed in their brown hair, which she wore in long ringlets and he in tight curls. They were fragile, agile and moved quickly, displaying in their movements a puerile and uneven grace that was

far from the serene beauty of a Greek statue and the Herculean musculature of Michelangelo's heroes.[32]

Their bodies, dressed in cherry-coloured silk netting covered in gold
sequins and bathed in the powerful brightness of the electric lights, twisted into strange contortions, conjuring the terrible sensation of both the
crunching of bones and the rustling of silk. In an absurd crossing of every
line, their disjointed bodies folded into unbelievable contortions that melt-
ed them into one—a monstrous caricature of Nature unhinged. And from
the reddish, shapeless mass emerged the two children's heads, their faces
contorted in a painful smile.

Suddenly, I had the strange sensation that *something* extraordinary was
happening in the theatre. Instinct, that strange and mysterious sentinel that
lies in wait while we rest in the arms of indifference, was sounding the
alarm. I looked around, and in a box seat spotted that strange couple that
had caught my eye at the Teatro Novedades[33] in Madrid. She, as always,
was dressed in black and triumphant in her luminous beauty, the square
neckline of her dress revealing the dazzling whiteness of her neck; her face,
of eucharistic[34] whiteness, was cut sharply by her red lips; between the
golden threads of her eyelashes sat her magnificent amethyst eyes; on her
blonde head sat a *renard bleu*[35] cap that matched the furs sliding down
her shoulders. And him . . . I hesitated for a moment, seized by a feeling of
unease. Was it him? It had to be. That was the same exaggerated elegance
of a romantic poet; the same floppy, ragged posture; the same heavy eyelids falling over lackluster eyes; but . . . was it the same man? He seemed
younger and, at the same time, more exhausted, more defeated, as if his
body were somehow crumbling. And yet, just like in Madrid, his eyes were
fixed on his companion, his entire body leaning towards her in an intense
yearning for control.

I shuddered in fright.

* * *

I met her by chance a few days later. Our meeting took place atop the Café
de París,[36] during a dinner where Clodahorlaomor, dethroned king of
Iskander,[37] was wining and dining some beauties. As we waited to sit down
for dinner, a group of us were laughing at the cynical quips of Francette
Dubois, a delightful *cabotin*,[38] when the door opened, leaving the laughter
petrified on my lips.

It was her!

For the first time, she was alone, and I felt this strange anguish. It was
like a premonition.

They introduced us, and we talked. Up close, she wasn't as remarkable.
She maintained, however, the most stunning aspects of her astonishing
beauty: the splendour of her figure, the triumphant glow of her complexion, the sparkle in her eyes; but above all else, a powerful life force, such an
intense joy, a reflection of passion, will, and power that I found both *fasci-*

nating and frightening at the same time. And as always, she wore neither a jewel nor a flower, nothing but her black dress; that day, it was a crepe de Chine[39] dress blooming with velvet roses of the same colour, and a splendid leather tunic. I observed her carefully. All of her movements, within the bounds of an exquisite harmony, had something energetic, wilful, determined about them: the magnificent haughtiness of a person who was born to dominate. Her contralto voice[40] was warm, at times inflected with passion and caressing sweetness, as if it were suddenly cloaked in desire, in a longing of exasperated voluptuousness.

She must have soon realised the weary impression she was having on me, for her beautiful eyes began to envelop me in wafts of desire. Without a doubt, her pupils had something hypnotic about them, which left me feeling uneasy. To push through the feeling, I started talking.

'I've seen you before in Madrid ... '

'In a theatre,' she interrupted. 'You were with Atilio, a dear friend of mine ... '

She also remembered seeing me at L'Olympia. Without question, she had a solid memory and could recall the most insignificant details of our previous encounters. Had she spotted me as potential prey? In that moment, my gut was telling me that, for this woman, men were just that: targets of her pleasure-seeking and greed, something that she would destroy, annihilate, and then abandon in a miserable wreck.

I again felt a chill.

* * *

Upon waking, I felt an odd happiness; something along the lines of an unusual lightness, an aery subtleness, in which the spirit, liberated from the confines of the body, wandered through imaginary spaces. Yet the longer I felt it the more painful it became, until it was finally unbearable. I forced myself awake. Confronted with reality, the feeling changed completely: the lightness was followed by an overwhelming heaviness, as if my legs and arms had turned to lead. I felt immense fatigue; such physical exhaustion that I feared that time had irrationally sprung forward, and I had reached old age. At the same time, my memory faltered. A confused fog surrounded murky thoughts and images, making it difficult for me to discern their origin. Where was I? Why was I there? What had happened to me?

Mad with terror, my hairs standing on end, my eyes wide with fright, and my forehead bathed in a cold sweat, I sat up. A terrible idea flashed before my eyes like a sinister lightning bolt, ripping away the darkness that clouded my thoughts. I was Mr Cadaver and lying beside me on the wide bed of a banal hotel room was Miss Vampire!

At first, I thought myself the victim of a nightmare. But no. I could now perfectly remember my exploits over the last few days, my besieging of the dangerous beauty, and finally, our meeting that ended in a night of passion. I recalled the fierce fits of insatiable desire, the erotic brutalities, the demonic whirlwind that had carried us away like a Dantean curse.[41] The cruel, endless, life-sucking kisses, and the deep, intense, knowing caresses that destroyed the bone marrow in spasms of painful voluptuousness that felt like dying.

I struggled to sit up, propping myself up with my elbow. Lying next to me asleep, she lost her principal charm: that wild overflow of life, that plethora of strength. Instead, sleep granted her an imposing statuesque majesty. I leaned over to get a better look at her. Her face was so white it could have been made of marble or alabaster; the eyelashes on her closed lids cast a shadow across her cheek, deepening the blue of the bags under her eyes; a strange rotting smell emanated from her scarlet lips.

My passion reignited, and I bent down to kiss the curve of her neck laced with blue veins. I pulled back in horror. She was cold, stiff. I had just kissed a recumbent marble statue, not the fiery woman that had pulsated in my arms the night before. Inadvertently, I thought of the tragic mystic legends of the Middle Ages, in which, by a miracle of God, beautiful women would become cold statues in the arms of sacrilegious monks tempted by Satan.[42]

But this was different. Hers wasn't the coldness of marble, nor the coldness of death. It was a viscous, reptilian glaciation; a repulsive iciness that was felt to the bone.

In a panic, I jumped out of bed and got dressed.

I set out for Constantinople that same night.[43]

The Cold Woman

CARMEN DE BURGOS

I

WHEN BLANCA ENTERED HER STAGE BOX at the Princess Theatre,[1] she caused the usual stir. The audience's attention shifted from the stage to her. From every seat in the house, binoculars turned toward Blanca. Even those who didn't know her—the ones sitting in the modestly priced seats in the upper balcony—followed her movements, dazzled by her beauty.

Tall and slender, her curves, silhouette and flesh were those of a statue. She shed her white cape like foam rolling off the sea, revealing a whiteish-blue hued neckline, face and arms. It was the colour that Russian ballet dancers' flesh takes under blue stage lights. Her face and body were those of a statue: colourless, only a perfect outline, and enough to seduce anyone. Her flaxen blonde hair, almost ashen, magnified that impression. Her brows and lashes were noticeable more so by the shadows they cast than by their colour. Her lips, also pale, were perceptible only by the pure and elegant edges of her mouth. Even her large sparkling eyes, an intense and crystalline green, were like two magnificent emeralds embedded in marble.

A red-orange dress, between brown and yellow in hue, clung to her body like a flame. And yet a cold sensation lingered in the retinas of those around her, produced by her flesh, hair, eyes and the magnificent emerald collar that adorned her neck.

A gentleman waved to her from a stage box. She reciprocated with an amusing gesture, more of a swing of the hand, and a subtle feminine smile that revealed sparkly alabaster-white teeth.

'Marcelo knows her,' said a fresh-faced bald man, turning back towards his companions. 'He waved to her from his sister-in-law's box.'

'He must tell us all about her,' his young male friends said, almost in unison. The loquacious group proclaimed themselves to be the censors and judges of all the socialites and stage beauties. They never passed up an opportunity to sit in the proscenium of any theatre and sport fancy tuxedos bespeaking the latest trends in the placement of a button or the cut of a lapel.

'I already know a thing or two about her,' said a thin young man. His head looked like that of a feather-plucked bird, with glasses resting on his beak.

'Do tell.'

'I believe her to be Basque,[2] and that she lived in a remote area of the Pyrenees.[3] A rich French nobleman got her out, but he had the good sense of dying and leaving her an immense fortune.'

'She's widowed?'

'Twice.'

'Considering how young she is, that's pretty fast footwork.'[4]

'It's impossible to know the age of a statue.'

'She went on to dedicate herself to travelling. India, Egypt . . . she finally settled down again with an Austrian nobleman, the count of something or other. He also died.'

'She's a magnificent woman!'

'Extraordinary!'

'Original!'

Blanca continued watching the stage, indifferent to the audience as they contemplated her through their binoculars.

The curtain fell. As the men stood, they exchanged glances and greetings to those around them, unanimously aware of how they were objectifying the newcomer.

Most of them either ended up exiting to the foyer for a cigarette or fulfilling the social obligation of going backstage. Few of them had actually watched the play.

What little was known of Blanca spread by word of mouth. The women in the balcony, who readily switched seats to stretch their legs, inquired about her to their male friends as they stopped by to greet them.

This was all anyone knew: she was Spanish, twice-widowed, rich, and of Basque breed and noble title. Having settled in Madrid,[5] she was now living a life of luxury in a magnificent garden-encircled hotel on Paseo de la Castellana.[6] She had carriages and motorcars, and even though she could be spotted at all the theatres around town, she kept to herself. She was always alone. This was why everyone was so surprised to see Don Marcelo, a gallant old senator and bachelor who had walked over to her balcony to greet her, conversing with her so affectionately.

A crowd waited for him in the corridor to enquire about her, but the warning bell sounded in urgency, letting everyone know that the curtain would soon rise and it was time to be seated. Marcelo wore a snide smirk on his face for the entire act, as though he knew he had left people waiting in disappointment.

'If I were to head over to the bar or the casino after the show, I'd be the centre of attention,' he said. 'Just being near you awakens everybody's curiosity. In the theatre, all eyes are on you.'

THE COLD WOMAN (BURGOS)

'Oh, I would find that awful. I want to live my life in peace and quiet, without anyone noticing me.'

'Madam, you are much too young and beautiful for that to happen, especially in these meridian countries,[7] so full of curiosity and passion.'

'Do you remember what they called me in Vienna,[8] where we first made each other's acquaintance?'

'"The Cold Woman."[9] Even more reason for my fiery young countrymen to enthusiastically throw themselves into the task of melting the ice. Let me assure you that this is the only time I've ever been glad to be old.'

'I don't understand.'

'My old age relieves me of the humiliation of not being able to satisfy you in bed.'

She laughed, then kindly said, 'Who knows! Perhaps I am the one who evades defeat with your reluctance to avoid the deed.'

'Oh, my friend, that condescending nature of yours is the worst indicator of all! Women only make such confessions to men that don't scare them.'

'You're the only person I know in Spain. It's such a pleasant surprise to have found you, but I beg that you be discreet. Don't say how little you know about me. Curiosity follows me wherever I go, never letting me feel at ease in any place, and I don't want that to happen here.'

'It's impossible to go unnoticed in Madrid. It's a small town in that sense.'

'The same thing happened to me in London[10] . . . in Paris[11] . . . It's my fate . . .'

Suddenly, as if overcome by some unsettling thought, she reached her gloved hand out and grasped his arm, saying: 'Do you sense something unusual about me, apart from my being so very blonde and pale?'

Sensing her fear, he lightheartedly responded: 'Just that you are too beautiful.'

She smiled and stood up, unsatisfied with what she could tell was an insincere response.

'You're leaving before the performance ends?'

'Yes . . . I want to avoid being surrounded by all of those people.'

The admired regard crowds with contempt, and there was an echo of that in her words.

Marcelo helped her into her foam-white ermine[12] coat and offered her his arm as he escorted her to her carriage. The group of friends, having left their box, greeted him with questions upon his return.

'Who is she?'

'Where did she go?'

'What do you know about her?'

'Would you introduce me?'

They were so curious, like a pack of dogs hot on the trail of a scent, and he began to feel somewhat annoyed at having always followed certain customs. Recalling her fear and annoyance at being a hounded woman, he decided to opt for discretion. He would not disclose the stories he had heard about her in Austria. He simply answered: 'I met the widow of Hozenchis and her husband in Vienna. She's a millionaire, and a beautiful one at that, as I'm sure you have all noticed.'

'She's magnificent . . . but strange. She provokes an inexplicable feeling . . . a coldness . . . '

'Bah! That's just your imagination! She's simply a little blonder and fairer than most. That's all. Goodnight.'

And after having squashed their excitement, he left.

II

Curiosity lingered around the elegant woman, her extraordinary beauty an impenetrable mystery. She declined all invitations and never received visitors. She went to the theatre alone, ventured out alone. Her jewellery, wardrobe, luxury hotel and train rides gave away how fabulously rich she was.

Don Marcelo was her only friend. He visited her, rode along in her carriage, was welcomed in her home, and invited over for dinner. Men and women besieged him daily, hoping to be introduced to the mysterious widow of Hozenchis, but he would always decline. He feigned knowing her well and referred to her only by her first name. And while refusing to make introductions, which she had strictly prohibited, he simultaneously feigned discretion, which only further sparked curiosity. In one of those conversations, he let the denominative 'The Cold Woman' slip, which caught on quickly. When her presence or the mere thought of her would provoke that cold ocular sensation, the nickname would come to mind. You could say that she wore a luminous halo, like that of lamp-posts on a freezing night, when their light appears cold, crystallised, milky white.

Her dresses were usually cold in hue. Her jewellery, always adorned with opals, pearls, emeralds, turquoise or diamonds, suggested something cold or ominous. They shone on her chest, on that opaque, white alabastrine flesh, like frost glittering in the light.

Those who had heard her speak said her voice was harmonious, yet penetrating, like a sheet of cold sharp metal. In the same way, those large green eyes were like an arrow straight through the heart. They could penetrate you with one glance, sending a shiver right up your spine.

The ladies were curious to know the brand of her perfume. A wonderful combination of something oriental and something strange, it left those she passed by with the faintest sensation of cold menthol.[13]

Marcelo had promised his nieces, Edma and Rosa, that he would find out about the perfume. The girls were two attractive little scamps, eighteen and twenty-two years of age, who eagerly encircled him as he entered the room.

'Did you find out her secret?'

'What brand does she use?'

THE COLD WOMAN (BURGOS)

He smiled contentedly, charmed like those good old men who feel caressed by the scent of a beautiful woman.

'Why so curious?' he replied.

'Because we want to smell like her,' Rosa said.

'You don't need to. You have the scent of youth seeping from your skin.'

'Oh, you're just being polite,' interrupted Edma. 'There's much talk of natural beauty, goodness and innocence, but I can tell that what men really want is a woman with experience. They leave their virtuous women for the "perverse" ones, or isn't that what you call them?'

'You're frightening me, child!' he replied. 'Where have you heard such things?'

'I don't need to hear them. I see enough . . . ' She continued, 'I want to know everything for myself . . . so that once I'm married my husband won't have to look elsewhere.'

'Don't pay her any mind, Uncle. She's being silly because she thinks Fernando is in love with Lady Haz . . . etc.'

'Jealous, are we?'

They had been slowly approaching a group of about a dozen young men and women drinking tea.

Edma murmured in his ear, 'Uncle, be discreet for God's sake.'

Rosa was chatting away with a group of four women that she had just approached.

'I need to know if you have the formula or not,' she said, redirecting the conversation.

'Yes, girls, I do,' said Don Marcelo, 'but it's such a complex formula that I may as well not even have it. Blanca's perfume is extracted from one of the most subtle of poisons, benzyl acetate,[14] which as we all know, is the active ingredient in asphyxiating gases. Through a costly process, it can be transformed into a scent similar to that of Arabian jasmine.'[15]

The group was left perplexed. How would they be able to take on a woman with such resources at her disposal? They almost began to hate her, to want to seek revenge for the superiority she cast that inadvertently put them to shame.

'Everything about her is odd,' one of the young women said.

'And she herself is the oddest of all,' replied one of the gentlemen. 'I know of nothing more original. She's a block of marble with a soul.'

'Yet,' added the young woman, 'maybe it's just a façade. We need to remember that she has purposefully closed herself off. She doesn't want to be seen up close.'

'If I were as gallant as you all think I am,' said Don Marcelo, 'I would agree with you girls and speak ill of "The Cold Woman," confident in that I were being well-mannered and kind, but Blanca is a close friend and I need to be loyal. She's more interesting up close than from afar.'

'But she has a coldness about her, doesn't she?'

31

'Yes, always. Just talking to her is like opening a window that faces snow-capped mountains. An invigorating, enchanting coldness.'

'So, something you want to keep your distance from,' Edma teased.

'I wouldn't say as much.'

'It's that she's in love with her name,' added another woman. 'Given how she dresses and accessorises, she clearly wants to live up to it ... Even her movements are icy. She glides ... '

'She can't help but be influenced by her name,' said an intelligent looking young man. 'Names have colours and properties. Blanca is a cold name.'

'And mine?' another young woman inquired, laughing.

'Mercedes is a blue name.'

'Ernesto is a romantic. Don't entertain his imagination,' said another dashing young man.

'Whereas Fernando has nothing to say.'

Edma fixed her jealous gaze on the young man. He raised his head, a kind and honest expression on his face, and simply said: 'I can't say anything about a woman I hardly know,' then looking at Edma, as if to reassure her, he added, 'and that doesn't interest me.'

As Rosita brought over Don Marcelo's cup of tea, he went over to sit near an opulent woman with large black eyes, saying: 'I should be safe from the cold over here.'

'But you seem so fond of snow,' she responded.

'I won't deny it. And while it's impolite to praise a woman in front of other women when she's not there, you are all too beautiful and intelligent to take offense. In private, Blanca is enchanting.'

'It's a shame you can't prove it,' teased Rosa.

'Maybe I can. I've managed to get Blanca to agree to meet you.'

The young men and women's excitement swept through the hall. Don Marcelo paused for a while to take it in, finally saying: 'That's right. When I asked Blanca about her mysterious perfume, I told her that you were the ones inquiring. She laughed a good deal at your curiosity, and since I had spoken so enthusiastically of your beauty and how much you wanted to meet her, she agreed to come with me. You'll meet her next time.'

'Great idea!' murmured Rosa.

'The truth is we won't know what to say to that woman who ... freezes the words out of our mouths.'

'Not to worry. People in Madrid find Blanca strange—to the point where you all probably think you're going to find a cloistered nun seeing the world for the first time. But Blanca is a refined, unbelievably dignified woman. Viennese society is rough, and she was one of the most respectable ladies there.'

But the girls, having gathered to deliberate, were no longer listening to Don Marcelo. It was crucial that they *toilette*[16] before their introductions. They couldn't let her upstage them.

THE COLD WOMAN (BURGOS)

The young men spoke enthusiastically to one another as well. It was obvious that none of them would miss the event. They were thrilled at the idea of solving such a perplexing riddle and then sharing it with the world of curious idlers that pursued her, more so than for her beauty, for how she remained in that privileged position of inaccessibility.

III

As they wandered around the great hall of Blanca's hotel,[17] they were taken aback by the strange aesthetic. It was of no time or place, and unlike anything they had seen. It was wholly international, an accumulation of every aesthetic from every time period. Yet despite being lavishly adorned with bibelots, it didn't have the hallmark of an antique shop. On the contrary, even the most distinct objects came together harmoniously.

The walls, lacquered in an angelic blue, were covered in a cornucopia[18] of framed paintings, Andrea della Robbia's[19] terracotta,[20] and Arras[21] and Gobelin[22] tapestries. Display cases on mantels and cabinets held Venetian and Murano glass,[23] designs by Gallé,[24] and ceramics from around the world, mostly blue and yellow in colour. Midnight-blue Chinese porcelain[25] adorned with flower petals falling from almond trees; Danish porcelain[26] with dreamy boats on clear blue sea foam on a sunny day; stormy-blue Delft pottery[27] with little Dutch girls in white hats. Talavera porcelain[28] in a parched-stalk yellow or the burnt green of a thirsty, dry plant, representing the ardent dryness of Castile.[29]

The furniture, if you could call it in this setting, was all so different from each other, so strange. Norwegian armchairs[30] with lightly painted wood and floral fabrics near a heavy, oversized, comfortable Spanish friar's chair.[31] Gold Louis XV chairs,[32] cretonne Pompadour armchairs,[33] Marie Antoinette's striped silk,[34] and crowns from the time of the Spanish Empire.[35]

They whispered to each other: 'It's too cluttered.'

'It's ostentatious.'

'It's like we're in a museum.'

Their initial curiosity satisfied, they looked around at each other. They had all tacitly agreed to wear white and other light colours. When they had previously gathered at Doña Matilda's house for tea, their display of expertly made luxurious frocks in an array of shades had been in vain. Blanca had one-upped them with her fairness, her white cloth dress, her stunning ermine fur coat, and her silver lamé[36] hat with a long matching veil. She was seductive, daring. All that piercing whiteness concealed the cold tone of her skin: pure white, without a trace of yellow or pink, but with possibly a hint of indigo, giving it a violet hue under certain lighting.

Now that they all imitated her like ladies in waiting, she arrived in all black, dazzling in a figure-hugging and gold-embroidered crepe de Chine dress[37] with black gloves. Both magnificent and funereal, it had long sleeves

33

THE FEMALE VAMPIRE IN HISPANIC LITERATURE

and a high neckline, neither of which were in fashion. Her marble head, encrusted with two emeralds, looked like a severed head resting on a black pedestal.

She took command and dismissed the customary greetings, neither kissing the ladies nor extending the gentlemen her gloved hand to be kissed. Two dozen tiny puppies, exceptionally white and perfumed, each smelling of a distinct flower, trailed behind her.

'You look beautifully tragic,' said Don Marcelo.

She shivered mildly, her pupils turning slightly pale.

'Never again speak of tragedy,' she declared. 'I'm superstitious and don't believe that words are meaningless. They represent real beings, and the evocations can be dangerous.'

'Spoken like a true Andalusian,'[38] said Doña Matilde.

'Andalusians aren't that superstitious. Quite the opposite. Ghosts can't live easily in all that light and sun. I'm from the North, from the mountains, where every legend has a home. You can find a witch on every peak in the Pyrenees.'

'Or a fairy,' intervened Ernesto.

She laughed, a laugh that carried the echoes of glacial waves crashing into each other, loud as a carillon.[39]

She made the rounds among the groups of her guests, extending a compliment and kind words to each one. She had the good sense to fawn over the plum satin dress embroidered with blue wooden beads, Doña Matilde's moleskin coat and the girls' adorable dresses. Edma was simply charming in a sweet red and black checkered dress with a little macaw tail[40] adorned hat. And then there was young Rosa, nervous in her pink dress and blue silk hat.

'Oh, to be young!' she said with a hint of coquetry, as if it were the only way she knew how. 'You are all so effortlessly beautiful.'

She knew it was vital that she talk to the women about their dresses and accessories. She complimented this one's *ciré* accessories,[41] that one's 'paradisal' black hat, another's beige and silver purse.

Everyone formed little groups around the different tables and played with the snuggly, unruly puppies. The toasty aroma of the tea warmed the room, making everyone feel comfortable. It was the kind of familiarity one feels at a tea party, the camaraderie at the table difficult to attain otherwise.

Despite her energy, laughs, and timely comments, something troubled Blanca. Her eyes would frequently turn towards the door. Finally, she said: 'It looks as though not everyone I had the pleasure of inviting the other day is here.'

They all looked around, as if taking inventory.

'That's right. Fernando isn't here,' said Ernesto.

'He won't be coming?'

Edma stepped forward and stated with extraordinary audacity: 'He promised me he'd come collect us.'

THE COLD WOMAN (BURGOS)

Her jealous brown eyes stared defiantly at Blanca's green ones, valiantly holding back the shudder that their coldness produced.

'I salute him,' Blanca answered dryly.

The confrontation between that strange dominating woman and the unassuming girl who was prepared to defend her love went unnoticed by the others. But those two had understood each other, and they were not to be deceived. They were fighting over a man.

IV

The hotel railing separated them from Paseo de la Castellana, making them feel as if it were far off in the distance. The carriages that passed by at that hour of the night were barely audible, moving slowly, as though the horse and coachman were asleep. The only ones awake, it seemed, were the couple inside, in love and immersed in a dreamworld, or the wandering romantics spellbound by the Madrid night or invoking the legendary city.

Blanca had ordered the lights be turned off in the garden, leaving the moon to cast those violet and silver hues particular to the lights and shadows of the countryside.

'Nights like these are my rivals,' Fernando said, sitting next to her. 'Instead of looking at me, you look up at the sky.'

'I love to gaze at the sky! The stars and I have known each other a long time. I know all their names ... Those who don't know first hand the loneliness of the mountains or who haven't sailed the world can't understand my passion for the stars. I spent my childhood in the ruggedness of the Pyrenees.'

'It must be from so much star gazing that your eyes have taken on that cold green light. While you look up at the stars, I'll look into your eyes. They are one in the same.'

'Something about them pulls me in. Those stars, having for so long lit the way for voyagers, make you want to travel. It's easy to understand the myth of the Magi following a star[42] as one pursues a chimera.[43]'

'Or, in other words, how I pursue your affection.'

'That's not fair. You know I love you .... I've loved you longer, perhaps, than you've loved me. Since I spotted you in the theatre that night with Don Marcelo. You know you're the only reason I agreed to go to the Melendez girls' home, but I probably shouldn't have done that!'

'Do you regret it?'

'It makes me sad to know the state of that poor girl. She was in love with you, and you were ungrateful.'

'Ungrateful, perhaps, but not a traitor. I never promised her I would marry her.'

'But you loved her.'

'I cared for her, but in the same way you care for a sister or a good person, someone intelligent, someone you know well. There wasn't that obsessive,

THE FEMALE VAMPIRE IN HISPANIC LITERATURE

burning passion. That's the kind of passion I feel now, and without having found you, I may have never known it.'

'So, you would have married her.'

'Perhaps.'

'But you weren't engaged?'

'No. It was as if something was telling me that "another woman" would arrive.'

'I regret being the cause of that young girl's despair. Don Marcelo, who since you and I fell in love is no longer my friend, came to tell me that she's falling apart . . . Her mother wants to come plead with me . . . and so does Edma. She thinks that I accept your affection only because I found her arrogant challenge offensive.'

Fernando shivered, then looked at her anxiously.

'But I'm not that depraved,' she said, 'and yet they must think me incapable of loving you as much as I do when they show up to demand I put another's happiness before my own. Is mine not as respectable as hers? Is there priority, or any rights at all, when it comes to love? No. It's that they don't understand that a woman who has been a wife and a mother can love with even more fervour than a girl who still doesn't know a thing about love.'

'They don't realise that you love me, Blanca. Don't forget that they call you "The Cold Woman." They believe that your august, serene, almost cold manner, is a reflection of your soul.'

She remained silent.

'Not even I,' he continued, 'could ever have dreamed that you would love me. I assure you that if you hadn't said it first, I wouldn't have been able to confess my love for you. You seemed so out of reach, so superior to every other woman.'

'Oh, please don't treat me like a goddess! I'd rather be a woman. If you saw me as a goddess, I'd be lost.'

'In all honesty, it was painful to see myself loved. That may be something I shouldn't confess, but I was convinced that the unapproachable "Cold Woman" was incapable of . . . . ever having . . . loved anyone.'

'That's true . . . You are my first and only love, Fernando.'

'Then why do you fill me with despair?'

'I don't want to be your lover.'

'Then be my wife.'

'No.'

'Why not?'

'Because I'm certain that our love would burn out as quickly as it was ignited. I'd prefer to leave with it intact, in my soul and yours.'

'How cruel.'

'It's less cruel than destroying what brings us both such joy.'

'But can't you see that I have given you every part of me?'

THE COLD WOMAN (BURGOS)

In his passionate outburst, Fernando managed to grab Blanca's hands and squeeze them between his own.

Those hands were frozen stiff. It wasn't the coldness of marble or of snow, but that of frozen flesh. The cold hand of death itself.

She tried to get away, but he grabbed her by the waist and pulled her into his arms. Seemingly defeated, she rested her head on his shoulder. Fernando delighted in how her ashen hair tickled his cheek like a shower of snowflakes. He kissed her cold face, purple in hue, a result of her features casting violet shadows under the light of the moon and the cold light of her emerald eyes. He kissed her wildly, passionately, as though he were trying to imbue her with warmth, with life, while his hands ran feverishly over the curves of her marble body.

As her eyes half closed, her pupils turned upward. They shone through the small opening like a ray of light straight from her soul. His lips drank up that cold light as he pressed his face against hers. Yet he was unable to transfer any warmth, and he couldn't feel her breath. It was as if she weren't breathing . . . Determined to consummate his passion, his pressed his lips to hers . . . then abruptly let go and backed away from her as she collapsed on the bench. He steadied himself against the trunk of a eucalyptus tree[44] as he wiped the sweat streaming down his face.

In that kiss of love, he had distinctly perceived the cold, pestilent smell of a cadaver.

When he regained his composure, he tried to conceal his shock. Upon seeing her so beautiful, so fair, abandoned as if in ecstasy, without having moved or uttered a single word, he regretted his reaction. His senses must have surely betrayed him. But now, infected with her coldness and unable to reignite his passion, he needed to convince her that he had pulled away out of chivalry.

'Blanca, my love,' he said, kneeling at the young woman's feet, 'forgive my outburst. Now you see that, despite everything, I can respect you.'

Blanca opened her eyes. If in her soul there had once been passion, and later any pain or turmoil, it wasn't evident on her face. She was serene, unaffected. She didn't complain about his outburst or his reasoning.

'The night, with its melancholy, is an accomplice to many things,' she said. 'Melancholy has more admirers than joy. The will subsides.'

She seemed to be apologising for her weakness. Clearly, she had not discerned the real reason behind Fernando's change of comportment. He wanted to be gallant and not acknowledge that she had surrendered herself to him.

'Your willpower never subsides, Blanca, except when it finds itself safe under my protection.'

She smiled, as though she were thankful for the compliment.

'But it's getting late,' she said. 'The stars tell me that the sun is about to rise . . . We must part.'

THE FEMALE VAMPIRE IN HISPANIC LITERATURE

She stood, and this time it was her who extended her stiff, cadaver-like hand, which he could not bring himself to kiss.

She walked him over to the gate herself, and, like always, followed him with her binoculars as he walked through the ivy glades, watching as each minute he would stop to turn and look back.

V

When he was far enough away to no longer be seen from the hotel, Fernando stepped off the sidewalk and went over to sit in one of those big iron chairs situated under the trees in Recoletos.[45] It was practically deserted at that hour. A couple of stragglers had made a makeshift bed and slept al fresco with their vests unbuttoned and heads exposed. The refreshment stands had all closed, but the buzz from that night's crowds still lingered in the air.

He was bewildered. He loved Blanca with an overwhelming, terrible passion that knew no limits. It was as if her green eyes emitted a cold and magnetic spark that enslaved him. Everything he did, his entire existence, was for her. It wasn't just a spiritual passion, but a burning physical one that, nevertheless, was impossible to satisfy. Each time that he got close to her, that he touched her, he would feel a strange scorching coldness, like he had just touched a cadaver. He hadn't noticed that penetrating iciness at first. He thought she had been denominated 'The Cold Woman' on account of her strange and expressionless form of beauty, as well as her reserved character, indifferent to the love she would awaken in others. This was how he interpreted her name, a name that had come to please him, for there would be such glory in procuring the love of one of those exceptional women supposedly incapable of it. Women like Cleopatra[46] or Lucrezia Borgia.[47] At the core of their love, there must be something akin to a drop of celestial liquor fit to drink by only a limited number of men—men who must feel glorious, just like Attis's priests[48] when the goddesses descended on them for a human child to carry back under their sashes.

Her cold touch had surprised him. Were he not so in love with her, he would have fled. At times, he looked at her with fear, with terror. Today, for the first time, he felt disgust. There was no doubt that from the depths of that mouth, from such a soft breath, emanated an odour of decomposing insides. It wasn't that common foul odour found in people with bad breath, but rather something more dreadful, more repugnant.

Now, replaying the scene in his head, he feared that Blanca had become aware of what was happening. Perhaps it wasn't the first time that she had caused such an impression on a lover, knowing full well how it would end. This must certainly be why she guarded her virtue with such austerity, as if she were ugly, despite her beauty. He was overcome with jealousy. He thought that she had perhaps experienced many similar romances, and for that reason she refused to be his, wishing instead to leave him longing, with

THE COLD WOMAN (BURGOS)

an insatiable dream. Maybe it was an act of revenge against all those who had abandoned her.

Had she always been that way as a wife and mother?

He was anxious to know, to unravel the mystery. He couldn't bring himself to stop loving that extraordinary woman. It was a torturous cycle, that of arriving anxious and trembling with passion for her, only to be stopped dead in his tracks, doused with that cold sensation. The coldness of her hands, her face, her entire body, horrified him in such a strange way.

And now, with his lips joined to hers, he shuddered at how the illusion of happiness had led him to feel this terror, this repugnance.

He eventually stood, walked up the length of the Recoletos promenade, and slowly found his way onto Calle de Alcalá.[49] Once outside the Casino,[50] he ran into a gentleman on his way out to his carriage who, despite the heat, was bundled up in a hefty coat with a collar pulled up to his eyes. He could tell it was the old senator by his manner.

'Don Marcelo!'

Without even realising it, he had called out to him. It was like a groan, like a cry from his soul, and the heartbreaking tone of his voice made the old man pause. He looked at him for a moment, and, without responding, gestured for him to follow. He got onto the coach, and with its door ajar, said to the young man: 'Please excuse me, but even in summer the elderly need to shield themselves from the night's breeze.'

'Don Marcelo, I wanted to speak with you.'

'This isn't the best time, my son. I got more carried away with playing cards this evening than usual. I had bad luck at the start, but I persisted, keeping in mind that like any female,[51] she's inconsistent, and sure enough, I won . . . I was pleased by the praise, but now I'm exhausted and dying to go to sleep.'

'Could we meet someplace tomorrow?'

'What for?'

From the old man's lips escaped a sound, almost a hiss, of indifference, that long dismissive sigh that so clearly suggests: 'And why should I care?'

But then he looked at him, taking notice of how pale and shaken the young man was, how much genuine pain he was in, and said: 'Fine. The best place to talk without interruption is at home. Come by mine later.'

'What time?'

'I'll sleep late. Come around two. Goodnight.'

The old man made one last sign of farewell but as Fernando went to close the door, he stopped him.

'Maybe it's best if you get in after all. I'm a bit nervous and won't be able to fall asleep easily. Let's ride around the outskirts of town, take in a Madrid sunrise and talk. After I go to bed, there's usually no sign of me until it's time to head back to the Casino.'

THE FEMALE VAMPIRE IN HISPANIC LITERATURE

VI

The coach passed through Puerta del Sol at its most dark and lonesome hour, giving it the impression of a riverbank, its asphalt shimmering with dew. It proceeded to go up Calle del Arenal,[52] passed by Teatro Real,[53] then through the old Plaza de la Encarnación, home to the legend of the Middle Ages.[54] Soon after it passed into Paseo de Rosales,[55] that 'border' that gives Madrid the slight air of a coastal province, like the memory of a wide sea covering the plain. The horses descended the hill and followed the path along Maria Luisa's gardens.[56]

The two men had remained silent during the ride. The city, even asleep, seemed to them like a crowd of people from which they had to hide their secret. They were instinctively quiet, like travellers traversing a tunnel. By the time they reached Moncloa,[57] in the middle of the countryside, there appeared to have emerged an unspoken trust between them. With the stars erased, the sky was lit up by a luminous pinkish gray that seemed to escape and penetrate under the trees, through their trunks, while darkness found refuge beneath the canopy above them.

The setting lent itself well to confidence. Maria Luisa's gardens added even more charm to the place named for a queen that despite having the face of a witch, which Goya[58] painted, was renowned for being a lover on account of the adultery she committed in the fronds of Moncloa.

Before Don Marcelo, Fernando made a general confession.[59] He knew that he had the ear of a big-hearted man of the world who would be capable of understanding the wild passion that had taken hold of him, driving him mad to the point of feeling almost indifferent towards the torments of the girl he had chosen to be his wife before meeting Blanca, and to whom he was bound by all the years they had spent growing up together.

As the old man listened, he tried to conceal his interest and the sort of pleasure he felt upon hearing such language, which was like forgotten music awakening echoes and memories in his heart.

He appeared to carefully contemplate the landscape, which revealed its lines and colours more brilliantly with each passing moment. They crossed paths with other carriages and automobiles that carried night owls from 'Casa Camorra'.[60]

Most of the carriages were packed with people. Out of them poured laughter and shouting, their accents worn out and phony. One could only make out their silhouettes and their heads bobbing along the route, like dummies[61] moving to and fro.

When Fernando finished, Don Marcelo replied: 'Alright, but why are you telling me all this? Is it that Blanca has rejected you, so now you find yourself thinking about Edma again, that poor girl who can't hide her love for you and who never hurt anyone?'

He hesitated to respond, and Don Marcelo added: 'If that's not it, then I don't know what you could possibly have to say to me. Don't forget that I'm

THE COLD WOMAN (BURGOS)

Edma's uncle, and that I blame myself for having been in some way responsible for what's happening.'

'It's that I don't even know what I want. I've managed to conquer Blanca's love, and I adore her, despite still loving Edma. Yet when Blanca fell in love and into my arms, I was overcome with an inexplicable repulsion and rejected her. I don't know if this feeling is a result of the duality of two women that lies in my soul, or if there's something real to it. You're the only person I know that's privy to Blanca's background, that can tell me about it, and I beg that you do.'

Don Marcelo remained silent. The coach had passed Puerto de Hierro[62] and was continuing in the direction of Cuesta de las Perdices,[63] as if the coachman had set out to reach the end of the world in a straight line, as long as he weren't called back. The sun had risen. The sky boasted a clear blue, burning with pink and silver to the east, like a promise of the rising sun. To the right, the hills of El Pardo[64] stood tall. To the left were the woodlands of Casa de Campo.[65] The foliage was sparse near the trail—anaemic and stunted pines and wispy weeds, between which rabbits could be seen jumping gracefully across, alert, their ears up, like two slippers, and their white tails standing straight up. From time to time a flock of partridges would join them, jumping and running around enthusiastically instead of flying. Already familiar with people, they would traverse without fear, as if they were aware of their protected status as royal game, and believed themselves untouchable.

Finally, Don Marcelo said: 'Blanca asked that I not disclose what I know about her, and although I never made any promises, I had the intention of keeping quiet. Wouldn't a revelation at this point seem like revenge? Despite everything, I feel very sorry for that rich and idolised woman.'

'I don't understand.'

'She's a woman to whom love is forbidden. Everyone is more in love with the idea of loving her.'

Fernando didn't dare ask any more questions.

They passed by the inns on opposite sides of the road that were open to travellers. The old man rang the bell to get the attention of the coachman, who, with an inexpressive and slumberous face, approached the door.

'Stop at the inn on the left.'

And turning to Fernando, he added: 'Here we can enjoy a *tortilla al ron*[66] and an excellent *chocolatito a la española*[67] in one of those private booths that overlook the garden. The view and the air are delightful, and we can talk as we please.'

VII

'I met Blanca in Vienna,' Don Marcelo said as he moved the alcohol's flames around with his spoon. He watched intently as they would change shape, as refined as the fire's spirit, and light up in flickers of blue, green, purple and

41

THE FEMALE VAMPIRE IN HISPANIC LITERATURE

orange that appeared to rise up from the root and then disappear into the air. 'I don't know whether to begin with telling my impressions at that time, or with what I learned later, arranging the events for easier understanding.'

'As you prefer.'

'Alright, then we'll begin with Blanca's childhood. Both her mother and father died from a mysterious malady a year after marrying, which the good people of the North believed to be rooted in supernatural causes, demons or witchcraft. The fact is that the mother died while giving birth to a being that was more icicle than girl. They could tell she was alive because she would open her eyes and move, but she was cold, frozen, and for as much as they bundled her up and tried to warm her, nothing worked. She forever remained cold, of that strange coldness. She confessed to me the doctors' surprise at taking her temperature for the first time and not being able to make it rise past thirty-five degrees.[68]

'But how did they explain such a strange thing?'

'They couldn't. There are many who would have liked to study her, but they weren't able to. The strange thing is that she doesn't feel the coldness she transmits. She feels fine, comfortable. You could say that she had no idea she's glacial; she ignores the cold sensation. There have been men of science who have thought that a strange, cold-blooded, reptilian organism took on the form of a female human. Others attribute it to the fateful transmission of her parents' mysterious malady; some people believe that one of her ancestors died in the Middle Ages from a strange illness that, while skipping generations, spread to her father and then to her. Whatever the case, it's a real phenomenon that cannot be denied; we can both see it and feel it. Needless to say, it was all spells and enchantment for her grandmother and the family that raised her. They've had the poor girl undergo hundreds of exorcisms, but religion has proved as unsuccessful as science.'

As he spoke, he finished his tortilla, then fixed his gaze on his friend's.

'Come on, Fernando. Don't be rude. Hurry up and eat that or I won't say another word. I won't wait for you to finish to drink my hot chocolate; it would get cold, and right now it's perfect. It's the most succulent breakfast in the world, and unjustly out of fashion. Like the work of friars, who were well aware of what they were doing.'

While dunking his sponge cake in the steaming cream that topped his hot chocolate, he continued: 'Blanca spent her childhood in a little Basque village, on Spain's border, buried in the foothills of the Pyrenees. I don't recall its name. The poor thing was bored to death on that old farm. She would pass the days caring for her favourite animals—chickens, rabbits, sheep. She would run up the mountain herself to find them grass and tender stalks, but strangely enough, the animals refused food from her hand. Cats would run off and dogs would bark at her. Mothers wouldn't dare think to let their children play with her. She couldn't even turn to agriculture. She would have loved to grow and care for plants, but they would wither at her touch, and she couldn't get the seeds to sprout. But this isn't as

42

THE COLD WOMAN (BURGOS)

strange as it sounds. There are many women who have this harmful effect on plants. In my country[69] they aren't allowed near the crops, especially during certain times of the year. I think they might be exaggerating about the animals. Poor Blanca told me all about the anguish she'd endure as she'd walk through the gorges and valleys of her country's mountain range and see one mountain after another. She would feel lost and imprisoned in the chain of them. Luckily, a French nobleman that was hunting in the area fell in love with her and they got married. He was old and must have been somewhat degenerate and sadistic. With him, this "Cold Woman," whose vital functions weren't at all defective besides her lack of a temperature, had two children: one an idiot[70] that didn't live long, and another that also died, of a tumour at two years old. Her husband died of another tumour. She was healthy, but she seemed like one of those rotten apples that spoil those who come in contact with their evil.'

'But that's terrible.'

'It is. Widowed and poor, she agreed to marry the Count of Hozenchis, an Austrian millionaire. He was widowed and had one child, which is why she doesn't have his title. He left her an immense fortune. She didn't have any more children. When I met her in Vienna, she was the most fashionable woman, entrancing with her beauty and luxuries. They had always called her "The Cold Woman," but after her husband died, they changed her name, calling her by that fateful name that made her flee the places she'd be recognised, and that she begged me, implicitly, not to repeat.'

'And what name is that?'

'The living dead.'

'Ah!'

'I can see that you're not surprised.'

'You should keep quiet.'

'No, it's better to get it all out in the open. You can't blame a beautiful young woman with no children, who never loved the husbands who saw her as just a curiosity capable of exciting their drained spirits, who spent her youth bored and lonely, for vehemently desiring to love. She had many suitors. She would choose some and romanticise them. It was difficult, and they shared in the fight . . . but she never 'gave in' to any of them. Everyone "respected" her; that is to say, they fled when they noticed the coldness and corpse-like smell of that beautiful body.'

'Did no one love her enough to overcome that misfortune?'

'Death rejects life. It creates a physical aversion that cannot be overcome. Blanca becomes an impossibility to any potential loves. That is, to anyone with a healthy body and soul.'

'How terrible. She's so beautiful, so majestic, so divine . . . '

'They talked about this a great deal in Vienna, attributing it to a spirit that incarnated in the little baby after the mother died giving birth. The spiritualists say that she's a spirit living in a corpse.'

'But what about the body's vital functions, its growth?'

'They are lent by the astral body.'[71]

'I don't believe those made-up stories about spirits. This to me seems like an isolated case.'

'No, my dear Fernando. That old saying "there's nothing new under the sun" is undeniably true. Everything exists, everything repeats itself, however uncommon it may be. Evidently, there are a lot of cases like these, people just don't hear about them; but there is a well-known historical precedent, as it concerns none other than a queen.'

'Pardon?'

'That's right. Catherine de' Medici[72] was also a living dead woman. She was orphaned after both her parents died from a strange illness, and Pope Clement VII,[73] who had come up with the plan of having her marry the king of France,[74] took care of her. He dismissed all her suitors, which including having to make his nephew Ippolito a Cardinal at the age of eighteen and sending him to Spain.[75] Catherine married Henry II when he was still the Duke of Orléans, and they had children, despite how repulsed her husband was by her. She mothered three degenerate kings. Her husband didn't disown her because she was savvy enough to befriend his favourite, Diane de Poitiers,[76] and he found that to be quite convenient. But Catherine de' Medici always had the cold body of a dead woman, and when she would remove her regal gowns, she smelled like a corpse.'

'And to what did they attribute the phenomenon back then?'

'Science couldn't explain it. The people thought her to be possessed by the Devil, who we've since replaced with avatars and reincarnations. It's all the same. The fact is that if it wasn't the Devil, it was an evil spirit in that dissolute woman, that poisoner that delighted in murder. She could curse people even unintentionally. There are those who maintain that the tragic story of Mary Stuart[77] stemmed from her having worn her mother-in-law's magnificent pearl necklace.'[78]

But Fernando was too horrified by that woman to listen to the historical digression.

VIII

Blanca, wrapped in a loose-fitting yellow crepe garment, standing near the balcony with her curly ashen hair falling over her bare shoulders, looked like a stone statue in a silk tunic. But that living statue suffered vigorously, reflected in her anxious look and green eyes that welled up with tears like glittering frost on the tender leaf of a tree.

She had gone to bed restless and anxious after seeing Fernando off at the gate's door. She still had her doubts about one thing, which she may as well have invented just to deceive herself. Time and again, the men who loved her fled after stealing a kiss from her cold lips. But this time she wanted to doubt, because it was the only time she loved in return. She hadn't lied when she assured Fernando that in him, upon spotting him on the Melen-

THE COLD WOMAN (BURGOS)

dez's balcony that night at the theatre, she had seen her destiny. It was to get close to him that she had spoken to the old senator about his nieces, agreed to have tea at his home, and invited them later to her own.

Edma's jealous defiance had only intensified her passion. Her attitude had let on that Fernando loved her; she had to have noticed for it to have bothered her so much. It was Blanca who had sought Fernando out, who had drawn him in. She was satisfied with how she had aroused his passion, making a show of it without ever taking pity on her rival, whose suffering overcame the pride that makes scorned women feign indifference. Edma felt she was dying without Fernando's love, and she didn't hide it. She spent her days crying, without the desire to eat or leave the house, plunged into a grief that was destroying both her health and her beauty.

Believing her to be suffering from jealousy, Don Marcelo had gone to beg Blanca that she restore her happiness by ceasing to receive Fernando. Yet far from what he expected, he found himself before a woman in love, determined to fight for her happiness, to make her passion triumph over any obstacle, no matter who was hurt in the process. She stifled his philosophical reasoning with the arrogant phrases of selfishness that existed within her own heart.

'Is others' happiness perhaps more respectable than one's own?'

But for the same reason that she was more in love than ever, she was also struggling more than ever. She didn't want to submit to Fernando's love for fear of watching him distance himself once his senses of touch and smell perceived the strange coldness of her body and that incomprehensible odour. She thought it best to flee, to take the memory of their love with her, to leave him with the fantasy of their happiness, the illusion forever maintained by the fever of a love unsatisfied.

But she had been unable to resist that mighty passion, stoked by the night's atmosphere. The aroma of honeysuckle and magnolia[79] from the garden excited her nerves. Magnolia is a treacherous flower for love—sensual, luxuriant, provocative . . . like those stars, buds of light burst open in the great magnolia tree of the sky.

She had let his mouth meet hers, moaning with passion. She wanted to fool herself into believing that such a brusque and incomprehensible reaction in a lover was the triumph of Fernando's chivalrous spirit. She clung to the hope that the young man loved her enough to overcome any negative impressions. If he truly loved her, as much as she loved him, it would overpower all else. The others, the ones who had fled, had chased her for the same prideful reason a woman follows the latest fashion. The opportunistic womanisers, the superficial frivolous lovers, the ones who aspired to marry her for her dowry or her beauty . . . Fernando was different. It was love. She was sure he would return.

She got all dressed up to wait for him the following night. Her alabastrine beauty, adorned with pearls, was superbly enhanced. An entire bottle of an angelica-based perfume[80] surrounded her with an intense, violent

THE FEMALE VAMPIRE IN HISPANIC LITERATURE

aroma that could mask any smell. Fernando was always on time. In the time she had known him, he had always arrived courteous and sweet, without ever making her wait. She knew when it was him ringing the doorbell because a strange vibration would course through her entire body. Then he would come in with his open-mouthed smile that smelled of rosemary and honeysuckle, which, just like the mountain air, lifted one's heart. He was of such healthy spirit that he spread healing and joy all around him. His body, impervious to the temperature, had never shivered as it did the other night when he had run his brawny hands over her glowing skin.

He was late. As Blanca waited in anguish, anxious, impatiently watching the clock, she thought up absurd things that could have happened to him, and equally absurd plans to go find him.

Finally, after a half hour of anguish, she saw him stop at the gate. He had walked up slowly, as if he were being led there by a force greater than his will.

After his conversation with Marcelo, he would have liked to walk away, to end things amicably with Blanca and not expose himself once again to that death-like sensation, the horror of which he could not overcome. And yet, every hour that passed only appeared to intensify his feelings for her. She was not to blame for her body's anomalies, of which she maybe wasn't even fully aware, seeing as it was pious to hide them from her as one hides their illness from those suffering from consumption[81] and cancer. He saw Blanca as an enchanted princess from a fairy tale who would only love the one who passed the test and lifted the spell. Surely, the other men who had courted her didn't love her as much as he, who would never hesitate to worship her with everything he had, even if that meant knowing that her blood were contaminated with a terrible contagious disease, even if her strange body were not human, even if the beloved spirit lived in an exhumed dead woman, even if she were the Devil incarnate ... he didn't care. She was who she was, and as a result, she became something ethereal, incorporeal, a dream, an idea ... love.

She looked so beautiful that he forgot about it all. His impression and Marcelo's stories, he almost found them laughable now. Those superstitions would influence people and make them look at Blanca as though she were a supernatural being. Her low temperature was an anomaly, but not enough to elicit such exaggerations, undoubtedly spread by those who were spiteful and jealous of her beauty. Perhaps the same phenomenon happened with Catherine de' Medici, and legends of witchcraft, demons and sorceresses were hatched up about her, with her enemies spreading the word.

That fairness, that admirable colour, that curvaceous flesh housed in such silky, smooth, satiny skin, enhanced Blanca's beauty. Her thick, loose blonde hair gave the impression of slumber, of coldness, that contributed to the legend.

But despite all his love, all his enthusiasm, all his intentions, he couldn't disguise how his body shook when she took his feverish hand in her own icy ones to have him sit down beside her on the divan.

THE COLD WOMAN (BURGOS)

The aromas in the air enveloped them.

'You arrived later than usual,' she said with affection. 'And today I was expecting you earlier!'

In those words, he could sense what she wasn't saying, sense the trepidation of every woman who has granted favours and then feared she's been a disappointment. She resented the lack of gratitude he displayed at not having come earlier to reassure her.

He was quick to explain himself, saying that he had been held up until now with affairs, family entanglements, and other matters.

'What's more, perhaps I am guilty of having taken my time,' he added. 'I felt you so strongly in my heart and in my soul that at times I was unaware of your absence.'

'How sweet!'

Unexpectedly relieved, she felt happy.

'Would you like a refreshment?' she offered. He was thirsty, the kind of thirsty that precedes states of anguish, but he feared drinking anything cold and increasing the cold sensation that overwhelmed him.

'No . . . I'm a believer in that only hot drinks cool you off.'

'Right, that's the latest theory, along with wearing wool in summer. I'm fortunate enough to not be affected by changes in cold or hot weather . . . I'm always comfortable.'

He listened eagerly to discern if her words contained an explanation to the mystery.

'You don't sweat?'

'Never . . . but never cold either . . . Look, I know how to make a special cocktail that you're sure to like. I'll prepare it myself.'

She rang the bell and gave the maids brief orders.

He looked at her with satisfaction. He liked the sense of familiarity he was establishing with a woman so beautiful and admired as a goddess, like she were his little housewife.

'I'm making you a Russian punch,'[82] she said to him as she poured a cup of cognac[83] in the shaker, then a cup of rum and a shot of curaçao[84] mixed with a few drops of bitters,[85] lime juice and sugar.

'My, that's a lot of ingredients!' he said, looking on with pleasure.

'And now some hot tea, and a few lemon wedges to give it that fragrance. There. You're going to like it.'

'And you.'

'I'm going to make something simpler for me. Just orange juice with sugar and a few drops of gin for aroma. I don't like alcohol.'

'No. Drink from this one.'

He wanted her to drink from that concoction, based on the popular belief that mixing different types of alcohol makes it go more to one's head. He hoped that she would drink, that she'd become intoxicated by those liquors, that the heat they'd produce would make her even more delightful, that her veins would light up by some unknown fire. Oh, how he wanted

THE FEMALE VAMPIRE IN HISPANIC LITERATURE

to see her cheeks flush and her eyes sparkle, even if were on account of the alcohol!

She agreed to try the drinks he frequently kept refilling for himself, which quickly left the shaker empty. It was he who felt light-headed and a new fire that made his blood circulate quickly and his temples and heart beat rapidly.

With every passing moment, she looked more beautiful, dressed in an elegant *déshabillé*[86] that bore a resemblance to a dance costume, revealing the contours of her statuesque body. Her beautiful head, with its perfect lines and colourless beyond her emerald eyes, was haunting with its whiteness.

Thoughts were fading from his imagination. He was forgetting Marcelo's story, the legend about her, everything, so that he'd only be able see her beauty and the enchantment that enveloped him.

Lying on the divan, Blanca appeared to be offering herself to him in sweet abandon. He was somewhat fearful of approaching her, an instinctive fear he was unaware of.

'What are you thinking?' she asked him.

'I'm not sure if I should tell you.'

'Two people in love shouldn't have any secrets.'

'I'm thinking about how you may have loved other men.'

'No. I was being truthful when I told you that I was driven to marriage by my circumstances, my indifference, by a lack of love that made me think the marriage proposals were practical.'

'It's not your husbands I'm jealous of . . . it's other men.'

'No one had ever noticed me before my husband.'

'And after?'

'I had suitors, flirtations that didn't mean anything . . . Nothing was ever made official . . . You have no reason to be jealous.'

He hesitated for a moment, then finally asked the brutal question.

'And why wasn't it ever made official?'

He saw her shudder in silence, as if searching for an answer that alluded her, bewildered by his audacity. Finally, she responded: 'When speaking to a lady, it should always be assumed that the reason nothing was made official is because she didn't want it to be.'

She had stood up and was giving him a haughty, cold look.

Fernando shuddered. He had gone too far and was afraid that he had offended Blanca, that his imprudence had created one of those wounds from which her love for him would bleed right out.[87]

He took her hand as he approached her, and yet despite his love and enthusiasm, he again felt a trembling deep down. He was unnerved by the coldness of her flesh, which, no doubt because of the accounts, reminded him of a corpse.

Her nerves were on edge. He noticed a stiffness to her joints, lodged in her hands, as if resisting surrender. Her spirit had distanced itself from him.

THE COLD WOMAN (BURGOS)

Anxious to conquer the love that seemed to be escaping him, he attempted to conceal his adverse impression by placing a kiss on her hand.

'Forgive me, Blanca, my life. I'm so jealous that I'm going mad. I love you so much!'

She seemed moved by his plea, and her stiff body softened.

'Blanca, my Blanca.'

He pressed her body against his chest, and instead of finding her lips, he kissed her on her forehead. The kiss did him good. It was as though he were feverish and had pressed his lips against marble, extinguishing the burn and soothing him.

Blanca, silent and with her eyes half closed, had surrendered herself in his arms. Yet he, despite his love, felt unsettled. Undoubtedly, touch is one of the great motivators of love. Perhaps children are so adored on account of their warm, soft, pink flesh, so soft to the touch. Love, in fact, cannot be extended without touch, just as sympathy cannot be extended without a certain timbre to the voice.

He kissed her madly, as if trying to extend her warmth through his kisses. He thought it imperative to put an end to those impressions, borne perhaps of his nervous state, of worry. He needed to fully give in to passion in order to reach a level of normality.

He kissed her eyelids closed, feeling how her eyes fluttered like doves under his lips. He then reached her mouth . . . . the stench of decomposing flesh! It was stronger than him, than his passion, than his will!

His arms opened and he stepped away from her with an involuntarily gesture of revulsion.

Silence reigned for a moment, which Blanca broke with a sob.

Fernando was indignant with himself. He couldn't understand what was happening in his soul. He still loved her and desired her madly, yet he couldn't overcome his revulsion at her touch and smell.

'What's wrong, my love?'

She looked at him with her beautiful emerald eyes. They were misty with icy dew and expressed an immense despair. Fernando hesitated. Could she be aware of the impression she was causing him? Was she innocent? Either way, letting her know how he felt would have been cruel. Her green eyes seemed to beg him not to deny his passion, to take her . . .

'You are so special to me, so sacred, that although I come to you trembling with passion, I'm unable to overcome how much I respect you,' he said, as if apologising.

She didn't accept his gallantry, and with sadness replied: 'No, Fernando. You don't love me that much.'

'How can you think that?'

'I see it.'

'You're wrong.'

'No.'

'Do you want me to swear to you?'

49

'It's pointless . . . I've told you so many times . . . I should go . . . '

'Don't say that.'

'I must.'

'I would follow you.'

'For what?'

'I've asked you to be my wife.'

'But I never accepted.'

'But you have, tacitly, in not avoiding my caresses.'

'It's true.'

'So?'

'I don't . . . I don't know . . . but there's something separating us. You come to me full of love but then pull back, as though I were guarded by a protective spirit.'

'It's just that I respect you, that you're so superior . . . that I feel unworthy of you.'

He approached her and extended his hand once more, determined to overcome all those neurotic feelings he was suffering from.

Perhaps the smell he perceived was no more than the smell of female flesh breaking through those of her perfumes, in contrast with them. Perhaps it was the scent of her race.[88]

In that moment, he vaguely recalled that certain people can have a special odour to their flesh, to their skin, that distinguishes them from others. Black people from different tribes were told apart by the smell of their bodies. Gypsies had their own smell that was different from the Indians, their ancestors. That scent of human flesh, like that of a hot chicken coop and unbearable in enclosed spaces, was found in all of them. People, like flowers, could be told apart by their perfume. Blanca's scent wasn't the stench of foul breath but the strange smell of decomposition, which, like her coldness, was reminiscent of a corpse; yet deep down, perhaps it was nothing more than the strange, marked smell of 'race,'[89] overemphasised by her perfumes. That misfortune had to be overcome.

He again joined his lips to hers, parting them so he could kiss her little white teeth.

He didn't know if it was that she was holding her breath, or that he was, but he was able to control the sensation. He didn't notice the odour.

Her white arms had wrapped around his neck like a circle of ice, which, now that he was used to it, didn't produce the painful sensation he had felt in the past. He was dazzled by her open eyes so close to his, and shuddered beneath the kisses that her cool lips reciprocated . . .

He wanted to drink up all her love, to breathe it in, store it in his chest . . . and then he got a whiff of it again. It was enveloping him, choking him, producing such anguish, such unbearable vertigo. He tried to overcome it, but he couldn't. He tried to break away from Blanca, who held him tightly against her heart. Meeting unconscious resistance, he obeyed his instinct,

THE COLD WOMAN (BURGOS)

stronger than any deliberation, and pushed her, brutally rejecting her in order to free himself.

He contemplated her for a moment as she lay crying on the divan. He said nothing. Why would he? It seemed that his love had dissipated with that smell just as ammonia dissipates intoxication.[90] It was impossible to try to overcome that physical repugnance. Smell and touch were integral to love, perhaps its most powerful auxiliaries.

He left without saying a thing, without turning to look back, and without Blanca uttering a single word.

The Vampire

HORACIO QUIROGA

THESE ARE THE LAST LINES I WILL EVER WRITE. Just a moment ago I was taken aback by the telling looks on my doctors' faces regarding my condition: the extreme nervous breakdown I was experiencing was taking me to the grave.

A month prior I had suffered an incredible shock, followed by brain fever.[1] I had not yet recovered when I suffered a relapse that brought me directly to this asylum.

Living graves. That's what soldiers who suffer from nervous system disorders call these secluded establishments tucked deep in the countryside. Patients lie motionless in the shadows, where every effort has been made to keep the place as quiet as possible. If a gun were to suddenly go off in the exterior hallway, half of the patients would die of panic. Incessant grenade explosions have turned these soldiers into what they are today. They lie in their beds absent-minded, inert, truly lifeless, the thick silence being the only thing shielding their broken nervous system. The slightest abrupt sound—a door closing, a teaspoon dropping—would prompt them to let out a horrible scream.

Such was their nervous system. There was a time when these men were revved up, wartime killing machines. Nowadays, the sudden drop of a plate would kill them all.

I've never been to war, but I wouldn't be able to withstand an unexpected noise either. A slight opening of the shutters that let in a glimmer of light would be enough to make me scream.

Yet even this controlled environment isn't enough to calm my nerves. I lay in the dimly lit, dead silence of the vast sitting room with my eyes closed, motionless and lifeless. On the inside, however, my entire being is lying in wait. My breakdown, my anguish, every part of me has become an exhausting and empty yearning for death, which I expect to befall me at any moment. Minute after minute, I anticipate a sharp crackling sound in the dizzying distance, beyond the silence. In the obscurity, I await the concentrated white spectre of a woman.

In a recent immemorial past, that spectre passed through the dining room and paused, then resumed course without knowing her fate. Afterwards . . .

* * *

THE FEMALE VAMPIRE IN HISPANIC LITERATURE

I was a robust, good-humoured man with my sanity intact. One day, I received an enquiry from a stranger regarding comments I had previously made about N1-rays.[2]

It was not uncommon to receive such requests, but what stood out to me was that a clearly well-educated man—one could tell from but the few sentences he had written—was so interested in a trivial research article.

I could barely recall the comments in question. Still, I responded with the name of the newspaper in which it was published and the approximate date of publication. I then forgot about the whole thing.

A month later, I received another letter from the same person. He asked if the experiment I mentioned in my article (he had clearly found and read it) had really been conducted, or if it was just a figment of my imagination.

I was a bit intrigued by this stranger's persistent questioning when he could have referenced more in-depth studies on the topic. I was merely a dilettante who dabbled in the sciences, and after all, it was evident that my comments on the strange effects of N1-rays were informed by another source. Whereas any man of science could have reassured him, my educated correspondent insisted that I be the one to verify the accuracy of certain optical phenomena.

As I stated previously, I could barely recall what I had written about the rays in question. I racked my brain and was finally able to remember the experiment in question. I wrote back saying that if he was referring to the phenomenon where bricks exposed to sunlight lose the ability to emit N1-rays when altered with chloroform,[3] this was indeed true. Gustavo Le Bon, among others, had verified it.

Such was the content of my letter. I sent it and soon forgot about N1-rays altogether . . . at least, for a little while.

A third letter arrived containing expressions of gratitude for my report, and the following lines, which I have transcribed word for word: 'It was actually a different experiment that I wanted to get your personal opinion on. I realise that you may find our continued written correspondence bothersome, so I ask that you grant me a few minutes of your time in person. Perhaps we could meet at your home, or wherever you find most convenient.'

Those were the contents of the letter. I had, of course, already dismissed my initial reaction at the thought of getting involved with a madman. I believe it was then that I began to suspect what he wanted from me, why he sought my opinion, and where my anonymous correspondent was going with all of this. It wasn't my poor scientific knowledge that interested him.

I finally understood. It was as clear as one's own reflection in the mirror when the next day, Don Guillén de Orzúa y Rosales—or so he called himself—sat across from me at my desk and began to speak.

I'll first describe his appearance. He was a man in the second stage of his youth whose countenance and refinement gave away that he enjoyed the spoils of old money. That he was *vieux-riche*[4] was the first thing one noticed about him.

54

THE VAMPIRE (QUIROGA)

The warm colour of the skin around his eyes, as though he were one of those people dedicated to the study of cathode rays,[5] stood out to me. He parted his black hair neatly to the side. His calm, almost cold, gaze expressed the same collected self-confidence and refinement as his demeanour.

Just a few words into our conversation, surprised by the lack of a peninsular or Latin American accent from a man with such a name, I asked if he was Spanish.

'No,' he replied. And after a short pause, he explained the reason for his visit.

'Although I am not of man of science,' he said, clasping his hands over my desk, 'I have conducted a few experiments on the phenomenon to which I alluded in my correspondence. My fortune allows me the luxury of a high-grade laboratory, which unfortunately exceeds my abilities. I have yet to discover a new phenomenon, and my aspirations are on par with those of a misguided mystery enthusiast. I'm familiar with the unique physiology— let's call it that—of N1-rays, and I would have left them alone had your article, referred to me by a friend, not reawakened my poorly dormant curiosity. At the end of your article, you suggest the parallels between certain sound waves and visual emanations. In the same way that a voice can be impressed on a radio circuit, so can the emanation of a face be impressed on a circuit of visual nature. If I have understood correctly that this has nothing to do with electrical energy, I kindly ask that you answer this question: did you have an experiment like this in mind when you wrote your article, or was the possibility of such materialisations just an imaginative speculation? This enquiry, Mr Grant, is the reason behind my writing you twice,[6] coming here and perhaps disturbing you.'

Having said that, he waited with his hands still clasped.

I responded immediately. Yet, with the same swiftness with which one scrutinises an old memory before replying, I remembered the suggestion that my visitor was alluding to: if the retina can impress a radiographic 'double' of a photograph through the ardent contemplation of the original image, then in a similar way, the active and emotional forces of the soul should be able to 'create' (not simply produce) a tangible optical image . . .

That was the thesis of my article.

'I don't know,' I quickly responded, 'if such an experiment has ever been conducted . . . This was all, as you rightly noted, an imaginative speculation. There is no validity to my thesis.'

'So, you don't believe in it?'

With his clasped hands still steady, he fixed his gaze upon me.

That look, which had suddenly come over his face, exposed his true motives for wanting to know my 'personal opinion'.

But I didn't respond.

'It's no mystery to us,' he continued, 'that N1-rays alone could never imprint on anything but a brick or a photograph exposed to sunlight. Another

THE FEMALE VAMPIRE IN HISPANIC LITERATURE

layer to the problem is what brings me here to take up your precious time . . . ,'

'To ask me a question with an answer already in mind?' I interrupted. 'Of course! And you, Mr Rosales, do you believe in my thesis?'

'You know I do,' he responded.

Has there ever been a moment when a stranger lays his cards out on the table and his gaze meets that of his opponent, who still holds his cards, and they both realise they are holding the same hand? That was the situation that my interlocutor and I had found ourselves in.

There is only one thing capable of stimulating the strange forces around us and altering our soul, and that is the imagination. N1-rays did not interest my visitor in the least. Instead, he was chasing the insane notion my article proposed.

'Then you believe,' I observed, 'in infra-photographic impressions? Supposing I am . . . the subject?'

'I'm sure of it,' he responded.

'Have you attempted it on yourself?'

'Not yet, but I will. I came to see you because I wanted to be sure that you wouldn't have suggested such an obscure idea without first knowing it were possible.'

'But suggestions and ideas are a dime a dozen,' I observed again. 'The asylums are full of them.'

'No. They are full of "abnormal" ideas, not ones viewed as "normal", such as yours. It's been said that only that which cannot be conceived is impossible. There is an unmistakable way of knowing how to convince people of the truth. You possess that gift.'

'My imagination is a little sick . . . ' I argued, retreating.

'Mine is sick, too,' he said, smiling.

As he got up, he added, 'I have taken up enough of your time. I'll end my visit with these brief words: how would it sound if you and I were to study your thesis together? Would you be up to running the risk?'

'Of failing?' I asked.

'No. We shouldn't fear failing.'

'Then what?'

'Just the opposite.'

'I agree,' I said, and after a pause, 'Mr Rosales, do you have confidence in your nervous system?'

'Very much so,' he said, smiling with his usual calm. 'It would be a pleasure to keep you updated on my experiments. Would we be able to meet again another day? I live alone and have few friends, and now that I know you better, I'd like to count you among them.'

'I'd be delighted, Mr Rosales,' I said, bowing.

A moment later, that strange man was gone.

* * *

THE VAMPIRE (QUIROGA)

A strange man, without a doubt. Educated and of vast wealth, without a homeland or friends, enthralled by experiments even more strange than himself. It was all enough to stoke my curiosity. He could have been paranoid, maniacal and on the brink of insanity, but it was evident that his willpower was something fierce . . . And for those who live on the border of the irrational, willpower is the only way to unlock the gates of the eternally forbidden.

Holing oneself up in the dark and contemplating a light-sensitive plate to impress the features of a beloved woman will not cost you your life. Rosales could pull it off successfully without condemning his soul to hell. What unsettled me about him, and why I feared for myself, was the inevitable fatal aftermath of such fantasies.

* * *

Despite his promises, I had not heard from Rosales. Then we happened to run into each other one afternoon in the main hallway of a cinema as we both left in the middle of a screening. Rosales exited slowly. The shadows and rays of light from the projector pierced obliquely through the room, landing on his head.

He seemed distracted by them. I had to call out to him twice for him to hear me.

'What a pleasure to see you,' he said. 'Do you have a few minutes, Mr Grant?'

'Just a few,' I responded.

'Perfect. Can you spare ten? Let's sit down somewhere.'

We found ourselves before two untouched cups of steaming coffee.

'Any updates, Mr Rosales?' I asked.

'No, not if you're referring to my creating a radiographic impression. It was a mediocre experiment that is not worth repeating anyway. Between us, there are more interesting things . . . When you saw me just a few moments ago I was following the beams of light pouring into the hallway. Does the cinema interest you, Mr Grant?'

'Very much so.'

'I knew it. Don't you think the projector's rays, once affected by a viewer, can carry more than just a lifeless large-scale reproduction? And please excuse my excitement . . . I haven't slept in days. It's as though I'm no longer able to. I drink coffee all night, but never sleep . . . I'll continue, Mr Grant: do you know what gives a painting life, and what distinguishes one bad painting from another? Poe's oval portrait[7] was alive because it was painted with "life itself". Do you believe there only to be a galvanic imitation of life[8] in the facial expressions of a woman who can awaken and excite an entire theatre? Do you believe that a simple photographic illusion can deceive men's deep understanding of the feminine reality?'

He fell silent and awaited my reply.

57

THE FEMALE VAMPIRE IN HISPANIC LITERATURE

People tend to ask aimless questions, but when Rosales asked something, it wasn't in vain. He genuinely wanted a response.

But how was I to respond to a man who always spoke with such restraint and courtesy? Nevertheless, after a moment I said: 'You're right, to a certain extent . . . There is clearly more to a film than just galvanic light, but it isn't life. Ghosts also exist.'

'Never in my life,' he objected, 'have I heard that a thousand men, sitting still in the dark, ever desired a ghost.'

After a long pause, I stood up.

'Your ten minutes are up, Mr Rosales,' I said, smiling.

He smiled back.

'It has been very gracious of you to hear me out, Mr Grant. Would you be so kind as to accept a dinner invitation for next Tuesday? We would dine alone at my home. I had an excellent chef, but he's fallen ill . . . Some of my servants may also be missing, but unless you're particularly demanding, we should be able to get by, Mr Grant.'

'Of course.'

'Delightful. Until Tuesday, then, Mr Rosales.'

'Until then, Mr Grant.'

* * *

I got the impression that his dinner invitation wasn't by chance, that his chef wasn't sick, and that I wouldn't find one servant in his home, but I was mistaken. A member of his staff greeted me at the door. I was then passed off to different servants as I made way to an area adjacent to the bedroom, where after a long wait, I received an apology: Mr Rosales was sick and would not be able to dine with me. He wanted to extend his apologies himself, but his attempts to get up were in vain. I could expect a visit from him as soon as he was back on his feet.

Behind the hieratical[9] servant, the door to the bedroom was slightly ajar, exposing its brightly lit carpet. Not a peep could be heard. You could have sworn that sick people had been tended to for months in that silent mansion, yet I had laughed with the house's owner just three days prior.

The next day, I received the following note from Rosales: 'Sir and friend, misfortune tried to rob me of the pleasure of your visit to my home yesterday. Do you recall what I told you about my serving staff? Well, this time I was the sick one, but no cause for alarm. Today I am well, and I expect the same to be true for next Tuesday. Will you be in attendance? I would like to make it up to you. Yours sincerely, et cetera.'

Again with the servants. Still holding the note, I pondered whether dining at the home of a man with a sick or partial serving staff, and whose mansion was lifeless but for the brightly lit section of carpet, would really happen.

I had been wrong about my peculiar friend once before, and I realised I had erred again. He and his environment were much too secret and reeked

THE VAMPIRE (QUIROGA)

too much of crime to be taken seriously. While Rosales thought himself to be of sound mind, it was clear to me that he had already stumbled over the edge of madness. I set out for the former sick person's palace the following Tuesday, praising myself once more for my misgivings in shaking up strange forces by partnering up with a non-Spaniard who endeavoured to sound like a Spanish nobleman. I was more prepared to be amused by what I heard than to enjoy my host's perplexing dinner.

Nevertheless, dinner was waiting for me, though not the serving staff. It was the doorman who escorted me through the house to the dining room door. He then knocked and promptly vanished.

A moment later, the owner of the house opened the door. He recognised me and let me in with a relaxed smile.

The first thing I noticed upon entering was the prominence of warm tones that, as if browned by the sun or ultraviolet rays, persistently coloured my friend's cheeks and temples. He was wearing a tuxedo.

The second thing I noticed was the size of the incredibly opulent dining room. It was so big that it swallowed up the table, which was covered in delicacies, but only three place settings. At the head of the table, I saw the silhouette of a woman dressed for a *soirée*.[10]

I wasn't, therefore, the only guest. We advanced through the room. Once I could see her more clearly, the strong sensation I experienced at the first sight of that feminine silhouette transformed into acute tension.

She was a ghost, not a woman—the smiling, translucent spectre of a woman in a low-cut dress.

I halted for a moment, but since Rosales acted as though everything were normal, I continued walking and took my place next to him. Pallid and tense, I waited to be introduced.

'I believe you're already acquainted with Mr Guillermo Grant,' he said to the lady, who smiled politely as Rosales smiled at me.

'And Mr Grant, do you recognise her?'

'Absolutely,' I replied as I leaned forward, pale as a ghost.

'Then please take a seat,' said the owner of the house, 'and help yourself to whatever you like. Now you can see why I warned you about my staff shortage. What a pitiful dinner, Mr Grant . . . . At least this lady's amiability and presence will make up for its shortcomings.'

As I already mentioned, the table was covered with delicacies.

In any other situation, the faintest sensation of terror would have been enough to make me bristle with fright right down to my bones. Yet, faced with Rosales's *parti pris*[11] of what constitutes normal, I let myself slip into the vague stupor that appeared to float over everything.

I turned towards her and noticed she hadn't touched her place setting.

'You won't be dining this evening, ma'am?' I asked.

'Oh, no, sir!' She responded in the tone of voice of a person who excuses themself for their lack of appetite. Then she clasped her hands under her cheek and smiled thoughtfully.

59

THE FEMALE VAMPIRE IN HISPANIC LITERATURE

'Do you frequent the cinema often, Mr Grant?' Rosales asked me.

'Yes, regularly,' I responded.

'I would have recognised you right away,' the lady said as she turned to me. 'I've seen you many times.'

'Not many of your films have been released here,' I observed.

'Yes, but you've seen them all, Mr Grant,' Rosales said smiling, 'which explains why she has spotted you more than once in the theatre.'

'Indeed,' I admitted, and after an extremely long pause I asked, 'Can you make out faces clearly from the screen?'

'Perfectly,' she replied. 'Why wouldn't I?' she added, slightly surprised.

'Indeed,' I repeated, but this time only to myself.

If I was certain I had not died on the way over to Rosales's home, then they should have acknowledged the trivial and mundane reality of a transparent woman in a dress.

The minutes passed by as we chatted inconsequentially. The owner of the house noticed that she kept raising her hand to her eyes: 'Are you tired, madam? Would you like to lay down for a bit? Mr Grant and I will attempt to fill the void created by your absence by having a smoke.'

'Yes, I am a little tired ...' our guest admitted, getting up from table. 'With your permission,' she added, smiling at us one after the other. Then she walked away in her beautiful dress, the glassware in the display case glistening softly as she passed by.

* * *

Rosales and I sat alone in silence.

After a while he asked, 'So, what do you think of all this?'

'I think that if I recently judged you twice in error, my first impression of you was correct,' I responded.

'You thought me crazy twice, right?'

'You can see how I would think that.'

We remained quiet another moment. Rosales seem unchanged; he was as polite and restrained as ever.

'You have enormous willpower,' I muttered.

'Yes,' he smiled, 'I can't hide it. I was certain of my observation when you saw me at the cinema. It was "her", without a doubt. Her face revealed an incredible amount of life, making me think that the phenomenon was possible. Everyone knows that a twinkling of life is imprinted on every still frame. Yet, from the moment a running film is stimulated by light, voltage and N1-rays, all of that is transformed into a vibrant trace of life that is more alive than our fleeting reality and the most vivid memories that guide the course of our life until we die. But only you and I know this.'

'I should confess,' Rosales continued slowly, 'that I experienced some difficulties up front. Perhaps my imagination drifted, but I brought an unnameable thing to life ... One of those things that should remain forever on the other side of the grave. It appeared and did not leave me for three days. The only thing it couldn't do was climb up on the bed . . . When you arrived last week, I hadn't seen it for two hours, which is why I had my staff let you in. But I spotted it at the foot of the bed, tense and trying to climb up, as soon as I heard your footsteps . . . No, it wasn't something of this world . . . It was my imagination run horribly wild. It won't be back. The next day, when I extracted tonight's guest from the screen, I risked my life . . . And I saved her. If you ever decide to extract the wrong life from the screen, be careful, Mr Grant . . . Death lurks just beyond this moment . . . Let your imagination run fully wild . . . as long as it doesn't veer off course. This is where willpower comes in. Neglecting it has cost many lives . . . Would you allow me a vulgar comparison? With a hunting rifle, your imagination is the projectile and your willpower is the scope. Aim well, Mr Grant! And now, let's go see our friend, who has surely recovered from her fatigue. Please, follow me.'

Thick curtains opened to a sitting room even larger than the dining room. There was a raised platform accessible by three stairs at the back of the room. It was arranged as a bedroom, and in the centre was a divan[12] almost as wide as a bed and as tall as a barrow. On the bed, under a diamond-shaped display of *plafonniers*,[13] laid the spectre of a beautiful woman.

Although the carpet absorbed the sound of our footsteps, she heard us climb the stairs and turned to look at us, revealing a soft smile: 'I fell asleep,' she said, 'Forgive me, Mr Grant, and you too, Mr Rosales. It's just so peaceful here . . . '

'Don't get up, ma'am, I beg of you!' exclaimed the owner of the home upon discerning her resolve. 'Mr Grant and I will pull up a couple of chairs so we can all speak at ease.'

'Oh, thank you!' she murmured. 'I'm so comfortable as I am . . . '

After we did as the owner of the house had directed, he continued: 'Now, ma'am, time is of no consequence. We're in no rush, nor do we anticipate any disruptions. Isn't that right, Mr Grant?'

'It certainly is,' I agreed, completely oblivious to the time and as stupefied as if someone had told me I had died fourteen years ago.

'I'm fine just like this,' repeated the spectre with both hands resting under her temple.

And I suppose we must have engaged in lively conversation because when I stepped foot outside, the sun had already been shining for hours.

* * *

I bathed upon returning home to prepare for my day, but I was so exhausted that I passed out as soon as I sat down on the bed. I slept for twelve hours straight, bathed again, and made it out the door this time. My most recent memories floated above me, ambulatory and looming, detached from place and time. I could have pinpointed each one of them, but all I wanted was to dine in a cheery, loud and bustling restaurant, because in addition to my

THE FEMALE VAMPIRE IN HISPANIC LITERATURE

tremendous appetite, I dreaded the idea of restraint, silence and contemplation.

I was on my way to a restaurant when I found myself in Rosales's dining room, sitting down before my designated place setting.

* * *

I dined at Rosales's home every night for a month, without my willpower intervening in the least. I'm certain that an individual by the name of Guillermo Grant continued to actively face his tasks and problems during the daylight hours, but night after night, from nine o'clock on, I turned up at Rosales's mansion. First in the dining room without servants, then in the sitting room.

Like the man who dreamed Armageddon,[14] my life under the sun's rays has been a hallucination, and I have been designated the role of a spectre. My real existence has slipped away, as if contained in a crypt, where in the company of another man we worship the spectre of a woman paraded on the slow-moving bedroom's wall under the bright *plafonniers*.

One night, as our friend appeared engrossed in thought, with her legs crossed and an elbow resting on her knee, Rosales interjected, 'It wouldn't be honest of me to let you believe that I'm completely satisfied with my work. I've taken serious risks to have this pure and loyal companion join me in my destiny, and I would give the remainder of my days to grant her just a moment of life . . . Mr Grant, I've committed an inexcusable crime. Is that how you see it?'

'I do,' I responded. 'All your pain and suffering wouldn't be enough to make up for even one of that young lady's blistering moans.'

'I'm perfectly aware . . . I have no right to justify my actions . . . '

'Undo them.'

Rosales shook his head: 'No, nothing could fix . . . '

He paused, then looked up with that same calm expression and tone of voice that seemed to carry him a thousand leagues[15] away from the topic at hand: 'I don't want for there to be any distrust between us,' he said. 'Our friend will never free herself from the painful fog she's in . . . without a miracle. With the exception of monsters, all creations are entitled to life, but only a small twist of fate can bestow it.'

'What kind of twist?' I asked.

'*Her* death, up in Hollywood.'

Rosales finished his cup of coffee. I added sugar to mine. Sixty seconds passed before I broke my silence.

'That wouldn't fix anything either . . . ' I muttered.

'You don't think so?' he said.

'I'm positive . . . I couldn't tell you how I know it, but I do. What's more, you're not capable of . . . '

'I'm capable, Mr Grant. Based solely on the sheer force that she exerts to survive each day, you and I both know that this spectral creation is superior

THE VAMPIRE (QUIROGA)

to any living offspring. Our companion is a work of consciousness. Do you understand, Mr Grant? She has an almost divine purpose, and if I stand in its way, I will be sure to meet eternal damnation before the tumultuous non-pagan gods. While I'm away, will you visit from time to time? Dinner is served at nightfall, as you know, and at that time everyone but the doorman leaves. Will you come?'

'I will,' I replied.

'That's more than I could have hoped for,' he said, bowing.

* * *

And so I went. I may have been on time for dinner one of those nights, but I mostly arrived late, though always at the same time; as punctual as a man who visits his girlfriend's house. At the table, the young lady and I would engage in lively conversation about different topics. In the sitting room, however, we barely spoke a word. We were too immersed in the stupor that flowed from the canopy of lights, whose glow seeped through keyholes and open doors, imbuing the mansion with a sluggish silence.

With every passing night, our brief exchanges were reduced to monotonous offhand observations about the same topic: 'He's probably in Guayaquil[16] by now,' I said absentmindedly.

And several nights later, at the crack of dawn, she said, 'He has already left San Diego.'[17]

One night, with a cigarette dangling from my fingers, I tried to pull myself out of a daze while she wandered the room in silence, her cheek resting in her hand. Suddenly, she stopped and said: 'He's in Santa Monica[18] . . .'

She continued wandering around for a moment, her face still resting in her hand, then climbed the stairs and into her divan. I sensed it without shifting my gaze, which continued to follow the walls of the room as they gave way with such speed that the lines converged without ever meeting. An endless avenue of palm trees appeared in the distance.

'Santa Monica!' I thought, bewildered.

I can't recall how much time had passed, but I suddenly heard her say from the divan: 'He's at the house.'

With the last bit of energy I could muster, I tore my gaze from the avenue of palm trees. The young lady lay as still as a corpse under the diamond-shaped *plafonniers* embedded in the ceiling. Before me, faraway on the other side of the ocean, the painfully harsh outlines of small palm trees stood out in the distance.

I closed my eyes and the image of a man flashed before me. He held a dagger over a sleeping woman.

'Rosales!' I muttered in fright. Then, in another flash, I saw the dagger plunge into her.

I don't know what happened after that. I managed to hear a terrible scream—possibly my own—and then I lost consciousness.

THE FEMALE VAMPIRE IN HISPANIC LITERATURE

* * *

When I came to, I was at home in my bed. I had been out for three days with a horrible case of brain fever that lasted for more than a month. Little by little, I was regaining my strength. Someone told me that a man had brought me home unconscious in the middle of the night.

I couldn't remember a thing, nor did I want to remember. I was lax in thinking about anything at all. For brief periods of time, I was permitted to walk around my house, which I did with a stunned look on my face. Finally, I was allowed to venture outside. I took a few steps without realising what I was doing, memoryless and aimless . . . And when I was in a quiet room and saw a man approach me whose face I recognised, I remembered who I was and what had happened. It made my blood boil.

'I'm finally able to see you, Mr Grant,' Rosales said, shaking my hand effusively. 'Since my return, I have followed the course of your illness with great concern, but not for a moment did I think you wouldn't make it.'

Rosales had lost weight. He spoke softly, as if he were afraid of being heard. Over his shoulder I saw the brightly lit bedroom and the divan I knew too well. It was surrounded with tall cushions, like a coffin.

'Is she in there?' I asked.

Rosales's eyes followed my gaze, then fell back on me. They were calm.

'Yes,' he responded, and after a brief pause, 'Come with me.'

We climbed the stairs, and I leaned over the cushions. All I saw was a skeleton.

I felt Rosales shaking my arm, and with the same soft voice: 'It's her, Mr Grant. It doesn't weigh on me, nor do I think I made a mistake. When I returned from my trip, she was no longer here . . . . Mr Grant, do you recall seeing her the exact moment you lost consciousness?'

'I don't remember,' I muttered.

'That's what I figured . . . When I did what I did on the night you passed out, she disappeared . . . When I returned, I tortured my imagination to bring her back again from the other side . . . and this is the result! When she belonged to this world, I was able to turn her spectral life into a lovely creature. I took the other one's life to animate her spectre, only for her to deliver me her skeleton . . . .'

Rosales paused. I detected the same blank expression on his face as he spoke.

'Rosales . . . ' I began.

'Psst!' he interrupted, lowering his voice even more. 'I implore you not to raise your voice . . . She's over there.'

'She?'

'Over there, in the dining room . . . . Well, I haven't seen her, but since my return she wanders from one side of the room to the other . . . I can feel her dress brush against me . . . Be quiet for a moment . . . Can you hear her?'

Across the still atmosphere of that quiet mansion, I couldn't hear a thing. We were completely silent for a while.

64

THE VAMPIRE (QUIROGA)

'It's her,' murmured a satisfied Rosales. 'Listen. She's skirting around the chairs as she walks . . . '

* * *

Every night for a month, Rosales and I sat vigil for the spectre of bones that once belonged to our resplendent guest. Behind the thick curtains that open to the dining room, the lights are on. We know she wanders around there, bewildered and invisible, uncertain and in pain. In the wee hours, when Rosales and I drink our coffee, she may have already been sitting at her usual spot for hours, her invisible gaze fixed on us.

The nights blur together. They are all the same. In the dazed atmosphere of the house, time itself appears to have stopped, as if before an eternity. There always has been and always will be *plafonniers* hanging over a skeleton, two friends dressed in tuxedos in the sitting room, and between the dining room chairs, a confined hallucination.

One night, I noticed a change in the atmosphere. My friend's excitement was palpable.

'I've finally found what I've been looking for, Mr Grant. Do you recall how I once told you that I had not made a mistake? Well, now I know that I have. You praised my imagination, no keener than yours, and my will power, which by contrast, is quite superior to yours. Between those two forces at work, I created a visible creature, which we lost, and a spectre of bones, which will remain until . . . Do you know, Mr Grant, what my experiment lacked?'

'A purpose,' I muttered, 'which you thought to be divine.'

'Exactly. I went from the excitement of a dark movie theatre to a moving hallucination. In the pulsating passion that a blown-up static photograph arouses in men, I saw more than just deception. I warned you that men get it right up to that point. There must be more life there than what beams of light and a metallic curtain can simulate. You've seen that for yourself. I was sterile in my approach, and that was my mistake. She would have made even the most insufferable spectator happy, but she found no warmth in my cold hands, so she disappeared . . . Love may not be necessary in life, but it's indispensable when knocking at death's door. If I had killed for love, my creature would be on the divan right now, palpitating with life, but I killed for the sake of creating, not for love, thus procuring life in its brutal state of origin: a skeleton. Mr Grant, would you leave me for three days, and then return to dine with us next Tuesday?'

'With her?'

'Yes. You, her, and I . . . . Trust me . . . Next Friday.'

* * *

I saw her again, dressed magnificently as usual, when I opened the door myself. I confess I was pleased to see that she had been looking forward to seeing me as well. She extended her hand, wearing the kind of welcoming

THE FEMALE VAMPIRE IN HISPANIC LITERATURE

smile one reserves for a loyal friend who has just returned home after a long trip.

'We've missed you a great deal, ma'am,' I gushed.

'And I you, Mr Grant!' she replied, cupping her face with both hands.

'You missed me? Really?'

'You? Oh yes, very much!' She extended me another prolonged smile.

At that moment, I realised that the owner of the house hadn't lifted his gaze from his fork since we had begun talking. Is it possible? ...

'And did you not miss our host, ma'am?'

'Him?' she murmured slowly as she turned to Rosales, leisurely dropping her hand from her face.

As she fixed her gaze upon him, I saw the most wild and passionate flame that any woman had ever felt for a man flash across her eyes. Rosales was looking at her, too. In the presence of such a candid and dizzying display of female love, he turned pale.

'Him, too ...' the young lady murmured, her voice quiet and weary.

During dinner, she chatted whimsically with me while pretending not to notice the owner of the house. Rosales rarely looked up from his fork, but the two or three times that their eyes inadvertently met I saw hers momentarily flash with the uncontrollable heat of desire.

And she was a spectre.

'Rosales!' I exclaimed when we found ourselves alone. 'If you have even the slightest desire left to live, you must destroy that! It's going to kill you!'

'Her? Are you mad, Mr Grant?'

'Not her. Your love! You can't see it because you're under her control. But I see it. No man could resist the passion of that ... spectre.'

'I'll tell you again, Mr Grant. You're mistaken.'

'No, you just can't see it! Your life has withstood many tests, but it will burn like a feather if you continue to excite that creature even in the slightest.'

'I don't desire her, Mr Grant.'

'But she does desire you. She's a vampire, and she has nothing to offer you! Do you understand?'

Rosales remained quiet. The young lady's voice could be heard from the sitting room, or beyond: 'Will I be left alone much longer?'

At that exact moment, I suddenly remembered the skeleton resting over there ...

'Rosales, the skeleton!' I cried out. 'What happened to her skeleton?'

'It went back,' he responded. 'It returned to the void. But right now, she is over on the divan ... Listen to me, Mr Grant. No creature has ever gained control of its creator ... I created a spectre, and, mistakenly, a skeleton in tatters. You've neglected some details of the creation, which I'll spell out to you. I acquired a lamp and projected our friend's films onto a screen that was sensitive to N_1-rays. (You remember N_1-rays, right?) Through an everyday device, I was able to keep her lingering photographic moments

66

THE VAMPIRE (QUIROGA)

moving . . . You know very well that sometimes when we speak, we experience moments of such certainty and timely inspiration that we can perceive within ourselves and in the faces of those around us that some part of us is being projected forward . . . That is how she came detached from the screen, at first oscillating just a few millimetres away from it. Then she finally came to me, just how you've observed her . . . This was three days ago. She's there . . . '

Again, the young lady's listless voice reached us from the bedroom: 'Are you coming, Mr Rosales?'

'Destroy it, Rosales,' I exclaimed, grabbing his arm, 'before it's too late! Don't excite that monstrous sensation anymore!'

'Goodnight, Mr Grant,' he said, bowing with a smile.

* * *

And so this story ends. Was Rosales able to find in this world the strength to resist? Very soon—maybe even today—I'll find out.

That morning, I was not in the least bit surprised to receive an urgent telephone call, nor to find the sitting room's curtains browned by the fire, a fallen projection camera, and remains of burned films scattered across the floor. Rosales was lying on the carpet next to the divan, dead.

The servants knew that the camera had been moved to the sitting room sometime over the last few nights. Their impression was that the films had accidentally caught fire, and that sparks had reached the divan. They attributed Mr Rosales's death to a heart injury brought on by the accident.

My impression differs. The calm expression on his face had not changed, and even in death, his face maintained its usual warm tone. But I'm certain that in the very depths of his veins, not a drop of blood remained.

Explanatory Notes

THE FOLLOWING NOTES ATTEMPT TO IDENTIFY sources, quotations, proverbial phrases and references to historical events and personages, as well as geographical locations and obscure or specialist language made in the five tales of this collection. Reference to contextual notes is by superscript arabic numerals that restart at each significant section of the volume, namely the five separate tales. In general, only the first occurence of a specific term is glossed, given the sequential nature of the texts, but terms occurring in each story are glossed fresh at initial appearance for each text. References to the Bible are taken from the Authorized Version, while the abbreviation *OED* indicates defintions that have been taken from the most recent edition of the *Oxford English Dictionary*, available online at *https://www. oed.com*.

THE FEMALE VAMPIRE

1. *colonel:* officer of high rank, whether of infantry or cavalry, typically in charge of a regiment of around 800 men; in the Spanish and Latin American army, the Colonel (*Coronel*) ranks below Brigadier General (*General de brigada*) and above Lieutenant Colonel (*Teniente coronel*). This detail further aligns his character with 'male impulses', violence and hierarchy.
2. *sphinx:* hybrid monster of ancient Greek mythology, usually possessing the head of a woman, the body of a lion and the wings of an eagle. The sphinx menaced the ancient city of Thebes in Central Greece, by devouring those who could not solve her riddles, until she encountered the city's lost prince, Oedipus, whose correct solution drives the sphinx to her death. The implicit meaning here is of a woman who is merciless and predatory.
3. *It was as if … those around her:* The original Spanish text states, 'Tenía, como una esfinge, la sonrisa y la garra, atemorizando con ésta las inclinaciones que con aquella producía'. *Garra* can be translated as 'claw', but it can also mean someone possessing a strength or strong sense of conviction that others find attractive. There is no reason to believe that this character has real claws, so I have opted for the latter meaning, translating it as 'spirit' for clarity and style's sake. With *garra*, Lugones is clearly playing into the animal-like qualities typically associated with female vampires, but unfortunately, double meaning as a literary device is lost in translation.
4. *Calvary:* hillside outside Jerusalem where Jesus was crucified.
5. *lachrymose:* tearful, weepy.

NOTES : THE WHITE FARMHOUSE

6. *crepuscular:* of or relating to twilight.

   opal: stone formed from silica—in its common occurrence, the opal is white or colourless; in its precious variation, its colouring varies from blue–green through orange to black, often displaying a colourful iridescence.

7. *pitiful:* This word is unintelligible in the facsimile of the original publication. The phrase has been interpreted as 'oprimíanle el corazón las cobardías lamentables de un condenado a muerte.'

8. *firmament upon firmament:* 'The arch or vault of heaven overhead, in which the clouds and the stars appear; the sky or heavens. In modern use poetic or rhetorical' (*OED*). In the original Spanish, this appears as 'firmaments'—translated here as 'firmament upon firmament' as a more fitting anglophone expression that captures the 'vastness' of the emotions explored in the story.

9. *Drop by drop ... and he died:* These last three sentences are one longer sentence in the original Spanish: 'Su alma caia gota á gota en el sér de la amada, transfundíase del pobre vaso de su cuerpo, en el magnífico vaso donde pusiera toda su vida para adorarla mejor, y asi, lleno de languidez suprema, se extinguió una noche en un doloroso desprendimiento de corazón.'

   For the sake of clarity and style in English, they have been broken up and some adjustments were made at the word level as well. Doing so rendered ambiguity as to the husband's active role in transfusing his soul into his wife's body, which is explicit in 'donde pusiera toda su vida'. Moreover, the sexual connotation of this transfusion should not go unnoticed, either, as the 'drops' of the colonel's soul that result in his 'listlessness' can be read as a reference to ejaculation and a resulting tired state. As such, this image parodies the medical and psychological discourses of the late nineteenth century that problematised female sexual desire and excessive sexual activity for their negative physical and moral tolls.

10. *Her soul was at war with itself:* The original Spanish reads, 'Habia inmensos derrumbes en el fondo de su alma', which could translate, among other similar options, to 'There were immense landslides in the depths of her soul.' To promote a smoother reading of the text, the English expression of being 'at war with oneself' has been employed, because it creates a similar image of destruction while averting the clunkiness of the literal translation.

11. *His hands were soaking wet ... made to cry:* a reference to her eyes, not his.

12. *fireworks go off in her soul:* another example of opting for an English expression proximate to the Spanish one created by Lugones. The original Spanish reads, 'en el alma de la amante hubo una emergencia de estrellas', which translates as 'there was an emergence of stars in the lover's soul'.

THE WHITE FARMHOUSE

1. *Lady Emilia Pardo Bazán:* Galician-born Spanish writer and feminist (1851–1921), known primarily as a naturalist whose novels and tales also employ gothic strategies such as vampire logic, suffering heroines and violent or eerie private spaces. She is regarded as one of the greatest Spanish authors of all time.

NOTES : THE WHITE FARMHOUSE

2. *Hegel's principle ... ideal is real:* Georg Wilhelm Friedrich Hegel (1770–1831), a German philosopher who wrote, 'What is rational is actual; and what is actual is rational.' See G. W. F. Hegel, *Elements of the Philosophy of Right,* ed. by Allen W. Wood, trans. by H. B. Nisbet (Cambridge: Cambridge University Press, 1991), p. 20. Replacing 'actual' with 'ideal' suggests the narrator's misreading of Hegel, who was an objective rather than subjective idealist. For Hege, the univese is the actualisation of God's rational mind.

3. *ultra-Kantian views:* The narrator's 'ultra-Kantian views' lead him to misrepresent Hegel because the narrator is even more of a subjectivist than the German philsopher Immanuel Kant (1724–1804). The play on words in this sentence thus cleverly represents the philosophical and ontological problem at the heart of the tale: do an individual's experiences determine what is 'real'?

4. *Königsburg:* Kant's place of birth; Baltic port city in Eastern Prussia, whose dominant language was German (since 1946 renamed Kaliningrad, when it became part of the Soviet Union and now Russian Federation).

5. *noumenon:* 'An object knowable only by the mind or intellect, not by the senses; spec. (in Kantian philosophy) an object of purely intellectual intuition, devoid of all phenomenal attributes' (*OED*).

6. *ontological problems:* questions related to the nature of being or existence.

7. *axioms:* generally accepted maxims or rules.

8. *ornamental flowers:* possibly, *Zootrophion griffin,* a species of the orchid family, native to the forests of Ecuador, in NW South America; its Latin name refers to the impression that its flowers resemble a griffin's head. These plants were cultivated for display in glass terrariums.

   gryphons: mythological creatures usually represented as bearing the heads and wings of eagles and the bodies of lions. The 'transformation' from beauty to chaos, or rational to irrational, represents the narrator's thoughts and mind appearing to become misshapen or contorted from the perspective of his tutor.

9. *Cordelia:* possible reference to the youngest daughter of King Lear in William Shakespeare's 1616 play of the same name. With a name deriving from the Latin *cor* (heart), Cordelia was honest, devoted, beautiful and brave, in contrast to her two ruthless and scheming elder sisters, Goneril and Regan; Shakespeare's Cordelia may originate in a legendary queen of the pre-Roman Britons, coming to power around 855 BCE.

10. *The Resurrection of Jairus's Daughter, by a Flemish painter:* depicts the reported miracle in the synoptic Gospels of Jesus healing a girl after she was thought to be dead (in Mark 5. 21–43, Matthew 9. 18–26 and Luke 8. 40–45). There have been many artistic representations of this biblical scene over the centuries: Palma is most likely referring to a painting supposed to have been by the Dutch artist Rembrandt van Rijn (1606–1669), but later attributed to Gerbrand van den Eeckhout (1621–1674), one of Rembrandt's pupils. Van Eeckhouts' *Resurrection of Jairus's Daughter* (*c.* 1663) formed the basis of numerous reproductions and engravings in subsequent centuries, and is currently located in Berlin's Gemäldegalerie.

11. *Beethoven's beautiful sonatas:* Ludwig van Beethoven (1770–1827), German composer and pianist, who wrote more than thirty piano sonatas—musical compositions with a distinct structure of three movements (*exposition, development, recapitulation*).

NOTES : THE WHITE FARMHOUSE

12. *Chopin's passionate nocturnes:* Frédéric Chopin (1810–1849), Polish composer and pianist, who popularised the nocturne—a single-movement composition 'suggestive of night, usually of a quiet, meditative character' (*OED*).

13. *entailed estate:* estate that was inherited by a settlement, usually by the nearest male descendant, which could therefore not be sold or passed on to a third party by the current occupier.

14. *fleur-de-lis:* lily flower.

15. *malaria:* 'any of a group of diseases of humans and other vertebrates caused by protozoans of the genus Plasmodium (phylum Apicomplexa), which are transmitted by mosquitoes and parasitize red blood cells, resulting in haemolysis, periodic fever, and various other symptoms' (*OED*). Diseases of the blood have special significance in vampire literature, as do bloodsucking insects and other creatures in Latin American literature. See Horacio Quiroga's 'El almohadón de plumas' ['The Feather Pillow'], found in *Cuentos de amor, de locura y de muerte* [*Tales of Love, Madness and Death*] (1917) as a prime example.

16. *Adam:* according to the Bible, the first man created by God.

17. *heliotropes:* 'A name given to plants of which the flowers turn so as to follow the sun; in early times applied to the sunflower, marigold, etc.; now, a plant of the genus Heliotropium (N.O. Ehretiaceæ or Boraginaceæ), comprising herbs or shrubs with small clustered purple flowers; esp. *H. Peruvianum*, commonly cultivated for its fragrance' (*OED*).

18. *evangelical legend:* in this case, referring to the biblical episode in which Jesus raises Jairus's daughter from the dead (see n. 10, above).

19. *wolves:* these animals often appear in vampire literature to foment fear and suspense, and to highlight a human's or vampire's connection to the 'savage' natural world. Such is the case in Bram Stoker's *Dracula* (1897), which appeared a few years before 'The White Farmhouse'.

20. *lugubriously:* in such a way that inspires sorrow.

21. *nacre:* irridescent off-white colour similar to that of mother-of-pearl.

22. *stoicism:* behaviour characterised by repressing one's emotions and indifferent to pleasure or pain, marked by patience; named after the Stoics, a philosophical school founded by Zeno around 300 BCE, who were marked by their austere ethical views and practices.

23. *Stein:* possible reference to the early 19th-century miniaturist and portrait painter, Carl Friedrich Stein.

24. *Hamlet ... Laertes ... Ophelia:* key characters in William Shakespeare's play, *The Tragedy of Hamlet* (c. 1599–1601). Hamlet, Prince of Denmark, plots his revenge against Claudius, his uncle's brother and murderer who has usurped the throne and married Hamlet's mother. Ophelia, the daughter of the court adviser Polonius, is drawn to Hamlet, but in seeking vengeance he cruelly neglects her, which combined with her father's death results in her insanity and apparent suicide. Convinced by Claudius that Hamlet is reponsible for both Polonius's death and Ophelia's madness, Laertes challenges the prince to a duel using a poisoned blade, which fatally injures both combatants. Hamlet's confession of his feelings for Ophelia referred to by the narrator occurs in *Hamlet*, v. 1. 285–87.

25. *positivist philosophy:* 'any of various philosophical systems or views based on an empiricist understanding of science, particularly those associated with the belief that every cognitively meaningful proposition can be scientifically veri-

NOTES : MR CADAVER AND MISS VAMPIRE

fied or falsified, and that the (chief) function of philosophy is the analysis of the language used to express such propositions' (*OED*).

———◆◆)◆◆◆◆———

MR CADAVER AND MISS VAMPIRE

1. *Baudelaire, Le Vampire*: 'You fool—if from her command | Our efforts delivered you forth, | Your kisses would waken again | Your vampire lover's corpse.' This is the closing stanza of the poem 'Le Vampire' by the French writer Charles Baudelaire (1821–1867), originally published in the 1857 poetry collection *Les Fleurs du mal*: the English translation above is taken from Charles Baudelaire, *The Flowers of Evil*, trans. by James N. McGowan (Oxford: Oxford University Press, 1998), p. 65.
2. *Plaza de la Cebada*: large square in a working-class neighbourhood of Madrid.
3. *Madrid*: capital of Spain since 1561, located approximately in the centre of the Iberian Peninsula.
4. *white cordovan hats*: wide-brimmed hats that originated in Córdoba, southern Spain.
5. *dressed to the nines*: 'dressed very elaborately or smartly' (*OED*)
6. *giant French hats*: the original Spanish reads 'grandes sombreros cocotescos'. The word *cocotesco* can be found in some Spanish magazines from the 1910s— e.g. *Actualidades* [Current affairs], 17 March 1910, and *La Esfera* [The social circle], 16 March 1918—while the word *cocotología* was coined by Spanish writer Miguel de Unamuno (1864–1936) in his essay 'Apuntes para un tratado de cocotología' [Notes on the study of cocotology], 1902), wherein *cocotología* refers to origami, or paper bird making. Both terms appear to be inspired by the French word *cocotte*, meaning a high-class prostitute or a hen.

   Given the exaggerated satirical representation of the crowd, de Hoyos's use of *cocotesco* can be interpreted to mean 'flashy' or 'gaudy', even 'bird-like' in terms of scale and the use of feathers on the large hats in fashion at the time. Since the term *cocotología* appears in the dictionary of the Royal Spanish Academy—the authoritative dictionary of the Spanish language—but the term *cocotesco* does not, I could not be sure about an exact translation and opted for substituting *cocotesco* with 'French' to maintain that connection. The allusion to prostitution is maintained in the remainder of the paragraph, while the allusions to excess and gaudiness are evident throughout the entire description of the crowd.
7. *tart*: sexually promiscuous woman or prostitute.
8. *début*: while the term is now standard in both English and Spanish, it is important to note that it appears in italics and with an accent over the 'e' in the original Spanish version, making visible the term's French origin.
9. *Poe*: Edgar Allan Poe (1809–1849), American writer of gothic literature, known for poems such as 'The Raven' (1845) and for tales such as 'The Fall of the House of Usher' (1839) and 'The Murders in the Rue Morgue' (1841). Poe was incredibly influential in Latin American and Spanish literature, having been directly referenced in tales by de Hoyos, Pardo Bazán, Clemente Palma and others.

NOTES : MR CADAVER AND MISS VAMPIRE

10. *Hoffmann*: E. T. A. Hoffmann (1776–1822), German author and composer who was also an important influence on the development of gothic and fantastic literature in Latin America and Spain. Some of his most influential and important works include 'Die Automata' ['The Automata'] (1814), 'Nußknacker und Mausekönig' ['The Nutcracker and the Mouse King'] (1816) and 'Der Sandmann' ['The Sandman'] (1817).

11. *dandy*: man of fashion, marked by his elegant clothing, groomed features and leisurely pursuits.

12. *defiant to British fashions*: suggests that Mr Cadaver's hair was not slicked back, as was the typical men's hairstyle in Britain around the time this tale was first published.

13. *lugubrious*: causing or expressing sorrow.

14. *great Rembrandt*: i.e. a large painting by the Dutch painter, Rembrandt van Rijn (1606–1669).

15. *Nice*: coastal Mediterranean city at the foot of the Alps, in the department of Alpes-Maritimes, within the Provence-Alpes-Côte d'Azur region of SE France, bordering Italy.

16. *Ostend*: coastal city in the province of West Flanders, NW Belgium.

17. *Venice*: picturesque capital of NE Italy's Veneto region; also known as 'the city of canals' because it was built on water as a refuge from invaders.

18. *Salome's Dance of the Seven Veils*: modern, explicit interpretation of a biblical scene, in which Herodias's unnamed daughter dances for her stepfather, King Herod Antipas (Matthew 14. 1–12; Mark 6. 14–27). The earliest adaptation may be Oscar Wilde's (1854–1900) one-act play *Salome* (1893), later adapted by the German composer Richard Georg Strauss (1864–1949) as an opera in 1905. These erotic adaptations clearly inspire the representation in this tale.

19. *chulos*: dance native to the Santander region of northern Colombia.

20. *apaches*: dance born of early 20th-century Parisian street culture.

21. *Herodias*: biblical character and princess of Galilee during the Roman Empire, born *c.* 15 BCE and died sometime after 39 CE; Salome's mother and King Herod Antipas's second wife.

22. *Herod*: King Herod Antipas (*c.* 20 BCE–39 CE), ruler of Galilee and Peraea, who promised to fulfil one of Salome's requests in exchange for a dance. At the encouragement of Herodias, Salome demanded the head of John the Baptist, who had condemned Herod's marriage to Herodias, as she had previously been the wife of his half-brother, Herod II.

23. *Persian red*: warm, deep red with a hint of brown.

24. *amphora*: tall jar with two handles and a narrow neck used by the ancient Greeks or Romans to hold mainly oil and wine.

25. *liturgy*: 'orm of public worship, esp. in the Christian Church; a collection of formularies for the conduct of Divine service. Also, public worship conducted in accordance with a prescribed form.' (*OED*)

26. *lives of holy ascetics*: The Ascetics of the early Christian church led abstinent lives often in retreat from civilisation, eschewing sensual pleasures in the pursuit of redemption or salvation.

27. *Bosch's paintings*: Hieronymus Bosch (*c.* 1450–1516), Dutch painter famous for works that often depicted nightmarish and macabre images.

28. *chimerical*: illusory or imaginary; derived from the *chimera*, a creature from ancient Greek mythology, which sported the head and body of a lion, a sec-

NOTES : MR CADAVER AND MISS VAMPIRE

ondary goat's head and a snake-headed tail; the chimera was slain by the hero Bellerophon.

29. *Herculean:* displaying excessive strength or muscularity, and referring to the classical demigod Hercules (Herakles), son of the god Jupiter (Zeus) and the mortal Alcmena.

30. *L'Olympia in Paris:* theatre and concert hall in the 9th *arrondisement* of Paris, France, which opened in 1893.

31. *promenoir:* walkway or promenade (French).

32. *Michelangelo's heroes:* Michelangelo di Lodovico Buonarotti Simoni (1475–1564), Italian sculptor, painter, architect and poet of the High Renaissance. His 'heroes' refer to his famous sculptures of young naked men, such as the statue of David, unveiled in Florence, Italy, in 1504.

33. *Teatro Novedades:* performing arts theatre in Madrid, founded in 1857; in 1928, nearly ten years after the publication of this story, it burned down, killing ninety people.

34. *eucharistic:* relating to the Christian Eucharist, 'the sacrament of the Lord's Supper; the Communion' (*OED*); in this case, emphasising the whiteness of Miss Vampire's skin (aligned with the colour of consecrated bread), or more symbolically her skin's 'sacred' quality.

35. *renard bleu:* fox fur with a blueish hue.

36. *Café de París:* There are Cafés de Paris all over the world, but given the date of publication of this tale, this is most likely a reference to the Café de Paris in Monte Carlo, Monaco, founded in 1868.

37. *Clodahorlaomor, dethroned king of Iskander:* Iskandar is a town in the Tashkent region of modern-day Uzbekistan, Central Asia. No information on 'Clodahorlaomor' or 'Iskander' has been located, so it is likely that this is not a historical reference. However, it is possible the king in question may be Emir Sayyid Mir Muhammad Alim Khan (1880–1944), who was absolute monarch (1911–1920) of the Emirate of Bukhara, a polity that spanned modern-day Uzbekistan, Tajikistan, Turkmenistan and Kazakhstan between 1785 and 1920. Emir Alim Khan was overthrown by the Red Army following a siege of the city of Bukhara that lasted four days.

38. *cabotin:* theatrical person; ham or show-off (French, from *caboter*, 'to coast', linked to the itinerancy of performers).

39. *crepe de Chine:* 'crepe of China' (French), a dress made of silk with a slightly wrinkled appearance. Note that one of Blanca's dresses in 'The Cold Woman' is made of the same material.

40. *contralto voice:* lowest female singing voice in classical music; suggesting here that Miss Vampire has a dark, low-pitched voice.

41. *Dantean curse:* Dante Alighieri (1265–1321), Italian poet, writer and philosopher, famous for *La Vita Nuova* [*The New Life*] (1294) and *Divina Commedia* [*Divine Comedy*] (*c.* 1308–1321). A 'Dantean curse' invokes the author's depictions of sinners' ultimate, eternal punishment in Hell, with this particular reference further suggesting the demonic or perverse nature of the couple's sexual encounter.

42. *tragic mystic legends ... monks tempted by Satan:* no reference has been located.

43. *Constantinople:* ancient city straddling the Bosphorus Strait between Europe and Asia. Following the collapse of the Western Roman Empire, Constantinople was the capital of the Byzantine Empire (330–1204, 1261–1453) and the

75

NOTES : THE COLD WOMAN

Ottoman Empire (1453–1922); in 1930, it was renamed Istanbul, and is now a large metropolis in modern-day Turkey, the second-largest city in Europe.

————◆◆◆◆————

THE COLD WOMAN

1. *Princess Theatre:* located in Madrid, the theatre opened in 1885; in 1931, it took its current name, Teatro María Guerrero.
2. *Basque:* Basque Country is a region that straddles the Pyrenees, spreading from northern Spain into parts of France. Basques were genetically isolated from the rest of Europe for centuries, and thus speak a language (Euskara) that is very different from other European languages. Basques are not typically considered Hispanic, but rather an indigenous European ethnic group, tending to have dark hair and pale skin. The southern part of Basque Country was annexed by Spain in the early 16th century: today, it is an autonomous community of Spain with its own parliament and president.
3. *Pyrenees:* mountain range that extends along the border of modern-day Spain and France for roughly 310 miles (500 km), reaching a maximum height of just over 11,160 ft (3400 m).
4. *pretty fast footwork:* I have borrowed the exact translation of this phrase from Abigail Lee Six's translation of the original Spanish, in her edition of de Burgos's *Three Novellas: 'Confidencias', 'La mujer fría' and 'Puñal de claveles'* (Manchester: Manchester University Press, 2016), p. 78. In the footnotes of her volume, she provides some excellent English translations for clarification purposes.
5. *Madrid:* capital of Spain since 1561, located approximately in the centre of the Iberian Peninsula.
6. *Paseo de la Castellana:* major avenue in Madrid that cuts across the city from South to North.
7. *meridian countries:* reference to the countries through which the Prime Meridian, an arbitrary line that divides the Earth into Western and Eastern Hemispheres, passes; countries include Spain, France, the United Kingdom, Ghana, Algeria and others.
8. *Vienna:* largest city and one of the nine states of modern-day Austria, located in the east; in 1804, it became the capital of the Austrian Empire (1804–1867), ruled by the Habsburg dynasty; in 1918, it became the capital of Austria and remains so to this day.
9. *'the Cold Woman':* At various points in the original Spanish text, 'The Cold Woman' is capitalised or not, and enclosed in quotation marks (either including or excluding the article). The present text standardises throughout as 'The Cold Woman'.
10. *London:* capital and largest city of both England and the United Kingdom, located in Kent, SE England; in the 19th and early 20th centuries, it experienced major population and industrial growth and became a global cultural, political and economic hub.

76

NOTES : THE COLD WOMAN

11. *Paris:* capital and largest city of France, located in the Île-de-France region of northern France; Blanca mentioning that she cannot go 'unnoticed' in these large, bustling cities further highlights just how much she stands out.

12. *ermine:* animal 'whose fur is reddish brown in summer, but in winter (in northern regions) wholly white, except the tip of the tail, which is always black'; 'the whiteness of ermine is often referred to in poetry as an emblem of purity' (*OED*).

13. *menthol:* 'crystalline terpenoid alcohol found in peppermint and other natural oils, whose odour and taste produce a characteristic cooling sensation, used medicinally in decongestants and analgesics, and as a flavouring' (*OED*).

14. *benzyl acetate:* identified in several fruits and flowers, including jasmine, it has been a component of perfumes and soaps since the early 1900s; it does not appear to be harmful to humans, unless one has prolonged or incredibly high exposure.

15. *Arabian jasmine:* species of tall evergreen climbing shrub (*Jasminum sambac*), originally native to Southern Asia but now widespread throughout the world; it has dark glossy leaves and clusters of white flowers, renowned for their sweet scent, which forms the basis of many perfumes.

16. *toilette:* French high-society ritual, referring to the process of dressing or grooming oneself.

17. *hotel:* 'originally and chiefly with reference to France or French-speaking countries: a large private residence, a town mansion. Now chiefly historical' (*OED*), Blanca's hotel appears to align more so with this meaning than with that of a large commerical facility open to many guests.

18. *cornucopia:* excessive amount, overflowing.

19. *Andrea della Robbia:* Italian Renaissance sculptor (1435–1525), who specialised in ceramics.

20. *terracotta:* 'hard unglazed pottery of a fine quality, of which decorative tiles and bricks, architectural decorations, statuary, vases, and the like are made' (*OED*).

21. *Arras:* city in the Pas-de-Calais department, within the Hauts-de-France region of northern France; famous for its highly sought-after tapestries in the 15th century.

22. *Gobelin:* reference to tapestries made, or like those made, at the Manufacture de Gobelins in Paris.

23. *Murano glass:* made in Venice and Murano, an island located very near Venice; renowned for its exceptional quality.

24. *Gallé:* Émile Gallé (1846–1904), an innovator in the French Art Nouveau movement.

25. *midnight blue Chinese porcelain:* known for its high quality, rich colours—especially cobalt blue, originally imported from Persia—and shiny glaze, the latter a result of firing at exceedingly high temperatures.

26. *Danish porcelain:* high-quality ceramics style produced in Denmark, recognisable for its use of bright blue, as well as its sleek lines and abstract forms.

27. *stormy blue Delft pottery:* also known as Delft Blue or Delftware, a reference to the renowned pottery produced in Delft, Holland in the western Netherlands.

28. *Talavera porcelain:* tin-glazed ceramics traditionally made in Talavera de la Reina, Toledo, a city in central Spain; later, introduced and made popular in Mexican pottery from the 16th century.

NOTES : THE COLD WOMAN

29. *Castile:* kingdom previously located in the centre of the Iberian Peninsula (1065–1230), today it comprises the regions of Castile and León and Castile-La Mancha, with Madrid at its centre; summers in the region are hot and dry.

30. *Norwegian armchairs:* early 20th-century style of quality, solid-wood chair decorated with paintings or engravings, as described in the tale.

31. *Spanish friar's chair:* made of wood, but solid only on the seat and part of the back; may also have armrests and decorative elements.

32. *Gold Louis XV chairs:* wooden, Rococo-style (highly ornamental, asymmetrical and sculpted) chair with curved cabriole legs; originally produced during the reign of Louis XV (1715–1774) .

33. *cretonne Pompadour armchairs:* type of furniture characterised by strong woven fabric, and named after Jeanne Antoinette Poisson (1721–1764), also known as Madame de Pompadour, an advisor to and chief mistress of King Louis XV.

34. *Marie Antoinette's striped silk:* gold-striped pale fabric, as seen in the oil-on-canvas portrait *Marie Antoinette in a Chemise Dress*, by French painter Élisabeth Louise Vigée Le Brun (1755–1842). Wife to King Louis XVI of France (1754–1793), the Austrian-born Marie Antoinette (1755–1793) was the last Queen Consort of France, from 1774 until her execution during the French Revolution.

35. *Spanish Empire:* Beginning in 1492 with the Spanish Crown-backed expedition of Christopher Columbus (1451–1506) to what was presumed to be India but would later be known as the Americas, the Spanish Empire became one of the most powerful colonial powers in history. Its downfall resulted from a combination of irresponsible financial decisions (i.e. not investing in infrastructure), Napoleon Bonaparte's (1769–1821) invasion of Spain (1808–1814), and other political events and decisions that weakened the Empire, encouraged Latin American independence movements and led to the loss of the last of their colonies in the Treaty of Paris, the culmination of the Spanish-American War (21 April 1898–10 December 1898).

36. *lamé:* 'material consisting of silk or other yarns interwoven with metallic threads' (*OED*)

37. *crepe de Chine:* 'crepe of China' (French), a dress made of silk with a slightly wrinkled appearance. Note that this is the same material used to describe one of Miss Vampire's dresses in Antonio de Hoyos y Vinent's tale, 'Mr Cadaver and Miss Vampire', originally published twelve years prior.

38. *Andalusian:* person from Andalusia, a southern province in Spain; as a 'southern' region, there are stereotypes associated with its residents, such as being superstitious.

39. *carillon:* set of bells.

40. *macaw tail:* bright, long tail feather worn as an accessory and taken from the macaw parrot, native to the Caribbean, Mexico, and Central and South America.

41. *ciré accessories:* 'having a smooth polished surface' (*OED*); the original Spanish reads 'plumas "cirée"', and while in modern-day Spanish *pluma* tends to mean either 'pen' or 'feather', it also used to mean 'accessories' or 'embellishments'.

42. *Magi following a star:* three biblical wise men or kings, foreign dignitaries who were led by a star from the East to Jerusalem, bearing with them gifts of gold, frankincense and myrrh to the infant Jesus (Matthew 2. 1–12).

NOTES : THE COLD WOMAN

43. *chimera*: illusion or fancy; derived from the *chimera*, a creature from ancient Greek mythology, which sported the head and body of a lion, a secondary goat's head and a snake-headed tail; the chimera was slain by the hero Bellerophon.
44. *eucalpytus tree*: also known as 'the gum tree' of Australia, as it produces gum, among other products, and has been introduced into various other parts of the world; the oil from its leaves is used for its medicinal properties.
45. *Recoletos*: one of the six *barrios* (wards) that make up Salamanca, a district in central Madrid.
46. *Cleopatra*: Queen of the Ptolemaic Kingdom of Egypt from 51–30 BCE, she was born in 69 BCE and died in 31 BCE, and is famously known for her lovers and husbands, including Julius Caesar (Roman dictator, 100–44 BCE) and Mark Antony (Roman politician and general, 83–30 BCE).
47. *Lucrezia Borgia*: (1480–1519) Italian noblewoman and governor of Spoleto, central Italy (1499–1502); the illegitimate daughter of Rodrigo di Borgia, later Pope Alexander VI, she was renowned for her beauty, intellect and political acumen, as well as being infamous for her numerous love affairs.
48. *Attis's priests*: In Phrygian and classical Greek mythology, Attis was the god of vegetation and consort of the Anatolian mother goddess Cybele. Attis castrated himself, as did the priests of Attis and Cybele known as the Galli.
49. *Calle de Alcalá*: lengthy major thoroughfare that runs through Madrid.
50. *the Casino*: reference to Casino de Madrid, a gentleman's social club inaugurated in 1836.
51. *like any female*: in Spanish, 'luck' (*suerte*) is a feminine noun.
52. *Calle del Arenal*: another lengthy major thoroughfare that runs through Madrid.
53. *Teatro Real*: famous opera house in Madrid that was built in 1850.
54. *Plaza de la Encarnación ... legend of the Middle Ages*: as noted by Abigail Lee Six, in *De Burgos, Three Novellas*, p. 95, most likely a reference to St Pantaleon's blood, which is kept in the Real Monasterio de la Encarnación, located in the plaza. St Pantaleon (275–305 CE) was martyred during the Diocletianic Persecution of Christians in the Roman Empire: legend has it that his blood liquifies each year on July 27th, and if it does not, a tragedy will ensue.
55. *Paseo de Rosales*: the full name is Paseo del Pintor Rosales, named after the Spanish painter Eduardo Rosales (1836–1873); it provided beautiful views of Madrid at the time and is now a street with some of the most expensive homes in the city.
56. *Maria Luisa's gardens*: A park with beautiful gardens in Seville was named after Maria Luisa of Parma (1751–1819), Queen of Spain from 1788 to 1808; hence, it is unclear whether this reference was erroneously made by the author or refers to a past garden that is no longer in Madrid.
57. *Moncloa*: now a district in western Madrid, and home to Casa de Campo, a large park about five times the size of New York's Central Park.
58. *Goya*: the artist Francisco de Goya (1746–1828) painted Maria Luisa several times for the court.
59. *general confession*: in this context, a figure of speech referencing the Catholic process of confession, wherein an individual seeks absolution for his or her sins to date.
60. *Casa Camorra*: well-known, high-end restaurant at the time; later destroyed during the Spanish Civil War (1936–1939).

NOTES : THE COLD WOMAN

61. *dummies:* The Spanish *pelele* has similar connotations as 'dummy' in English, and can mean both a doll-like figure or effigy as well as an imbecile. Given the author's clear criticism of aristocratic and upper-class practices in the tale, *pelele* can be interpreted as a play on words that engages both meanings, and so 'dummy' was selected as opposed to other options.

62. *Puerto de Hierro:* Spanish for an 'iron gate', a monument in NW Madrid built 1751–1753.

63. *Cuesta de las Perdices:* stretch of road that connects Puerto de Hierro and the Hipódromo de la Zarzuela, a racecourse on the outskirts of Madrid.

64. *hills of El Pardo:* large, forested area that extends across roughly one quarter of Madrid.

65. *Casa de Campo:* once a royal hunting estate, now the largest public park in Madrid.

66. *tortilla al ron:* traditional flambé dessert from Galicia (autonomous community in NW Spain), which originated in France and is finished by burning off the rum (*ron*).

67. *chocolatito a la española:* Spanish-style hot chocolate beverage, made up of chopped dark chocolate, cornstarch, whole milk and sugar, which are whisked together.

68. *thirty-five degrees:* The average human body temperature is 36.5–37.5 °C (97.7–99.5 °F); a typical human body with a core temperature of 35 °C (95.0 °F) would be suffering from hypothermia.

69. *country:* taken to mean a different territory in Spain, not a different nation; the same holds true when, two sentences later, Marcelo refers to Blanca's country, the Basque region of northern Spain.

70. *idiot:* derogatory term used in the 19th and early 20th centuries for a person with a cognitive disability or impairment.

71. *astral body:* in Theosophy, 'the ethereal counterpart or shadow of a human or animal body' (*OED*). As mentioned in the Introduction to the present volume, Blavatskian Theosophy was a major influence on occult beliefs in the late 19th and early 20th centuries, observable in *modernista*, gothic and fantastic literature of the time (see pp. xxx–xxxi, above). In 1875, the Russian mystic and author Helena Petrovna Blavatsky (1831–1891) cofounded the Theosophical Society and authored one of Theosophy's foundational books of esoteric philosophy: *Isis Unveiled*.

72. *Catherine de' Medici:* Caterina (1519–1589), born into the powerful Florentine House of Medici, became Queen consort of France (1547–1559) and Queen regent (1560–1563), and mother of three kings: Francis II, Charles IX and Henry III. Don Marcelo's account of Queen Catherine, also known as the 'Serpent Queen', plays into how she has been maligned throughout history, but the historical facts are true.

73. *Pope Clement VII:* Catherine's uncle; born Giulio de' Medici (1478–1534), he was head of the Catholic Church and ruler of the Papal States from 1523 until his death.

74. *king of France:* Henry II (1519–1559), who reigned between 1547 until his death; he married Catherine in 1533 while still the Duc d'Orléans, through an arrangement made between his father King Francis I of France and her uncle Pope Clement VII.

NOTES : THE COLD WOMAN

75. *Ippolito a Cardinal ... to Spain:* Catherine had a long line of suitors seeking an alliance, including James V of Scotland. Ippolito de' Medici (1511–1535) became Lord of Florence when his cousin (not uncle) Giulio was elected pope as Clement VII in 1523. To assist him with church business, Clement created Ippolito as a cardinal and named him first Archbishop of Avignon in January 1529—a decision Ippolito resisted throughout his life, preferring the secular rule over Florence. Rumours suggested he was sent to the church to put an end to an illict relationship with his cousin Catherine de' Medici.

76. *Diane de Poitiers:* French noblewoman (1500–1566) and King Henry II's head mistress from 1535, when she was thirty-five and Henry fifteen, until his death in 1559.

77. *Mary Stuart:* Mary, Queen of Scots, the daughter of James V (1542–1587) and Queen Mary I of Scotland from her birth in 1542 until her forced abdication in 1567, and Queen consort of France (1559–1560) following her marriage to Francis II (1544–1560), which was cut short by his death aged sixteen. She was also Catherine de' Medici's daughter-in-law.

78. *her mother-in-law's magnificent pearl necklace:* reference to the Hanover Pearls, handed down from queen to queen; Catherine de' Medici passed them down to Mary, Queen of Scots.

79. *magnolia:* 'plant of the genus Magnolia (family Magnoliaceae), which consists of large (rarely shrubby) trees, native chiefly to eastern North America and eastern Asia and bearing usually large, cup-shaped, white, pink, or purple fragrant flowers' (*OED*).

80. *angelica-based perfume:* fragrance derived from the aromatic plant native to northern and eastern Europe, *Angelica archangelica*; its seeds and stems are used for flavouring and in confectionery, and its roots are extracted for medicinal uses.

81. *consumption:* historical term for tuberculosis, an infectious disease caused by the bacillus, *Mycobacterium tuberculosis*, which affects the lungs and other parts of the body; typical symptoms include a chronic, bloody cough, fever and weight loss. The term 'consumption' derives from the Latin *consumere*, 'to take over completely from within', emphasising the initially hidden symptomology of the disease. Consumption appears frequently in naturalist and gothic, especially vampire, literature of the time, such as in various stories by Pardo Bazán.

82. *Russian punch:* while the classic Russian Spring Punch uses vodka, this version with cognac includes other similar ingredients, including sugar, lemon juice and liqueur.

83. *cognac:* 'French brandy of superior quality distilled from Cognac wine. The name is sometimes extended (for trade purposes) to any French brandy' (*OED*). Cognac is a commune in the Charente department of the Nouvelle-Aquitaine region, western France.

84. *curaçao:* liqueur made from spirits flavoured wih sweetened orange peel.

85. *bitters:* 'infusion, typically in alcohol, of a bitter substance or substances (usually of botanical origin), originally used medicinally and later mainly as an aperitif or a flavouring, esp. for cocktails' (*OED*).

86. *déshabillé:* slip or nightgown, typically made of silk or another light fabric.

87. *He had gone too far ... would bleed right out:* In the original Spanish publication, this sentence reads: 'Había ido muy lejos y temía haber ofendido a Blanca, haberle causado en su amor propio, por su imprudencia, una de esas heridas por las que se desangra el amor.' It was important to maintain the blood-letting

NOTES : THE VAMPIRE

metaphor here because it transfers the vampire logic to Fernando, further contributing to Blanca's sympathetic portrayal.

88. *scent of her race*: see n. 89, below (and p. lxii, n. 144, above).

89. *yet deep down ... smell of 'race'*: In the original Spanish, this reads: 'tal vez no era más que un olor "de raza," acentuado, extraño, que se exageraba entre las esencias.' It felt important to keep the quotation marks around the word 'race', as it implies the lack of evidence behind the assumption that certain races have distinctive smells, as if it were something merely overheard in conversation.

90. *ammonia dissipates intoxication*: colourless alkaline gas with a strong smell, compounded from hydrogen and nitrogen (NH_3); smelling salts that released pungent ammonia fumes could be used to restore an unconscious person's respiratory flow and thus revive consciousness.

<hr style="width:30%"/>

THE VAMPIRE

1. *brain fever*: catch-all term for symptoms associated with a nervous breakdown, recurring in gothic and Victorian literature: e.g. it is the fictional ailment that kills Heathcliff's love, Catherine Earnshaw, in Emily Brontë's *Wuthering Heights* (1847).

2. *N1-rays*: 'discovered' through the polarisation of X-rays in 1903 by French physicist René-Prosper Blondot (1849–1930), which supposedly increased illumination generated by hot bodies without increasing their temperature. It was later concluded that N- or N1-rays did not exist, as it the only evidence was subjective and it was impossible to replicate the effects of Blondot's experiment. Indeed, Blondot's experiment was debunked by the American physicist Robert W. Wood in 1904.

3. *chloroform*: trichloromethane ($CHCl_3$), a dense colourless liquid used as a form of inhaled anaesthetic, first produced in the 1830s by mixing chlorinated lime (calcium hypocholrite) with ethanol (ethyl alcohol).

4. *vieux-riche*: 'old money' (French), derived from land ownership though inheritance, and associated with good breeding. The term was opposed to *nouveau riche* ('new money', French), with wealth being recently gained through mercantile and other speculative practices, thereby limiting the amount of refinement its possessors could develop. The Spanish edition has several terms in French that have been conserved in this translation, as their inclusion by Quiroga speaks to the great influence of and admiration for French literature and culture by Latin American authors. From the early nineteenth century, and as several scholars have noted, Latin American authors spent time abroad in France immersing themselves in literary circles where they familiarised themselves with new literary trends and the 'masters', and later brought French ideas and trends back home.

5. *cathode rays*: beams of electrons emitted by passing electricity through the cathodes (electrodes) of vacuum tubes.

6. *my writing you twice*: Rosales says he has written to Grant twice, but Grant previously said he had received three letters, adding to the narrator's unreliability already hinted at in his being treated in an asylum.

82

NOTES : THE VAMPIRE

7. *Poe's oval portrait:* reference to 'The Oval Portrait' (1842) by the American writer Edgar Allan Poe (1809–1849); the tale-within-a-tale describes how an artist who paints his wife's portrait turns to find her dead once the painting is completed. The artist has been so enthralled by his work that he failed to notice that his artwork was 'sucking the life' from her: the story can be read as, among other things, a critique of love, marriage and the addiction to art, and is often-times read through the lens of vampirism.

8. *galvanic imitation of life:* named after the Italian scientist and philosopher, Luigi Galvani (1737–1798), whose theory of 'animal electricity' (galvanism)—that all living creatures emited electricity generated by the chemical processes of their bodies—inspired the motif of renanimated corpses in science fiction and horror narratives, most famously Mary Shelley's *Frankenstein; or, the Modern Prometheus* (1818).

9. *hieratical:* 'appropriate to sacred persons or duties' (*OED*).

10. *soirée:* social gathering that occurred in the evening, and consisting of refreshments and interesting or convival conversation.

11. *parti pris:* bias or prejudice.

12. *divan:* day bed, or couch arranged as a bed.

13. *plafonniers:* ceiling lights.

14. *Armageddon:* originally, the Last Day of Judgement—the end of the world in biblical tradition—and subsequently global destruction owing to some major catastrophe. This may be an intertextual reference to H. G. Wells's short story 'A Dream of Armageddon' (1901), in which the protagonist reveals to the narrator (whom he has just met on a train) that his dreams are killing him.

15. *thousand leagues:* 3000 miles (5500 km).

16. *Guayaquil:* Santiago de Guayaquil, largest city in and main port of western Ecuador, located on the banks of the Guaya River, which flows into the Pacific Ocean.

17. *San Diego:* city on southern California's Pacific coast, approximately 19 miles (30 km) north of the Mexico–United States border.

18. *Santa Monica:* Californian coastal city, approximately 135 miles (215 km) north of San Diego.